DON'T
TELL A
SOUL

.

DON'T
TELL A
SOUL

DAVID ROSENFELT

St. Martin's Minotaur ✿ New York

Please e-mail David Rosenfelt at dr27712@aol.com with any feedback.
Your comments are very much appreciated

This is a work of fiction. All of the characters, organizations,
and events portrayed in this novel are either products of the author's
imagination or are used fictitiously.

www.minotaurbooks.com

Book design by Spring Hoteling

ISBN-13: 978-0-312-37395-5
ISBN-10: 0-312-37395-3

First Edition: July 2008

10 9 8 7 6 5 4 3 2 1

For Debbie

DON'T
TELL A
SOUL

Prologue

Friends have asked me why I'm telling this story, and for a long time I had no intention of doing so. For one thing, it's already been told so many times. Television has covered it endlessly, newspapers and magazines have made it a staple on their covers, and the inexhaustible blogosphere has grown exhausted in the rehashing.

Everyone remembers where they were the day it all went down. It is seared into the public consciousness, and nothing I can write will change that. Nor would I want it to.

But I have something new to tell, information that citizens have not heard, but perhaps can benefit from hearing. I was there; I had a front-row seat, and that separates me from the other chroniclers of history.

After having told my story for months to every imaginable branch of the federal government, they have mysteriously and arrogantly insisted I maintain a public silence. This I will not do.

I will tell it as it happened, and I hope the picture I paint will be as unbiased as possible. It will be daunting for me, or painful, or cathartic, or a great relief. Probably all of the above.

So why am I telling the story? I guess I just feel like you should know the truth.

"It's the little things that change your life.
They change your life, Timothy Wallace."

Whenever Tim Wallace's mother, Carol, had something important to tell him, she ended it with "Timothy Wallace." She always called him Tim, everybody called him Tim, but when she was imparting some special wisdom it was "Timothy," as if his formal name would lend it some additional credibility and significance.

She was a small woman; by the time he was eleven Tim had matched her height of almost five two. But she would put on her most solemn face and stare straight at him. The sadness in her eyes would make Tim want to look away, but to the best of his recollection he never did.

"The little things can change your life, Timothy Wallace."

What she was really talking about was fate, and how fate was dictated by moments you could neither expect nor control. And then she followed it with the story he had heard so many times. If her friend Donna hadn't taken a bus downtown that day, if she had taken a cab instead, she wouldn't have met Charlie, the man Donna eventually married.

And then, since Donna would not have known Charlie, he could never have fixed Carol up with Kenny Wallace. And then Carol and Kenny would never have had their son, Tim. And Kenny couldn't have abandoned them when Tim was only six months old, never once contacting them in all the years since.

So Donna's deciding to take the bus that day was the "little thing" that changed Carol's life for the worse, but in turn literally gave life to Tim.

That was what was strange about the "little things," and how they changed your life. They could be good or bad, and sometimes you didn't always know right away.

For Tim, and especially for Maggie, the "little thing" was the hat.

It was an important, even symbolic, moment for both of them.

Tim and Maggie had been married for almost five months, and while Tim had sworn "for better or for worse, in sickness and in health," that hadn't as yet included his boat. His pride and joy. His sanctuary.

He had owned the modest thirty-foot motorboat for six years, having bought it for himself on his twenty-fourth birthday. It was his place to decompress, to read, to be alone, to think, to get away from whatever might be bothering him, or to focus and reflect on that which was good.

Tim's close friends, Danny and Will, had been out on the boat with him a few times, but never a woman. Not even Maggie.

Not until that day.

The fact that this milestone didn't happen for the first four months after their marriage was more a function of the calendar than anything else. It isn't until early May that things start warming up on Long Island Sound, which is where Tim kept the boat. He was waiting for a decent day, and while the weather forecast for this one wasn't perfect, it would have to do.

"Why don't you keep it docked down there?" Maggie had asked on more than one occasion, pointing down at the Hudson River from the window of their twenty-third-floor apartment in Fort Lee, New Jersey.

Fort Lee is living proof of the old joke that the three most important things in real estate are "Location. Location. Location." It wraps around the New Jersey side of the George Washington Bridge, and is therefore wildly valued for its proximity to, and view of, New York City.

It was inevitable that high-rise apartments would spring up along the water, and just as inevitable that the prices would rise even higher. Tim and Maggie lived in Sunset Towers, as prestigious an address as Fort Lee possesses, and used that vantage point to take easy advantage of the theater, restaurants, and energy that New York provided better than any city in the world.

They were just leaving their apartment when Maggie unveiled the hat. He assumed it had to be a hat, because it was sitting on her head. But in reality it looked like a manhole cover on steroids, with a round brim so large that the Third Infantry could find shade under it.

"What the hell is that?" he asked, when she put it on. He knew that sounded a little harsh, so he added, "Honey."

"My new hat," she said, turning slightly to show it off in its full glory. "They only had one left."

"So other people beat you to that?"

She nodded. "Isn't it great?"

"And your plan is to carry that around on your head all day?"

"I'm sensing that you don't like it."

"No, I like it," he said, smiling. "It's just that it's among the ugliest things I've ever seen."

She nodded. "That's good, I was afraid you'd want to borrow it."

The drive out to the pier, with no traffic, was about forty-five minutes. Of course, as far as Tim was concerned, this was merely an untested theory, since there had never yet been a day in New York without traffic.

On this particular day it took an hour and fifteen minutes, much of it spent on the Cross Bronx Expressway, though the name "expressway" must have been given by someone with a particularly cruel sense of sarcasm. During the ride, Tim suggested Maggie hold the hat in her lap in deference to the fact that they were in Tim's convertible. Were it to blow out into the open road, he opined, it could take out a tractor trailer.

So instead Maggie's hair blew in the wind, and she was characteristically unconcerned about it. Maggie had dark, curly hair, and in Tim's view it would look good even if she put her head through a car wash. In fact, he always thought she looked best when she got out of the shower, when her hair was wet and unbrushed. Of course, she was also naked then, and that may have contributed to his bias.

Halfway into the ride, Maggie reached out, took his hand and squeezed it. "Did you tell Danny and Will you were taking me on the boat today?" She was referring to Danny McCabe and Will Clampett, Tim's best friends, who often mocked his "sanctuary" concept.

He shook his head. "No, I didn't tell anyone. I figured I'd surprise people after the fact."

Once they arrived at the pier, Maggie was so anxious to see the boat that she kept walking ahead of Tim. It wasn't completely logical, since there were hundreds of boats lined up, vertically parked along the pier, and she had no idea which one it was. She therefore had to keep waiting for him to catch up, and since he was carrying lunch and other supplies, he wasn't moving that quickly.

But when she happened upon it, she recognized it instantly. He'd had the idea the week before, and hadn't told her, relishing the surprise. He had renamed the boat *The Magster*, his nickname for her, and she stood there staring at the inscription on the hull.

Finally, still looking at the name and not Tim, she said, "You think I'm going to cry? Well, I'm not. I love it, and I love you, but I'm not going to cry."

"I wouldn't expect you to," he said. Maggie had a thing about crying; she wanted to save it for the "really important stuff." Which had always been fine with him.

As soon as they got on the boat, Maggie made it very clear that she wasn't there as a passenger. She wanted to know how it all worked, and insisted on doing everything from starting the motor to steering out into the Sound. She seemed to relish the entire experience and got thoroughly into it, even calling out "Ahoy!" to a nearby boat as they navigated out on the water.

After the first hour they just relaxed out there, drifting with the motor off, and reading the Sunday *Times*. They each had their own favorite sections; Tim was a Sports and Week in Review guy, while Maggie started with News, and then moved on to Arts and Leisure. Tim had once commented that this routine made them seem like an old married couple, and Maggie said that one day they would be, so they might as well start now.

Not long after, the wind started to pick up, and knowing what Tim did about the weather patterns on the Sound, he was aware that there was a chance the day would have to be cut short. He suggested they have lunch, and Maggie got up to prepare it.

Tim was the type that could happily eat his dinner standing next to the refrigerator, but to Maggie each meal was an event. It always amazed him; he had a constant struggle with his weight, stuffing 180 pounds onto his five-foot-eleven frame, while the five-foot-seven Maggie wouldn't weigh 120 pounds if she were carrying a barbell.

Maggie's insistence that each meal be treated as something special was actually one of the few areas of friction between them. Tim wanted to be far more casual about it, to eat pretty much whenever he felt like it, and to watch TV or read the paper while they ate. Maggie viewed mealtime differently, considering it an important time to talk and connect with each other. Tim had once pointed out the illogic of this; it made no sense for people to talk at the exact times they were filling their mouths with food. Of course, the observation got him nowhere.

Within five minutes the small table was set with an enormous amount of food. There was a dazzling array of dishes to sample, each in its own special serving piece. No plastic containers for Maggie. She even brought champagne to toast a new, substantial federal contract that Tim's construction company had won recently.

She looked at the table with satisfaction. "What do you think?"

"I think it should be enough," Tim said. "Actually, if a navy destroyer floats by, we can invite the crew to lunch."

"What about them?" Maggie asked, pointing to a large boat about five hundred yards away. She waved in their direction, but there didn't seem to be anyone out on the deck. Tim had seen it periodically during the morning. It was a boat he was very familiar with, a ninety-foot Oceanfast 360, retail price close to two million five. He had a dream of owning a boat like that, albeit not painted an ugly green with a white stripe as this one was. It was a goal that was only slightly more likely than his dream of becoming a Super Bowl MVP.

"Anybody who would paint a boat like that such an ugly color doesn't deserve lunch," he said. "Besides, they're rich enough to buy their own. Let's eat."

Eat they did, and after Tim had consumed enough food to sink *The Magster* from his weight, Maggie asked, "You want some dessert?"

"I can't," he said. "I do not have a single cubic inch of internal space left."

"That's a shame. I made crème brûlée."

"Unless I use my emergency space," he allowed. "That's always an option."

She nodded her understanding. "If this isn't an emergency, what is?"

Maggie got up and walked over to the cooler to get the dessert, but as she leaned over, a gust of wind blew the hat off her head and out into the water.

"Damn!" she yelled, as she reached out but just missed catching the hat.

"Don't worry about it," Tim said, looking at the huge hat floating on the water. "A freighter will find it and tow it back to shore. Or I'll get you another one."

"I like that one."

He nodded. "And it was indeed beautiful. But as you can see, it's going off on its own. All we can do is wish it well."

"Tim, it's right over there." She pointed to the hat, which by that time was already almost thirty yards away.

He tried to put on his most incredulous look. "You mean you want me to go out there . . . to get that ridiculous hat?"

"Of course, I do," she said. "Come on, Tim, it's drifting away."

"Maggie . . ." he said, though he was going to have to come up with something a lot stronger if he was going to get out of this. He looked up at the gathering clouds as if for inspiration.

"It's going to start raining soon."

She nodded. "Don't worry about it; you'll be wet from getting the hat anyway." She pointed behind them. "Besides, there's still sun, you'll dry out fast."

Logic like that was hard enough to deal with, and then she came in with the clincher. "I'll give you my undying love."

He muttered, "I thought I already had that." This was not a battle he was going to win, so he walked over to start the engine. The hat was moving away from them, taunting him, and he would at least pull the boat as close as he could before jumping in. The water was getting slightly choppy from the increasing wind.

He restarted the engine, and was not happy that it made a strange noise. He made a mental note to get it checked once they went back to the pier. He pulled the boat about ten yards from the hat, and prepared to go in to get it.

"Put on your life jacket," Maggie said.

"What for? I can swim like a fish."

"Tim, please put it on."

He sighed his continuing defeat, and put on the bright orange jacket, fastening the straps under her watchful eye. He jumped in the water, which sent a cold chill through him, and swam with powerful strokes toward the hat. It had already moved another fifteen yards away; clearly the hat was trying to elude capture.

In the distance Tim could see the Oceanfast 360, and hoped

that the people on board did not see him. This hat retrieval was embarrassing, and not his finest moment on the high seas.

When Tim finally reached the hat, he put it on his head and turned back toward the boat so Maggie could see him wearing it. "What do you think?"

Maggie wasn't looking at him; she was standing near the side of the boat, looking at the motor. "Tim," she called out, "I think there's something . . . Tim, there's something wrong with the motor!"

"TURN IT OFF!" he yelled. "TURN IT OFF!"

"It's smoking!"

"MAGGIE! TURN—"

The next thing he saw was a flash of white, so quick that it almost didn't register.

And then nothing.

"It went South."

That was the entire message that came in the form of a handwritten note, slipped to Roger Blair in the prison mess hall during dinner. He was seated at a long table, twelve seats on each side, and he looked around at the other inmates seated with him. No one seemed to be interested, which was not surprising. In this place, it took all available energy to worry about yourself.

"It went South."

That's all it said, but Roger didn't need any further explanation. He realized immediately that it meant something had gone terribly wrong. It also meant something else, an unwritten, secondary message that Roger also understood very well.

He was going to die.

It was the kind of death sentence from which there was no appeal, no "habeas corpuses," or whatever the hell else his asshole attorney always talked about. And no anti–death penalty liberals were going to march outside the prison when he died; he was going to go unnoticed.

There was nowhere to go for help, no stay of execution that could be granted. Roger even smiled to himself at the prospect of going to the prison authorities for help; if anything, that would hasten his demise.

The only remaining questions were when and how. Roger hoped it was soon; days spent in prison waiting to die were days not really worth living. The "how" was almost certain to be a sharp blade in the back, or across his neck, or maybe a garrote. Whatever was chosen, his killer would certainly have a different technique than the state; there would be no "lethal injection," no offered "last meal."

For the rest of the day he looked around warily, waiting for them to make their move. He did this although he was not sure he even wanted to see them coming; it might be better if he were unaware. That way it would be quicker, and hopefully less painful.

Roger worked in the prison laundry, which was considered to be a relatively good assignment by the inmate population. Well, Roger knew, pretty soon there was going to be an opening, and like all prison jobs, this one was going to be filled "in-house."

For the first time in a very long while he thought about his wife, and felt the urge to talk to her. Not that he had the capability of doing so; she had stopped coming to see him a while back, and his attempts to find her had turned up nothing. With the end approaching, he wasn't feeling resentful toward her; he just wanted to say goodbye.

Nothing happened the entire afternoon, which in itself was not a great surprise. These things were better done in darkness than in light; no one would be around to witness it. No matter when it was done, Roger knew, no one would be around who cared.

As always, lights went out at ten o'clock, leaving Roger lying on his bed, alone and awake. He listened for an approach, but it was not forthcoming, and he drifted off to sleep.

The cell was seven by ten, and at this hour was completely dark. But somehow prison darkness never fazed Roger. He thought it must be because this place in which he spent every minute of every day was always so grey, so dreary, that pitch-blackness seemed only a shade darker.

With no clock in the room, he did not know what time it was when he heard the cell door rattle slightly. The lock was sufficient to keep him in, but he harbored no illusions that it could keep them out.

Within moments Roger could sense that his executioner was inside, his identity but not his purpose shielded by the darkness.

"Took you long enough," Roger said.

If the intruder was surprised, his voice did not betray it. "It's time."

"Yeah," he said. There was no fight in his voice, nor was there any resistance planned. They would keep coming at him, as many as it took, and they would kill him. Might as well get it over with now. "You even know why you're doing this?" Roger asked.

He heard a slight laugh of surprise. "Yeah. For money." There was a click and a small beam of light appeared out of the intruder's hand. Roger could still not see his face, and really didn't want to.

Roger said, "I don't mean that. I mean—"

The blade swept across his neck, ending his sentence and his life.

A life that had long ago gone South.

From the moment he heard the facts, Detective Jonathon Novack realized exactly what he had.

It was a cold-blooded murder; and he knew who'd done it. He knew it in his gut, and he could count the times his gut was wrong on very few fingers.

There are a bunch of things that homicide cops in urban areas do not have, at least not in Novack's experience. They don't have long weekends off, they don't have secure, happy marriages, and they don't have coincidences in their work. And in this instance, for Novack's gut to be wrong, this would have to be the mother of all coincidences.

Novack had long ago learned to strip away all the bullshit and focus on the facts, and in this case the facts were clear. Tim Wallace had taken his wife, Maggie, out on his boat, a boat he had been out on, without incident, at least a hundred times. While drifting on Long Island Sound, he turned on the motor, and decided to swim to retrieve a hat his wife had lost overboard. At that very moment, the motor blew up in a massive explosion, obliterating the boat and his wife.

Quite a coincidence.

And a slam-dunk, no-doubt murder if ever there was one.

Except it didn't turn out quite that way, and if there was a more frustrating case, Novack couldn't remember it.

The Coast Guard had been on the scene of the explosion

within minutes, and they found Wallace floating, held up by his life jacket, in a state of what the doctors called convulsive shock. That lasted ten days, long enough to miss his wife's funeral, or more accurately her service, since the body was never recovered. When he finally regained full consciousness and coherency, he claimed not to remember anything after reaching the hat and seeing the flash of white.

Unfortunately, experts determined that the blast could conceivably have been an accident, based on a defect in a similar motor that caused an explosion a week earlier off the coast of Florida.

That was followed by a surprising willingness on the part of Wallace to take a lie detector test, and his just as surprising refusal to hire a lawyer. He passed the test with flying colors, and while that is not admissible in court, it certainly had an effect on both Novack's boss and the district attorney.

To complete the annoying trifecta, Novack could find no evidence of problems in the marriage. They had met eighteen months before, had had a whirlwind courtship, and no one would say anything other than they seemed completely in love.

The media jumped on the case, immediately joining Novack in the suspicion, almost the certainty, that Wallace had engineered his wife's death. Half of Larry King's panel all but had Wallace convicted, and Nancy Grace accused the police, and by extension Novack, of incompetence for not having Tim in jail on day one. But as day one became month one, the pundits ran out of unsubstantiated charges, and there were simply no revelations to support the media onslaught, or to add any fuel at all to the fire.

The simple fact was that Novack had uncovered nothing. And while his gut didn't require any evidence, his bosses, the courts, and every other part of the justice system did.

It was enough to make him and his gut nauseous.

But not enough to make him stop. This case would never get cold, not in Novack's mind. He would work it whenever he could, probing it from every angle, until he put away the son of a bitch who literally blew his young wife out of the water.

December thirty-first held absolutely
no special significance for Tim Wallace.

It was simply another day to be in pain over the loss of Maggie, a sorrow that was not about to be affected either way by the fact that it happened to be a holiday.

The aching had not lessened in the months since that awful day out on the water. And if truth be told, Tim didn't really want it to lessen. In his mind it would be stupid and illogical to be happy, or content, or pain-free. Maggie was dead, blown to bits while he went swimming for a fucking hat, and the knowledge of that was supposed to hurt.

He wanted it to hurt.

He also wanted to work; it represented an impersonal world, a place he could be without feeling Maggie's constant presence, or more accurately, lack of presence. And here he caught a break; the small construction company, Wallace Industries, that he began six years prior was thriving, and they had more work than they could handle.

Soon after 9/11, Tim was among the first to recognize the boom that was about to hit in security construction. Many buildings, especially those owned by the government, were found in need of reinforcement and specially constructed concrete perimeters. They simply had not been built in the expectation that they would someday be bombed, or that a plane might be flown into them.

Tim was shrewd enough to declare himself and his company to be expert in this area, and it did not take long for him to start receiving very healthy contracts. The federal government had money to spend, and Tim's company was one of the places they spent it.

The irony was that this last year was by far the most successful year ever for Tim's company. They were nearly finished with their part of a massive U.S. Government complex of buildings in downtown Newark, called the Federal Center, a project costing in excess of three billion dollars. Their portion of it was relatively small, but Tim and Danny recognized that it was just the beginning.

The Federal Center complex would be a model of its type, with each building possessing state-of-the-art security, and was planned as the forerunner for similar projects around the country. They were virtual federal cities within cities, the idea being that it was easier to provide security for one large complex, rather than for buildings spread out in different locations, as was currently the case. The future for any company on the ground floor of such an enterprise was potentially unlimited.

Almost two years ago, Tim had brought Danny McCabe in as his partner. They had met when first starting out at a large construction company, and became fast friends. Danny didn't quite have the nerve to join Tim when he started his own firm, but he did come over later, when it was obvious that the new company was a solid one.

Danny was both hardworking and talented, a problem solver in a business that had round-the-clock problems. But the most significant asset he brought to the company was a crucial contact. His uncle was Fred Collinsworth, senior United States Senator from New Jersey, and the ranking member on the Senate Appropriations Committee. Uncle Fred had proven to be invaluable in steering federal work to his nephew's company, most notably the Newark project, and that was a huge factor in the company's growth.

Granting the project to Danny and Tim's company was not strictly nepotism. Many smaller construction companies were given substantial contracts, and the senator pointed to it as a new way of doing business, as opposed to the recent practice of enormous companies controlling everything.

It was a politically wise move on his part, both because he could claim that he was helping small business, and because in reality it was creating a large group of businessmen who were beholden to him, and who would show their appreciation in campaign contributions. It also earned him the enmity of the Franklin Group and its chairman, Byron Carthon. Franklin was a huge, multinational corporation that was used to getting these kinds of gigantic government contracts.

But Collinsworth was unconcerned with Carthon or the Franklin Group. He was well aware that when the contracts were granted to many smaller companies for similar Federal Center complexes around the country, he would immediately have a huge national base of political and financial support from which to draw, the kind of situation that could help propel a politician, if he were ambitious, to the highest of national offices. And Collinsworth was nothing if not ambitious.

Tim was pleased and a little surprised when the friendship between him and Danny was not in any way harmed by the partner dynamic. He could rely on Danny, which was especially vital during the months directly following Maggie's death.

Danny and Tim's other very close friend was Will Clampett, who worked for them as an independent contractor handling the computer issues so vital to modern construction. Danny and Will frequently attempted to draw Tim back out into the social world. They just felt it would be better for him to get out more, take his mind off things, even if he had no interest in dating.

Tim's efficient thirty-one-year-old assistant, Meredith Tunney, shared this feeling and joined in the gentle persuading, but Tim remained firm. He was not going to do anything until he was ready, and "ready" seemed light-years away.

But New Year's Eve, while of no significance to Tim, was considered very significant by Danny, Will, and Meredith. They were plainly worried that it would be a particularly difficult night for him, despite his protestations that he'd be fine.

Meredith had been a godsend for Tim and the company. Hired just two months before Maggie's death, she had kept Tim's life in order ever since. She had the uncanny ability of anticipating his needs, whether it was paying his bills, or making all of his appointments and reservations, and this enabled him to keep his life only on the brink of chaos, without crossing the line.

So Meredith spent the day with Tim in his Englewood office, stealing glances at him and wondering how she could broach the subject of his plans for New Year's Eve. She was going out with friends, and had already pronounced it unacceptable that Tim stay home alone.

By three-thirty in the afternoon it was obvious Tim was not about to introduce the subject. She wanted to take off to get ready for her own evening, so she took a deep breath and plunged ahead. He was at his desk doing some paperwork, when she walked in and said, "So, Tim, what have you got going on for tonight?"

He didn't even look up. "A couple of parties, then into the city to watch the ball drop, then probably clubbing until morning."

She frowned, knowing full well who she was talking to. "Come on, really."

He finally looked up and nodded. "Pizza, half pepperoni, and a DVD of *Godfather I* and *II*."

"You're not going out?"

"No, this year I think I'm going to go in," he said. "Everybody else will be 'out,' so I'll have 'in' all to myself."

She shook her head sadly and looked at her watch. "Well, I've gotta go get ready; anything you need before I leave?"

"Can you track Danny down? I need to talk to him; he's probably at the site."

"He went home an hour ago, Tim." Then, pointedly, "It's New Year's Eve; he has plans. Plans that I'm sure he would love to include you in."

Meredith got nowhere with that and left, while Tim spent a

couple of more hours doing work before heading home. He stopped for a take-out pizza, something that had become so routine that he considered it likely that his car would do it on its own if he relinquished the controls.

His apartment felt as barren and unwelcome as always, except for the incredibly soothing presence of Kiley, his golden retriever. It was obvious that Kiley missed Maggie terribly, but she seemed to try and compensate by providing comfort for Tim.

Danny and Will had suggested repeatedly that he move out of this apartment, as a way of putting the memories behind him. He hadn't done so, partially out of a vague feeling that it would be disrespectful to Maggie, as if he were moving on without her. This same feeling had caused him not to change a single thing about the place, not even so much as moving a picture.

He realized that he was living in the past, but the past seemed a hell of a lot better than the present. As far as the future . . . well, he didn't want to go there . . .

Kiley and Tim shared the pizza, though she only liked the crusts. There was very little on television, so he followed his original plan and popped in the *Godfather* DVD. On his large plasma screen, it looked at least as good as it had ever looked in any theater.

Tim had seen these movies so many times that the characters felt like old friends. Even though he didn't want real-life company tonight, he wouldn't have minded if Clemenza came over and made him some pasta, especially if he brought some cannolis with him.

It was getting close to nine o'clock, and Tim was in the process of making his nightly decision as to whether to fall asleep on the couch or trudge into the bedroom, when the doorbell rang. Kiley looked at him from her vantage point on the recliner chair, as puzzled and annoyed by the intrusion as he was.

"This can't be good," he said, and she seemed to nod in agreement.

Tim opened the door, and Danny and Will came barging in. "Happy goddamn New Year," said Danny. "Let's go."

"Go where?" he asked, though he knew exactly where they were talking about.

"Oh, I don't know . . ." Will said, "maybe the same place we go every New Year's Eve. Duuuuuhhhh."

Will and Danny were demonstrating the feigned upbeat attitude they had maintained around Tim since shortly after Maggie's death. They were fully aware that their friend was in agony, and somehow instinctively felt that if they were in an obvious good mood around Tim, it would brighten him up as well.

The fact that it hadn't worked for all these months somehow never led them to a conclusion that their strategy was ineffective. It wasn't that their approach was flawed and didn't work, it was simply that it hadn't worked yet.

Tim knew that Will was talking about a bar in nearby Teaneck called the Purple Rose. It was a place that was always just very comfortable to be at, and they never considered going anywhere else.

Tim had not been back to the Rose since Maggie died, and certainly had no plans to change that anytime soon. "It's not going to happen, guys," he said.

"Tim, here's the deal," Danny said, putting his arm around Tim's shoulder. "You're my partner, and you're my friend, and even though you're a complete pain in the ass, I love you. But tonight you walk into the Rose under your own power, or you get carried in under ours."

"Try and understand this," Tim said. "I don't want to go. It doesn't feel right, not yet, and I don't want to do it."

Danny nodded. "We know that, Tim. And we know how hard it is. But you're not getting there on your own, and tonight's the night we give you a push."

Usually Tim easily fended off these kinds of efforts by his friends, but this time they were coming on more strongly, probably because it was New Year's Eve. He knew that if the roles were reversed he would do the same, since the impulse came from friendship. "Guys, I appreciate this, okay? You think it will make me feel better, but it won't. It really won't."

Will had already nudged himself into the recliner chair with Kiley, and was petting her head. "Maybe you're right," he said. "And if you're miserable, you bail out. Besides, everybody will be so drunk, they won't even know you're there."

"And the French fries," Danny added. "Remember the French fries?"

The Purple Rose had the world's greatest French fries, thin and crisp, a taste Tim wouldn't have minded reconnecting with. "I remember," he said. "And someday in the future I will have them again."

"Tonight," said Danny. "Tonight is the night."

Will came in for what he hoped would be the clincher. "Tim, until now I haven't said this to you, and Danny hasn't either, but it's time to put it out there. Tim, Maggie would want you to do this. She would want you to go out and have some fun."

Tim would ordinarily have rejected that out of hand, but for some reason, this time he thought about it. Tim had recently been thinking about the possibility of spending a night with the guys at the Rose, and he had been annoyed at himself even for the thought.

He also knew that what Will said was the absolute truth; Maggie would want him to go. So maybe now was the time . . .

He finally nodded. "Okay . . . you're right. I'll go." Then he turned to Kiley and said, "Let me know what happens to Luca Brazi."

Danny put his arm on Tim's shoulder. "This is great. And by the way, Will and I talked it over, and since this is your coming-out party . . . you're buying."

The Purple Rose apparently never got the memo that everything had changed since Maggie's death.

At least that's the way it struck Tim. He found it somehow jarring that the place was the same as always, sawdust on the floor, wooden tables carved with every possible initial, a wood-burning fireplace in the center, and at least thirty televisions strategically positioned throughout, usually showing sports. Of course, on New Year's Eve the televisions were tuned to the Times Square holiday festivities, though on a human-per-square-foot basis, the place was every bit as crowded as the streets on which the ball would drop.

Tim, Danny, and Will had their own reserved table, in deference to their years as loyal patrons, and it was there that Tim positioned himself. They ordered food and beer, and while Danny and Will headed off to try their luck with the countless single women milling about, Tim remained behind.

The music from the vintage Wurlitzer jukebox was loud but bearable, but not even if Springsteen showed up to do a live concert would Tim have been glad that he came. He was there for less than a minute when he realized that he simply was not ready for this, and he was more than a little angry with himself for giving in.

He just sat at the table and watched everyone else celebrate having successfully made it through another year, an observer of the human condition from an outsider's perspective.

New Year's Eve had never really been Tim's thing anyway; the revelry had always seemed forced, as if partygoers were trying to live up to a mandate to have a great time. He had often used alcohol in an attempt to overcome his natural reticence, usually with good success, but had no plans to try that technique tonight.

Danny and Will occasionally came by to check on him, and Tim told them without enthusiasm that he was fine. He looked at his watch repeatedly, trying to decide if he should stay until midnight. There was just a half hour left, but it was going to feel like forever.

"Hi. Happy New Year."

Tim looked up and saw an attractive woman standing right in front of him, a pleasant smile revealing perhaps the whitest teeth Tim had ever seen. They actually gave off a glare. "Mind if I sit down?" she asked, but did so without waiting for him to answer.

"Which one of them sent you over?" he asked.

She smiled again, and pointed back into the crowd. "The drunk one in the blue shirt; I think his name is Danny. He said you needed cheering up."

"Trust me, it's not a job you want to tackle."

"What's wrong?" she asked with apparent sincerity.

"I'm sorry. Don't take this the wrong way, but I've never been one for opening up to strangers at bars."

She was undeterred. "I'm not a stranger," she pointed out, holding out her hand. "I'm Janice."

Tim shook her hand. "Hello, Janice. I'm Tim."

"Nice to meet you, Tim. So will you tell me what's wrong?"

"My wife died," Tim said, and immediately regretted it. He mentally berated himself for not making up some other reason for his funk.

"Oh, God, I'm sorry," Janice said. "That must be so hard for you."

"It was harder on her," Tim said, standing up. "Excuse me for a second, will you?"

Tim left the table and headed toward the back of the bar. He wasn't sure where he was going; he just had a need to get away from Janice and her sincerity and her white teeth.

There was a phone booth back near the restrooms, and Tim got in it and closed the door. He leaned his head forward, against the phone, and took deep breaths to try and get control of himself. He felt like he was losing it, hyperventilating, and was scared by the feeling.

Tim had no idea how long he was in there, though it couldn't have been too long, because he didn't hear anyone outside yelling "Happy New Year!" yet. He was slowly getting himself together, feeling better, and thinking that perhaps he should take the phone booth home, since it seemed to have a soothing effect on him.

"You making a call?"

He looked up and saw a heavyset guy with his face pressed close to the glass, fogging it with his breath. He was signaling his desire to use the phone. About to lose his refuge, Tim took a deep breath and opened the door. He wanted to say, "Why don't you get yourself a goddamn cell phone?" but instead quietly got up and let the intruder take his place.

Tim headed back into the main room and saw Will standing near the bar, his left arm around a woman and his right arm around a beer. He made his way over to him. "I'm going to take off, Will."

Will looked at his watch. "It's five of. Just give it ten minutes, okay? Start the New Year with friends."

Tim felt wiped out, too much so to even argue. Ten minutes was not the end of the world; it just seemed like it. "Okay. I'll be at the bar."

He found a place at the end of the bar to wait out the time, alone in a room full of people. Unfortunately, this solitude lasted less than a minute, when a man came over to him. He was probably forty, tall and good-looking, with one of those square jaws that projected authority. Tim had no way of knowing that his face was altered by a heavy prosthetic makeup, the kind they use in the movies, and that he was wearing a wig of a different style and color from his normal hair.

He was dressed in a suit, with his tie loosened at the neck, as if he had just gotten off from work and stopped by for a drink. Except in this case it was many drinks, because the man was clearly very drunk. As he held out his hand to say hello, Tim thought that if he didn't take it, the man could conceivably fall over.

"Hey, how's it goin'? Name's Jeff. Jeff Cashman."

Tim tried to make his response as unenthusiastic as possible, in the hope that it might deter him, though Cashman was in no condition to detect subtlety. "Tim," he said.

"Good to meet ya, Timmy. Happy goddamn New Year."

"You too."

Tim hoped that Cashman would move on to meet other new friends, but instead he leaned in toward Tim. "You a good guy?"

Tim didn't answer, and looked up at the closest television as if he couldn't hear him. They seemed to be ready to drop the ball on the freezing Times Square crowd. Unfortunately, when Tim looked back, Cashman was still there.

"Hey, Timmy," he said again, "you a good guy?"

Tim nodded with resignation; these ten minutes were going to be even longer than he feared. "Yeah."

"Can you keep a secret? A really big one?"

"No . . . I think you should tell someone else."

"No, I wanna tell you. I wanna tell someone this year." He looked at his watch, exaggeratedly, as if to make sure it was still this year. "So I gotta hurry."

"Look, Jeff, I'm not the guy you—"

Cashman interrupted him. "You know where Kinnelon is?" When Tim didn't answer, he took it as a sign that he couldn't be heard over the din. He shouted, "Kinnelon! You know where it is?"

Tim was well aware that Kinnelon is a town in northwest Jersey, about thirty miles from where they were standing. "Yes, but—"

He interrupted Tim again. "I murdered somebody there. A girl . . . three months ago."

"That's not funny," Tim said.

Cashman nodded, as if he could see that truth through his alcohol-induced haze. "No, it's not funny," he said. "It's definitely not funny."

Then he paused, as if reconsidering. "Well, it's sorta funny. Before I killed her, I cut off her middle finger. Her fuck-you finger. Then I buried her behind the swing set at this little park they have on Maple Ave."

Cashman had finally accomplished what no one else had been able to. He had cut through Tim's funk and pissed him off. "What the hell is the matter with you?" he asked.

All Cashman did was laugh. "Nothing. Not any more. I actually feel much better now. Now it's your problem."

Suddenly the entire place was counting down, and the televisions confirmed that the ball was dropping. "TEN . . . NINE . . . EIGHT . . . SEVEN . . . SIX . . . FIVE . . . FOUR . . . THREE . . . TWO . . . ONE . . . HAPPY NEW YEAR!"

Everybody in the place started screaming and hugging and kissing each other. Everybody except Cashman and Tim. Cashman finally got up to leave, but put his finger to his mouth in a signal that Tim should keep quiet. "This is our secret, okay, Timmy?" he asked. "Don't tell a soul."

He laughed again as he walked away, but it was a silent laugh, drowned out by the noise of all the normal people having fun.

"Trust me, I freaked him out...totally freaked him out,"

said the man who twenty minutes before had pretended to be Jeff Cashman. He was talking to his employer for the evening.

The employer laughed. "But he believed you?"

"Damn straight. You should have seen his face."

"I wish I had . . . it must have been great." He laughed again, vicariously enjoying the moment.

They were talking at a rest stop near exit 156 on the Garden State Parkway. They stood next to their cars, about fifty yards from the highway, close enough to hear the cars whizzing by them.

"Cashman" could see there was someone in the passenger seat of the employer's car. It looked like a woman, but it was dark and hard to tell for sure. Other than that they were alone, because at that hour, and with the temperature down near fifteen degrees, nobody else seemed inclined to stop to rest.

"It was," "Cashman" agreed, wrapping his arms around himself to ward off the cold. He wished he had actually been drunk, rather than faking it. He'd be a lot warmer now.

"Was he scared?" the employer asked. "Or annoyed?"

"Cashman" was freezing and not terribly in the mood to chat much more. This was supposed to be a fifteen-minute job. "Scared . . . freaked out. I don't know what you have planned for him, but this part of it worked."

"That's great. Nice work."

"It'll be nice to get home and get this shit off my face," he said.

"I can imagine."

Cashman nodded, anxious to wrap this up. "Yeah. So if you'll give me my money . . ."

"In the trunk."

"What do you mean? Cash? You could have given me a check."

"Sorry, I'm not being clear," the employer said, seemingly amused over the misunderstanding. "There is no money. I want you to get in the trunk. Now."

"What are you talking about?" Cashman asked.

This time the man's voice took on a slightly harder edge. "That time I *was* clear, but you're being difficult. I want you to get in the trunk."

"Come on, what's going on here?" asked Cashman, unable to keep fear from creeping into his voice. "Quit joking around."

"In the time you've known me, have I ever joked around?" Not waiting for an answer, he continued, in a matter-of-fact tone of voice, "Now, I want to kill you while you're in the trunk. Otherwise I have to do it out here, and then lift you in. That shouldn't be so hard for you to understand."

"Cashman" started to respond, but panicked and turned to run. He made it about a foot and a half before what felt like a clamp grabbed his neck from behind.

The last thing he felt was not pain, but an overwhelming fear from the knowledge that what grabbed him was not a steel clamp, but an incredibly powerful hand.

And the last thing he heard was the snapping of his own neck.

Once the body was wrapped in plastic and put in the trunk, the man took out his cell phone. He would have preferred to make the call from the warmth of the car, but he didn't want the woman to hear what he had to say. If she did, he'd have to kill her sooner than he planned.

He dialed the number he was given, fully aware that the man

who answered could at that moment be anywhere in the world. Washington, London, Monte Carlo . . . there would be no way to tell.

"Talk to me," was how the phone was answered.

"Our friend did what he was supposed to do. The message has been delivered."

"Good. And where is our friend now?"

"We won't be hearing from him again."

"You are as good as advertised. Maintain your high standard."

Click.

The man put away his cell phone and smiled to himself. It wouldn't be long before he too was rich enough to be anywhere in the world, doing anything he wanted, at any time.

Not long at all.

If the night out was meant to ease
Tim's entry back into the world,

it didn't quite go according to plan. It was a completely uncomfortable experience, capped off by an encounter with a raving lunatic.

At least Tim hoped he was a raving lunatic, because the alternative was that he was a brutal killer. He didn't look like the killer type, but then again Tim had never really met one in the flesh.

Tim had turned his phone ringer off when he got home, and in the morning he saw that the message light was flashing. That light represented the outside world, so he showered, dressed, and had breakfast before reluctantly pressing the button.

It was Will, saying, "Hey, Tim, I hope last night wasn't too painful. Danny and I are going down to the Rose to watch the Bowl games. How 'bout meeting us down there? Just beer, burgers, and football; I promise."

Spending New Year's Day watching the games was another tradition that Danny, Will, and Tim observed religiously, and Maggie was there last year as well. They would bet on the games among themselves, and Maggie, with no football knowledge to speak of, had an interesting way of picking her teams. She researched which football program had the best graduation rates, and her bet on them would reflect her support for education. Suffice it to say that education and football prowess did not often go hand in hand.

Tim hadn't been following football much during the year,

probably just a reflection of his general malaise. He certainly had no desire to go back to the Purple Rose, at least not in this decade, so if he was going to watch any football, it would be at home.

Tim took a few minutes to Google the terms "Sheila," "murder," "missing person," and "Kinnelon" in various combinations, and came up empty. This was probably more reassuring to him than it should have been; like many other people, Tim had come to believe that if something wasn't on Google, it didn't exist. Having performed that cursory investigation, he turned off the computer, put Kiley in the car, and drove to the dog park.

Dog parks are a creative invention of the late twentieth century, which basically provide dog parents a chance to arrange a mass canine play date. They are usually a very large enclosed area in which dogs run and play together, off leash. Their human owners, mostly female, stand off to the side and talk primarily about their dogs. Occasionally tennis balls are thrown, creating an absolute frenzy.

Not all dogs like it, and Tim suspected that Kiley had mixed feelings. She had always seemed reserved in her enthusiasm, not joining in with the main crowd, but occasionally sniffing and being sniffed by certain dogs that she knew and liked.

Maggie and Tim used to come here every Sunday morning, and it was one of the few things that they did together that he continued. It just didn't seem fair to Kiley to deprive her of enjoyment and exercise, so he took her there whenever he could, which was every Sunday.

When Maggie was there, she did most of the socializing with the other humans, and Tim became the designated tennis ball thrower. There were a few people he spoke to regularly, one of whom was Eden Alexander, a woman two years younger than him.

As always, Eden was there when Tim and Kiley arrived, and she greeted them with her ever-present smile. Tim had a tendency to think that people who were relentlessly upbeat were probably not all that bright, but Maggie told him once that Eden had a Ph.D. in art history from Stanford. If so, she was certainly one of very few

Stanford Ph.D.s who always wore a Mets cap with a blond ponytail pushing through the opening in the back.

Kiley made no secret of her friendship with Eden's German shepherd, Travis. Her tail started wagging the moment she saw him, a certain indicator of affection. Human smiles and apparent warmth can be insincere, but Kiley's tail-wag could be taken to the bank.

When Eden saw him he separated from the group of eight women she was standing with. "What are you doing here?" she asked.

Tim had no idea why she should be surprised at seeing him there, since he was certainly a regular. "I come here every Sunday," he pointed out.

She looked puzzled. "But isn't this New Year's, male, sit on the couch, drink beer, watch football, and fart day?"

He snapped his fingers. "Damn, I completely forgot."

She laughed. "There might be hope for you yet."

Eden had been helpful to Tim in the weeks after Maggie's death. She came by his apartment occasionally, just to say hello and ask if he needed anything. He was almost obsessive in not letting friends help in any way, yet he'd let Eden take Kiley to the park a few times. She was there without being intrusive, and when it comes to providing comfort, Tim quickly learned that was a talent not to be taken lightly.

Since Tim had been coming to the dog park without Maggie, he hadn't felt particularly comfortable. He was aware that his reluctance to socialize and converse came off as more aloof and unfriendly without Maggie's amiability to provide cover. He hadn't lost his skill as a tennis ball thrower, but it somehow now seemed more one-dimensional.

"Really cold today, huh?" he asked.

Eden did a double take. "Wait a minute . . . was that . . . was that chitchat?" she asked, exaggerating her surprise.

"I'm making conversation. It's a New Year's resolution."

"No, that wasn't conversation," she said. "That was chitchat.

And since I've never heard you chitchat before, there must be something going on."

"Nothing's going on."

She didn't believe him. "Come on, you can talk to Auntie Eden."

For some reason that he couldn't identify, he did feel able to talk to her. "Something weird happened last night," he said. "Actually, a step beyond weird."

"You mean besides my date?"

"I went to the Purple Rose with some friends . . ."

She nodded her approval. "Good. Did you have fun?"

He shook his head. "Not even a little . . . but I didn't expect to. What was a surprise happened just before midnight. Some guy I never met before told me he committed a murder three months ago."

"Oh, my God!" She said this a little more loudly than she would have liked, and a few of the women looked over. Eden smiled at them and lowered her voice as she talked to Tim. "Just like that?"

Tim nodded. "Just like that. He asked if I could keep a secret, and then told me about it. Like he was getting it off his chest and onto mine."

"Was he drunk?" she asked, lightly taking his arm to move him away from the women, two of whom appeared to be trying to eavesdrop on them.

"Very."

"Then maybe it was the alcohol talking."

"I hope so."

"Did he tell you who the victim was?"

"He said her name was Sheila, and that he killed her in Kinnelon. I'll spare you the gruesome details."

Eden thought about it for a few moments, weighing the possibilities. This was not an area in which she had a great deal of expertise. "You think he could have been telling the truth?"

Tim shrugged. "I doubt it, but obviously I can't be sure. I Googled it, but didn't find anything."

"Are you going to go to the police?" she asked. "Just in case?"

"I don't know; it's probably just a drunk in a bar spouting bull-shit. I was thinking I could check a little more on my own. Maybe drive out there."

"Today?"

"I guess so. I haven't really thought it through."

She seemed dubious. "You're going to go try and dig up a body?"

"You think I'm nuts?" he asked.

She smiled. "Pretty much; just be careful. Hey, why don't you leave Kiley with me? She'll have a great time with Travis."

It was a good idea, and Tim accepted the offer. Eden said that they could meet back at the dog park at four o'clock, and promised that Kiley would have a wonderful day.

While Tim went looking for a body.

Kinnelon is in the most rustic part of New Jersey.

It's an affluent residential community that borders the state's ski resorts, and is particularly beautiful in the winter, with snow everywhere except on the well-plowed roads. It is snow that remains white, as opposed to city snow, which almost immediately turns grey, and then black. Tim knew it to be an immutable law of meteorology that the length of time snow stays white is directly proportional to the distance it falls from an urban area.

As a teenager, Tim used to ski at Great Gorge, about twenty minutes down the road, but the years had eroded whatever familiarity he had with the area. Fortunately, he had a GPS satellite navigation system in his car, and he set it for Maple Avenue in Kinnelon, without providing a street number. He figured he'd just drive along Maple looking for a park with a swing set, and maybe a headstone that said HERE LIES SHEILA. MURDERED BY CASHMAN. That was pretty much the extent of his plan.

The route took him through the center of the quaint town, which while never bustling, was particularly quiet on the holiday. He saw that there were two cars parked in front of the small town hall, and decided to park, just in case anybody was there.

He was surprised to find the front door open, having expected that it would be closed for the holiday. There was a woman sitting at the general information desk across the large room. She was at least in her mid-seventies, and probably hadn't been out partying the night before.

Tim walked over to her, self-conscious that his sneakers squeaked on the spotless wood floors, a noise accentuated by the otherwise totally silent surroundings. She watched him every step of the way, perched on a high chair behind the elevated desk, as if she were looking down on her kingdom. She did not greet him, instead waited for him to state his business.

"Hello . . . Happy New Year."

She nodded slightly, which he took as a major concession.

Tim continued, "I was wondering if you had any information on missing persons in this area within the last six months, actually in Kinnelon itself."

She looked at him as if he were insane. "We don't keep records like that here, young man. That would be a police matter."

"Right. Of course. I understand that, but I'm just doing some research on small-town crime, and I wouldn't want to bother them."

"But you were willing to bother me?"

It annoyed Tim that he found this little, old, and obnoxious lady intimidating. "I'm sorry about that. I didn't even think you were open on the holiday."

"I've worked every holiday for forty-five years."

"Very admirable . . . thank you. Have a good day."

He started to leave, and then stopped. "The thing is, I'm not asking for official information, but are you yourself aware of a young woman that might be missing in this area, or perhaps a recent murder?"

She huffed, as though he had insulted her personally. "I should say not."

Tim smiled pleasantly and left, actually feeling that even while being rebuffed he had learned something. If there was a recent missing person or murder in this town, he was quite sure that this woman would know about it.

Tim got back in his car and drove slowly along Maple Avenue, looking for a park with a swing set. He only had to go about four blocks before he saw the place; it was across the street from a grammar school, and took up a full square block. The swing sets and other similar equipment were set up all the way on the other side from where Tim was.

Tim drove around to get closer to it, and parked the car. The entire park was snow covered, and it was cold enough that the snow barely showed indentations when he stepped on it. It had been there a while, at least a few weeks, and would likely remain until April.

There were five kids, bundled up in ski jackets, playing on the swing set. Four women stood nearby, talking to each other while casting wary glances at Tim and then their children. It struck Tim as a dog park for humans, absent the tennis balls, biscuits, and barking.

Tim could see where his presence would cause the women alarm, so he smiled and gave them a little wave. They neither smiled nor waved back.

Tim walked behind the swing set, therefore near the kids, and he could literally see the women's alarm levels elevate. They all walked closer to the swing set in a protective maneuver, a synchronized movement that Tim thought made them look like bundled, frozen Rockettes.

"I dropped something around here . . . I figured maybe I'd come and look for it," he said lamely, but it seemed to have no effect. These women were at Defcon 4, heading for 5, and he was the suspected enemy missile.

Actually, there was no need for him to be there at all. It wasn't like he was really going to take an ice pick and shovel out of his car and dig up the area. In the unlikely event that there was a woman buried under the ground, there was no way for Tim to know where.

He stared at the ground for a minute or so, then got in his car and drove back home, thankful that no one he knew had witnessed his investigative prowess in action. The only one who was even aware he was going there was Eden, and his plan was to give her a recounting that would make it sound less pathetic than it really was.

He drove back to the dog park, where Eden was waiting for him. "So?" she asked.

"So, what?"

"Was there a murder or wasn't there?"

Tim proceeded to tell her the events of the day, leaving out the part about the women staring at him in horror, as that didn't seem terribly integral to the story.

"So what do your instincts tell you?" she asked, after he finished.

"That a drunken asshole sent me on a wild-goose chase, and I wasted a day in the process."

"You don't think you should at least tell the police, so you can put it behind you for sure?"

He knew that he probably should do exactly that, but didn't want to. "If I thought there really was a Sheila . . . but there's no evidence of any kind that Cashman was telling the truth."

"Except for the fact that there is a park with a swing set on Maple Avenue in Kinnelon."

She was right, of course. While Cashman's identifying a real place proved nothing, it did add at least something to his credibility.

He felt a need to defend his reluctance to bring the story to the police. "My recent experience with law enforcement was not the most pleasant."

Eden knew at least some of his dealings with the police after Maggie's death, and their clear suspicion of him, so she didn't press the issue.

"You'll make the right decision," she said, then smiled. "Or maybe you won't."

Tim's leaving for work in the morning
was delayed five minutes

by the standard, end-of-the-weekend phone call from his aunt
Joyce. His mother's only sibling, Joyce had long ago assumed the
role of official worrier about his welfare, a job that had taken on a
far greater importance after Maggie's death.

As always, the conversation consisted of meaningless and not
very revealing chitchat about how their weekends went before she
got to the key question.

"So, did you meet anyone?"

He used to fend off the question with a joke about meeting
the mailman or some golfing buddy, as if not understanding what
she meant. But he soon grew tired of that; it took too long and it
didn't dissuade her from asking the same question over and over
again.

"No."

"So you're not dating at all?"

"No." Aunt Joyce could not stand his being in pain, and she had
latched on to his dating as a potential cure. "I'm not dating," he
continued. "This is the nondating, working phase of my life."

"I'm sorry . . . I hate to be an interfering aunt. But this is not
healthy."

"It's very healthy," he said. "Actually, these days dating is not
healthy. People who don't date live to a hundred and eighty." Tim

wanted to make her happy, to say something to convince her that he was doing well, at least by her standards. But that would necessarily entail having a girlfriend, or better yet, a fiancée. At one point he considered creating a fake girlfriend to tell her about, but then he'd have to spend the rest of his life avoiding dinner invitations on behalf of the happy couple.

He finally managed to extricate himself from the call and left. He was only five feet out the front door when he saw it, stapled eye-level to a telephone pole.

It was a missing persons flyer, with a picture of a young woman, identified on the flyer as Sheila Blair. It said that she had been missing for three months, and was last seen in the Kinnelon area. Anyone with information was to contact the state police.

It had to be Cashman's Sheila, Tim knew. There are no coincidences that enormous.

Tim took down the flyer and put it in his briefcase to take to work with him. Danny had beaten him in, a phenomenon that only happened on days that his aunt called and delayed his departure.

Tim brought him up to date on his weird conversation with Cashman, and his resulting fruitless trip out to Kinnelon.

"So you think it was bullshit?" Danny asked.

"I did until this morning. Then I found this." He took out the flyer and put it on the desk. "It was tacked on to a telephone pole in front of my apartment."

"That's her?" Danny asked.

"It sure fits. He didn't give me her last name, but the first name, and the time, and Kinnelon . . . how could it not be her?"

"You've got to talk to the cops about this," he said.

Tim nodded. "I know; I'm dreading it."

"It doesn't have to be Novack. There are other cops in the world."

"Yeah," Tim said. Danny knew all about Novack, the cop with the Javert-like, relentless certainty that Tim was Maggie's murderer. In the months since, Novack had called Tim occasionally, to ask about some innocuous detail of that awful day. It was his way of telling him that he was still on the case, and therefore Tim had not gotten away with his crime.

"You want me to go with you?"

Tim shook his head. "No . . . I'm just going to go and get it over with."

He decided to avoid any chance of dealing with Novack by going to the local Fort Lee police precinct. A nondescript building in the center of town, which looked like it could have been a small library, except it would be unusual to find ten police cars parked in a library lot.

Tim approached the desk sergeant and told him that he had information about a possible murder. This is not the everyday Fort Lee occurrence, and Tim was immediately whisked in to see Detective Joanie Patrick, an attractive, petite woman about thirty years old. If you gave Tim five hundred guesses as to her occupation, homicide detective wouldn't be on his list.

Tim had spent more time than he cared to in police stations, and had never been in a conversation with a detective that couldn't be heard by other detectives sitting nearby. It was always disconcerting; Tim never knew whether to talk softly and try to keep it private, or loudly and let everybody in on it. This time he went with softly.

He told Detective Patrick the story in pretty much the same fashion he had told it to Eden and Danny, concluding with the flyer. She was quiet and mostly expressionless throughout, though Tim thought he detected a lip curl of disapproval when he mentioned going out to Kinnelon.

When he finished, she asked, "Could you identify Jeff Cashman if you saw him again?"

He nodded. "Definitely."

"But you never met him before?"

"If I did, I certainly don't remember it."

"Your wife never mentioned him?"

The question hit him like a punch in the gut. She knew who Tim was, had known it all along, and she was already considering the possibility that this new situation was somehow related to Maggie's death. Tim tried to make his voice as cold as possible, which was easy considering how he was feeling. "No, my wife never mentioned him. Are we finished here?"

She let him go after finding out how to reach him if she had further questions.

"What are you going to do about this?" Tim asked.

"We'll contact you if we need you," said Patrick dismissively.

He could have kept asking questions, but she was not going to tell him anything, and the truth was he really didn't want to hear about it anyway. He had done what he was supposed to do. He had told the authorities about it, and now it was their problem. Cashman had gotten it off his chest, and now Tim had as well.

The van was a three-year-old Chevy Caravan,

and it looked exactly like tens of thousands of others on the road every day. Like everything else involved in this process, that was by design. Nothing would be done to attract attention, or stand out in any way.

The drive up from Florida had so far taken three days. Ricardo Vasquez had been instructed not to exceed sixty-five miles per hour, and to obey every traffic law to the letter. He was not about to disobey; the downside of being stopped by the police would be a hell of a lot worse than a traffic ticket.

On the New Jersey Turnpike, sixty-five seemed like walking. Ricardo stayed in the right lane and watched the world whiz by him. That's okay, he thought. He would take the money he'd get for this trip and buy a Porsche, and then they could eat his dust.

Until then he would be very careful, just like he had been so far. Only Lucia had any idea where he was, and she wasn't nearly smart enough to know what he was doing. And she wouldn't tell anybody anyway; she knew what he would do to her if she did.

Lucia was going to be out of his life soon anyway. Ricardo would be able to afford much classier women, women he could show off. The only thing he'd lacked in the past was money, and in a few days that just wasn't going to be a problem.

Ricardo had been on the road since seven o'clock in the morning, and hadn't had breakfast before he left. As it was approaching eleven o'clock, he was starving.

His instructions were very specific; he was to get all his meals at the fast food places along the highway, and eat them in the car. Until this point he had done exactly that, but he was getting sick of it. He wasn't looking for anything fancy, maybe just some blueberry pancakes, with sides of bacon and hash browns thrown in. And hopefully some coffee that didn't come in one of those damn Styrofoam cups.

Ricardo figured that it shouldn't be too hard to locate a diner capable of satisfying his needs, so he got off the highway near a town called Cedar Grove. Sure enough, he found a perfect place within five minutes. It was called Grandma Patty's Pancake House, and as he parked the van, Ricardo hoped that Grandma Patty had been up all night cooking.

Ricardo didn't bother to look around when he got out of the car. Even if he had, he would not have noticed the grey minivan that had been following him since he entered New Jersey. Ricardo did not know about it, just as he didn't know about the GPS transponder on the bottom of the car, which made following at a safe distance easy.

Ricardo did make sure the van was entirely locked before going inside. This seemed like a sleepy little town, but he imagined its citizens would wake up pretty quickly if they learned that there were filled barrels of illegal drugs worth many millions of dollars sitting outside Grandma Patty's.

Patty proved to be a disappointment. The portions were large, but generally tasteless and greasy. The blueberries were not even mixed in the pancakes, as he liked them, but rather dumped on top. Ricardo would have complained, he would have told Grandma Patty what she could do with her blueberries, but he was not about to draw attention to himself. He even left a standard tip, though it bothered him to do so.

Annoyed with himself that he had wasted time, Ricardo got back in the van and pulled out onto the road. He did so quickly, without really looking, without seeing the teenaged boy stepping out into the crosswalk with his five-year-old brother.

He felt the thud before he realized what had happened, and watched in horror as the little boy was thrown off the fender onto the grass along the side of the road. The teenager didn't seem to be hurt, only shocked, and his first instinct was to run to his brother, lying dazed in the grass.

Ricardo had only a moment to decide what to do. To stop and get out was to invite disaster; the cops would find out that the van was stolen, and would then impound and examine it. Ricardo would be finished. To take off was his only chance, and a quick glance did not seem to reveal any bystanders who had witnessed the accident. Even if they did, and got his license number, he'd be okay. The van had fake Florida plates, and he would just steal new ones at the next rest stop.

So his decision was an easy one, no matter how it turned out. And within a minute, it was obvious that it was not turning out well. He heard the siren before he saw the police car in his rearview mirror. The van was not about to outrun it, especially in its loaded-down condition, but Ricardo hoped that the equalizer would be his prowess as a driver. He sure as hell was better than any small-town cop.

Ricardo did not head back for the turnpike; that would draw in the state police and choppers, ending any chance for a successful escape. Instead he wanted to make it through the town and out onto the back roads, where the playing field might be more in his favor.

He was nearing eighty miles an hour when he reached into the glove compartment and took out the .44 Magnum. This cop probably thought he was dealing with some young idiot who panicked when he hit the kid. If it came to it, he wouldn't be ready for what Ricardo had in store for him.

The sound of the siren was getting louder, and Ricardo realized with some concern that this was due to an additional police car entering the chase. They were coming at him from different directions, closing on him in a sort of pincer movement designed to cut off any chance of escape.

Ricardo almost relished the moment. He had been getting out of close shaves all his life, and it had taught him not to panic, but rather to wait for the opportunity when it presented itself. This situation was not different, and his senses were keenly tuned, waiting for his chance as he flew down the streets.

Suddenly, as the cars were closing in, he saw it. It was a narrow alley that could get him out of the vise he found himself in. If he could get to it, there seemed a chance he could leave the pursuers behind, since they did not have the advantageous angle that he did.

Ricardo went for it, hitting the brakes and taking the turn on two wheels. He made it into the opening in what could only be described as a brilliant piece of driving. He actually smiled at the realization that the only people in position to appreciate the maneuver were the cops left behind by it. Too bad they would never get to meet him and offer their congratulations.

Ricardo headed back toward the turnpike, driving quickly but not so fast as to attract renewed attention. It was no more than a few minutes away, and he was confident that once he got there, he'd be home free.

The first bullet, the one that missed, ripped through the base of his neck and severed his spinal column. For all intents and purposes, he was dead by the time the second bullet tore through the back of the van.

Ricardo was obviously not able to witness the resulting explosion. He was therefore not aware that it was powerful enough to level half a city block, and blow out windows in a paper factory three blocks away. He was also not aware that the plan was for him not to make it to New York alive anyway, and that the chase only hastened his demise by less than an hour.

The timing and manner of Ricardo's death also prevented him from having the surprise of his life, which would have been the discovery that the size of the explosion meant that what he was carrying in the van wasn't drugs at all.

For Jonathon Novack, the phone call was
the best Christmas present he had gotten. Ever.

It was far too soon to know how the bizarre trip to the Fort Lee police by Tim Wallace fit into his wife's murder, but it certainly had to
be connected. And whatever this latest twist was, Novack was going
to use it to nail Tim's ass to the wall.

Novack was at his ex-wife's house in Fair Lawn when he got the
call from Lieutenant Patrick. Cindy had divorced him three years
ago, but in some bizarre way the divorce hadn't taken. Novack was
simply not willing to give her up, and even though he had moved
out, he still came around every chance he could.

Cindy had initially viewed this as a significant problem. For
one thing, potential suitors were less likely to visit knowing that her
six-foot-three detective ex-husband was on guard. It just was not
what Cindy had envisioned when she got the divorce; her expectation was that she would no longer be married.

Over time Cindy had gotten used to the arrangement. Novack,
which was how she and everybody else referred to him, could still
be a major pain in the ass, but he was at least more attentive in this
new arrangement. He also had his own apartment, so she could
more easily throw him out of the house than when he lived there.

Back when she thought she had secured a real-life divorce,
Cindy had finished her master's in speech therapy and had gotten a
job in the local school system. She also started an after-school

private practice so that she could better support herself. She became quite successful, but never shared with Novack that she was making more money than he was. His ego would have had a tough time handling it.

Even the sex, while never a problem between them, had actually gotten better since their split. So all in all, the divorce had done quite a bit for their marriage, and Cindy could see no reason not to recommend it to other married couples.

Within thirty seconds of getting the news about Tim, Novack was in the car and on the way to pick up his partner, Detective James Anders. Anders had only been partnered with Novack for four months, and therefore hadn't been involved with the Wallace case. But he sure as hell had heard about it; Novack saw to that.

Over the years, Novack had never actually liked any of his partners, but Anders had an easygoing style that was close to acceptable. For Anders, things had been slightly more difficult. Soon after coming to the department, he had had an emergency appendectomy, and when he returned he inadvertently left a copy of his medical records on his desk . . . the desk that he shared with Novack.

Novack had accidentally read every word of the file, and saw the notation that said Anders had been born with only one testicle. Somehow that tidbit of information then found its way into an e-mail to the entire department. It resulted in Anders's acquiring the nickname "One Ball," and in his swearing to exact revenge on Novack if it took him the rest of his life.

Novack and Anders immediately went to Tim's office, and since Meredith said he was out to lunch, they decided to wait. Meredith was not happy about this, knowing that Tim would be upset, but there was nothing she could do about it.

Tim was in fact not at all surprised to find them there when he arrived. "That was quick," he said.

"You were expecting us?" Novack asked.

"Yeah, you could say that."

Novack introduced Anders, and Tim brought them both back

to his office so that they could speak privately. "You want something to drink?" Tim asked.

"What have you got?" Novack asked.

"Mineral water."

"What is that . . . like . . . water with minerals in it?"

"Right."

"Sounds great, but we'll pass," Novack said. "So tell us all about this Cashman guy."

It was a story Tim was getting tired of telling, but he went through it one more time. Neither Novack nor Anders interrupted, just as Lieutenant Patrick hadn't. Tim chalked that up to a police listening technique.

When he finished, Novack asked, "And you're sure you never met him before?"

"As sure as I can be. And I haven't seen him since that night."

"So he comes up to a perfect stranger and confesses to a murder."

"Apparently so."

"Any idea why he would do that?" Novack asked.

"He said it was his way of getting it off his chest. He said that now it's my problem, which I'm starting to believe is the truth."

"Tell me about the flyer," he said.

"I left it with Lieutenant Patrick."

"I don't mean what it looked like. Where did you find it?"

"I told you . . . on a telephone pole in front of my apartment."

"Right," Novack said. "Had you seen it there before?"

"Not that I remember. But I would have more reason to notice it after hearing what Cashman had to say."

"Have you seen others, or just that one?"

"Just that one." Even as Tim said this, he knew how ridiculous it sounded. The only flyer for the murder Cashman had told him about happened to appear in front of his apartment. "Look—"

Novack interrupted him. "Did you see any of the flyers in Kinnelon when you were there?"

"No, but—"

"So somebody in Kinnelon goes missing, they wait three months, print one flyer, and post it thirty miles away in front of your apartment?"

"Maybe they printed ten thousand flyers and posted it everywhere; I don't know. Maybe Cashman posted the one I saw; maybe he didn't. Why don't you catch the slime ball and ask him?"

"You seem nervous," Novack said.

"I'm not nervous; I'm annoyed. I did what I was supposed to do and reported this. You can do with it whatever you want."

"And we appreciate your cooperation," Novack lied. "And right now I'd like you to come with us. You don't have to, but it would be helpful if you did."

"Where to?" Tim asked, though there was no answer that could please him.

"Kinnelon. To look for Sheila."

"What do you need me for? I've told you everything I know."

Novack shrugged. "Maybe you'll think of something else when we're there."

The drive in Novack's car out to Kinnelon was a very uncomfortable one for Tim. He couldn't see how he could be of any real value to them once they got there; they could find the park and swing set as easily as he did. Tim assumed they had to be harboring the ridiculous hope that he'd somehow trip up, make a mistake, and in the process reveal himself to be a murderer.

Anders drove and Novack sat in the passenger seat, with Tim in the back. They didn't ask him for any directions, just drove directly to the park, further proving that they were not seeking any help from him whatsoever.

Other than the fact that it was still snow covered, the park looked nothing like it did the last time Tim was there. Replacing the women and their kids were six police cars, at least fifteen officers, and some digging equipment. Since it had only been about five hours since Tim told his story to Lieutenant Patrick, it was an impressive mobilization.

Novack directed Tim to stay nearby, and he and Anders headed

for Sergeant Conway of the Kinnelon police. They did not introduce Tim, nor did anyone acknowledge him.

Conway was not happy to be there, which was understandable,
since the temperature was hovering in the mid-teens. "I'm Conway," he said. "You're late."

"That's because we drove all the way here from civilization,"
Novack said. He motioned toward the activity behind the swing
set. "Find anything?"

Conway shook his head. "No, but then again there's nothing to
find. Nobody's heard of this woman, and it's sure as shit that nobody reported her missing. And there's not a damn flyer within fifty
miles."

They started walking toward the swing set, and Tim followed
along. "Is this the only swing set around here?" Anders asked.

Conway nodded. "It is, but we can dig up the entire town if
you'd like."

"You think we shouldn't have called you?" Novack asked.

Conway shrugged his response. "We're small-town . . . we
don't think. We just keep our shovels ready and start digging when
and where you big-city guys tell us."

Novack nodded. "And don't think we don't appreciate it."

They all stood off to the side, about twenty feet from where the
digging was going on, trying to keep warm. After about thirty minutes, none of them had any feeling in their extremities.

"Sergeant . . . over here." It was one of the diggers calling to
Conway, and there was an urgency to his voice. Conway, Novack,
Anders, and Tim hobbled over on frozen feet to see what might be
going on.

When they got there, one of the officers didn't say anything,
just pointed down into the ditch.

It was the skeletal remains of a hand, pointing up out of the
frozen ground, the middle finger missing.

"Holy shit," said Novack.

The discovery of the body immediately
turned the park into a crime scene.

Anders led Tim away and into the back of the car, where he was
forced to wait almost two hours by himself. The situation was not
without its upside; Anders left the car running and the heat on. The
downside was that it was boring as hell, and Tim did not get to see
what was going on, or hear what was being said.

Novack and Anders finally came back to the car, and began the
drive back. They weren't saying anything to each other, and certainly not to Tim.

"Did you learn anything?" Tim asked.

Novack nodded. "Sure did. Every day is a learning experience."

Tim was all too aware he was going to get nothing from Novack. "Okay . . . my car is at the station house. If you need my help
again, call me."

Novack's response was immediate. "We need your help again."

When they got back to the station house, Novack brought Tim
to the office of Sergeant Robert Taveras, the sketch artist for the
department. Taveras's office, no more than eight by ten, was set up
like an artist's studio, but rather than have a chair behind a desk, his
was facing an easel.

Taveras had an easygoing way about him, and went to some
lengths to get Tim to remain calm. "I want you to tell me everything you remember about Cashman's face, but don't try too

hard . . . don't try to push it. Just relax and remember him natu-rally, as you would anyone else."

Tim had always been very visual and attentive to detail; it was one of the reasons he trained as an architect before moving into the construction end of things. He directed Taveras confidently and expertly, and a likeness of Cashman immediately started to take shape.

"Jesus Christ," Taveras said, impressed by Tim's direction. "Have you done this before?"

Tim shook his head. "First time. Square off the chin a little bit . . . not too much."

Taveras did as he was told, then asked, "Like that?"

"Almost," Tim said. "Can I show you?"

Taveras gave him the pencil, and Tim made a slight adjustment in the chin before handing it back. "That's it, except the cheeks were a little fuller."

Taveras did a little work on the cheeks, and then stepped back so Tim could get a head-on look. As far as he was concerned, he was looking at Jeff Cashman. Obviously, he had no way of knowing that the likeness was of the makeup- and wig-altered version of Cashman, since that was all that he had seen.

"That's him."

"You sure?" Taveras asked.

"Well, I only met him once, but I don't think you could get a much better likeness with a photograph. It gives me the creeps all over again just to look at him."

Taveras sprayed the canvas to prevent it from smearing, and then picked up the phone and called Novack, who came right in. "So, how's it going?" Novack asked.

"We need more witnesses like this guy," Taveras said.

Novack looked at the drawing. "So that's your Jeff Cashman?"

Tim didn't like Novack's use of the word "your." It implied that Cashman was Tim's creation. "That's Jeff Cashman."

Novack turned to Taveras. "Okay, let's get it copied."

"Will do."

"Can I go home now?" Tim asked Novack. "Do you need me any more?"

"Are you planning any trips?"

The question, like pretty much everything Novack said, got under Tim's skin. "What if I was?"

"Then I would tell you to change your plans," Novack said.

"Why?"

Now it was Novack's turn to be annoyed. "Why? Because we just dug a woman out of the ground. She was killed and very probably tortured. And if I decide it'll help me catch the scumbag who did it by talking to you, I don't want to have to go looking for you at a Club fucking Med."

"I'm not planning any trips."

"It's refreshing to meet such a concerned citizen. You're free to go."

Once Tim left, a copy of the Cashman drawing in hand, Novack went into Anders's office to rehash the events of the day. He often found it helpful to do so while things were still fresh, or as fresh as they could be at ten o'clock, after a very long day.

"He killed her," Novack said. "He killed her and he's rubbing our noses in it."

"Why would he do that?" Anders asked.

"How the hell do I know, One Ball? Maybe he's a sick fuck." The truth was that the recent events didn't fit with Novack's view of Wallace, which was not of a serial killer, but of a guy who for whatever reason killed his wife.

"Sick fuck? Is that the technical term for it?"

Novack nodded. "It's from the Latin *sickamus fuckamus.*"

Anders smiled. "I thought that's where you were from." He got up and grabbed his jacket.

"Where are you going?" Novack asked.

"Home. Just in case my girlfriend still lives there." Anders had a girlfriend that he mentioned occasionally, but that no one in the department had ever met. When Novack described the situation to Cindy, she had speculated that perhaps Anders was gay, and that the girlfriend was either nonexistent, or actually a "guy-friend." Novack told her she was crazy, but wasn't really sure himself.

"Aren't you going to Cindy's?" Anders asked.

Novack shook his head. "Nah . . . it's Tuesday."

"So?"

"So lately she doesn't want me to come over on Tuesday. I'm not really sure why."

"Maybe she has a normal, emotionally stable, nondegenerate guy come over on Tuesdays. Just for a change of pace."

Novack shook his head again. "Nah . . . last Tuesday I hid out in the bushes by her house, just to make sure."

Tim made a quick stop at home to walk
Kiley before heading back out.

His destination was the Purple Rose, a place he hadn't planned to frequent again for a very long time. But Tim didn't like where this Cashman situation might be headed, and he certainly didn't trust what Novack would do with it.

It was not a time to sit back and wait.

Danny and Will were at their regular table when he arrived; it would have been a news event if they weren't. But Tim's first stop was the bar, to talk to Frank Lester, the bartender.

Frank was a smallish man, in his late fifties, who always had a smile on his face and a calm, "this too shall pass" demeanor, no matter how chaotic the bar got.

He also knew how to make every drink ever invented, and many that weren't. Danny suspected that Frank just claimed to know what the drinks were, but actually made them up in the moment, assuming correctly that his customers were too drunk to know the difference.

Danny tested him once, ordering a "dishtowel" on the rocks. Frank had simply nodded and prepared a pretty damn good drink, which became one of Danny's favorites.

"Hey, Frank."

Frank brightened noticeably when he saw him. "Hey, Tim, good to see you. We miss you around here."

"Thanks . . . I was here New Year's Eve."

"You were? I didn't see you. Wild night, huh?"

"Yeah . . . I was the one hanging from the chandelier." Tim reached into his jacket for the drawing of Cashman. "Were you here all night?"

Frank nodded. "Until around three in the morning." He motioned toward the table where Danny and Will were sitting. "I put your drunken friends in a cab."

Tim put the picture on the bar. "Did you see this guy that night?"

Frank stared at Cashman's face, trying to place it. "It's possible . . . I mean, he looks a little familiar. But I just couldn't be sure. There were so many people here."

"So you don't know who he is?"

Frank shook his head. "No. I don't think so. You want to leave it here and I'll ask some other people?"

"No, that's okay. Thanks."

Tim started to walk toward Danny and Will's table, stopping when Frank said, "Hey, Tim?"

He turned. "What?"

"It's really good to have you back here, buddy."

Tim nodded his thanks and continued on to the table to see his friends, and their surprise and delight at his arrival was obvious. They made a big show of bringing over another chair for Tim, and positioned it in the center, thereby affording him the best view of the televisions. As shallow males go, it was a poignant and heartfelt gesture of friendship.

"What happened with Novack?" Danny asked, when Tim was settled at the table.

Tim proceeded to tell them about the trip to Kinnelon and the discovery of Sheila's body. "No shit?" Will asked, amazed. "She was where Cashman said she'd be?"

Tim nodded. "Yeah. With a middle finger missing."

He took out the picture of Cashman. "You guys recognize him?"

"That's Cashman?" asked Danny.

"Yeah."

Neither Danny nor Will recognized the picture, but both admitted that they were drunk that night.

"Do they know who this Sheila was?" Will asked.

Tim shrugged. "I don't think so, but I'm not sure; Novack's not exactly confiding in me. He doesn't believe a word I say."

"Cops aren't supposed to believe people," Will said. "It happens all the time."

"Damn," Danny said, still staring at the picture. "What if this scumbag gets away with it?"

"Then he'll get away with it," Will said. "That's another thing that happens all the time."

"I just feel like I owe Sheila more than this," Tim said. "Hey, what about the women you guys were with? Maybe they'll recognize the picture."

"Tim, it was New Year's Eve, remember? Alcohol . . . ?"

"So I was the only one in the place who was sober that night?"

Will raised his glass of beer. "Pretty soon you'll be the only one sober tonight."

"I think it's subject-changing time," Danny said. "Did you catch the news today?"

"No. Why?"

"Some guy crashed his car after a police chase down in South Jersey. It exploded."

"So?"

"So it took out windows three blocks away. They think it was Cintron 421 . . . at least a hundred pounds."

"Jesus . . . where was he going?"

"North."

The partners didn't need to verbalize why this was especially meaningful to them. Their job was to construct buildings that could withstand significant explosives, and Cintron 421 was about as significant as you could get without a mushroom cloud.

"Did you find out any of the particulars?"

"Not yet, but I called my uncle. If we're lucky he'll call me back." Senator Collinsworth would certainly get information faster than they would, but he was not exactly quick to respond to requests.

"Let me know what you hear," Tim said.

Danny got up and headed for the bathroom, and Will said, "Hey, Tim, I'm sorry about the other night. We were just trying to get you to have some fun, and—"

"Not your fault, Will. You couldn't have known."

"Yeah, but now you've got all this shit to deal with. I'm just sorry about it, you know? You of all people shouldn't have the aggravation."

Will, while outwardly the gruffest of the three friends, actually possessed the most sensitivity, though he took pains to hide it. A genius with computers, Will did all the computer work for Wallace Industries, helping to design the programs that governed such things as temperature control and the ventilation and alarm systems in the buildings.

He had met Tim and Danny when they played on the same team in a local weekend softball league. He was all-hit, no field, but the "hit" part was extraordinary, as Will had tremendous power. Tim, Danny, and Will combined for eighteen home runs that season, and Will hit eighteen of them.

Will professed to be rigidly self-ruled by logic, leaving no room for emotion in any decisions he made. Tim had seen cracks in that façade, but was not about to point it out. If that was how Will wanted people to see him, Tim saw no reason to challenge it.

Danny returned, and Tim said his goodbyes and went straight home. When he got there, the phone was ringing. "You get it," he said to Kiley. "It's probably Novack."

But Kiley was not inclined to answer the phone, so Tim did so. "Hello?"

"You told them, Timmy."

The voice was filtered through a computer, and therefore not recognizable, but Tim knew very well what the words meant. "Cashman?"

"I trusted you. It was our secret."

"You murdered her."

"Right . . . Just like I said. But you shouldn't have told them, Timmy. It was our secret. I'm very disappointed in you."

"You're right . . . I'm sorry," Tim said. "Why don't we meet somewhere . . . tomorrow . . . so we can talk about it."

"Oh, we'll definitely meet again. Pleasant dreams, Timmy."

Click.

"If Cashman lived within two hundred miles
of here or Kinnelon, he changed his name,"

Novack said, as he paced around the office of his boss, Captain
Mark Donovan. He and Anders were there to bring Donovan up to
date on events so far, and what they had learned about them.

Donovan represented everything that Novack ordinarily would
have expected not to like in a cop. The son of former commissioner
and permanent legend Stanley Donovan, he was groomed from day
one to move smoothly to the top of the department. The fact that
he was just an average cop was almost an irrelevance, and everyone
who wore a badge knew that this precinct captain position was just
another check mark on a résumé.

What made this surprisingly palatable to Novack was that
Donovan was quite open about his political ambitions, and agree-
ably deferential to cops like Novack and Anders. He knew who he
was, he knew who they were, and he blended it all quite nicely. He
gave respect and in turn received it, even from the normally disrespectful Novack.

"Jeff Cashman doesn't seem like that unusual a name," Donovan said.

Novack nodded. "It isn't; there are seventeen of them in the
target area, but none are our boy."

"What about the victim?"

Novack turned to Anders to provide the information. "Just as dry; if her name really was Sheila Blair, nobody's reported her missing. It's possible that Cashman didn't know her real name, and just made one up."

"DNA?" asked Donovan.

Anders nodded. "Running it now."

"You want to go public with the Cashman sketch?" asked Novack.

Donovan thought about this for a moment. Obviously it would get the public involved in the manhunt, which was a positive. The downside would be that Cashman would be aware that he was being hunted. "No . . . I don't want to let him know we're looking for him yet."

"That's if he exists," said Novack.

Donovan's face registered his surprise. "You think Wallace is lying?"

"Damn straight. I think Cashman is Santa Claus and the Tooth Fairy," Novack said, and Donovan noticed that at the same moment Anders could not conceal a slight grimace. Obviously the two partners were not in complete accord about this. "Look . . . you're Cashman," Novack continued. "You commit a murder months ago, you completely get away with it, and then you give it up to some stranger in a bar? Does that make sense?"

As if he were refereeing a Ping-Pong match, Donovan turned to Anders. "You don't agree?"

Anders shook his head. "I'll admit it's possible, but I look at it a different way. You're Wallace. You commit a murder, get away with it, and then you go to the police with a made-up story about some guy confessing in a bar? That make any more sense?"

"Maybe Wallace was feeling guilty, couldn't stand it, and had to let somebody know where she was," Novack said. "So he makes up this story."

"The same could be true of Cashman," Anders said. "But if I'm Wallace, I know you've been after my ass for months. So if my conscience makes me tell the cops about Sheila, I make an anonymous phone call."

"Not if Wallace wanted to fuck with my mind," said Novack.

"Come on, you're the one who's obsessed here. Not him."

"And you've got less brains than testicles," Novack said.

Novack's apparent obsession represented an area of concern to Donovan; he had known for a long time that Novack was overboard in his unrelenting focus on Wallace. Donovan had never completely shared his view that Wallace must have killed his wife, despite his substantial respect for Novack's instincts. To have a detective on his team maintain a vendetta that never bore fruit would not be good for any of them.

Nevertheless, he decided to jump in for the moment on Novack's side. "The flyer is a significant piece here."

Novack nodded vigorously in agreement. "That's right; the only flyer gets posted outside Wallace's apartment. And only Wallace's prints are on it."

"Maybe whoever hung it wore gloves," Anders said. "Last time I checked it was wintertime."

"And who printed the damn thing? We can't even find anybody who's ever heard of Sheila, so who printed it? And it says to notify the state police, but we know nothing about her. Wallace printed and hung the damn thing himself."

"There's another possibility. Maybe Cashman did it, but he's setting up Wallace. Maybe he has a grudge against him."

"Did you go to the police academy?" Novack asked. "Or did you just see the movie?"

Before Anders could respond, Donovan's intercom buzzed, and he answered it. He listened for a moment and then hung up. "Wallace is here to see you," he said, to Novack.

Anders was surprised. "He's here again?"

Novack was already standing up as he turned to his partner and grinned. "Sickamus fuckamus."

Tim was waiting in Novack's office when he and Anders got back. "Well, good morning. Glad you stopped by," Novack said.

Tim was not in the mood for chitchat, particularly when it was of the insincere variety. "I'm in a hurry to get to work, but there's something I had to tell you."

"You want some coffee?" Anders asked.

"No. He called me."

"Who called you?" Novack asked.

"Cashman. His voice was filtered through a computer, but it had to be him. He knew that I told you about him, and about Sheila."

"How did he know that?' Anders asked.

"He didn't say, but he was angry."

Anders again, "Did he threaten you?"

"Not exactly. He said he was disappointed in me, that we'd meet again, and he told me to have pleasant dreams."

"The animal," Novack said, shaking his head in mock horror.

Tim was immediately pissed. "Hey, this isn't funny, you know? We're talking about a murderer here."

"That's for sure. We're definitely talking about a murderer."

It was a veiled reference to Novack's suspicions of Tim, and it did not escape him. "You think I'm making this up? Maybe you think I killed Sheila?"

Novack was not about to back down. "I'm still working on what I think, so for now I'll just tell you what I know. I know you've been involved with the violent death of two women in less than a year."

As always, the reference to Maggie's death in a criminal light angered Tim, and he started to object, but Novack cut him off.

"Two in one year; that's pretty unusual. You can go out on the street and check out a thousand people . . . fifty thousand people . . . and none of them will have that track record. Two murder cases for one innocent citizen is a lot."

"My wife's death was not a 'case.' It was an accident."

"Yeah, well . . . I have my doubts about that," said Novack, with a slight smile on his face that was meant to disconcert Tim and piss him off.

It succeeded at both goals. "That's because you don't know shit. I know what happened; I was the only person there."

Anders seized at that. "Which is why you're the only person who can answer questions about it."

"Check his notes," Tim said, indicating Novack. "I answered every stupid question he had ten times. I even answered them when I was hooked up to a lie detector. Look, am I being held here? I have work to do; do I have to stay here, or can I leave?"

"This time you can leave," Novack said.

Tim stood up and moved toward the door, then stopped and turned back to the detectives. "There's a maniac out there. He kills women and cuts off their fingers. I don't know why he drew me into this, but you might want to stop wasting your time and find out."

Tim's next few days were "Cashman-free,"

which is to say that he heard nothing from either Cashman or Novack. Tim enjoyed the respite, and though he was quite sure that he had not heard the last of it, he was able to mostly block it from his mind as he went about his business.

Tim thought of that blocking ability, which was called "compartmentalizing" when Bill Clinton was said to be able to focus on the nation's business during the Lewinsky controversy, as having saved his sanity in the months after Maggie's death. It enabled him to concentrate on work, or a World Series game, or taking Kiley for a walk, without being tortured by constant thoughts of Maggie and that awful day out on Long Island Sound.

Tim usually spent the bulk of his time in his office, leaving Danny to supervise most of the work at the Federal Center site, but events lately were preventing him from doing that. They were in crunch time, with the center scheduled to be opened in just four weeks with a gala reception. It would be rather embarrassing if everyone showed up and the building had no roof or floor.

As it came together, the Federal Center was an immensely impressive project. It was a crowning achievement for Senator Collinsworth, bringing in a huge amount of money and jobs to the state. It didn't take someone with Collinsworth's political savvy to know that money and jobs mean votes, but it did take someone with his political power to make it happen.

Tim and Danny's company had a huge stake in the success of

the complex. If things went according to plan and budget, they could naturally expect a substantial amount of work when the complexes went national, springing up in virtually every state of the union. The overall money the government would be spending would be in the hundreds of billions of dollars, and any piece of that, however small a percentage, could not be other than very significant.

The car explosion in South Jersey had no direct effect on Tim's work, but it had a psychological effect on anyone who was in any way involved with the business of combating terror. After two days it had succumbed to the ever-changing news cycles and the lack of new information, so the media and the public moved on. But for people in the know, it was scary as hell.

Federal authorities had identified Ricardo Vasquez as the ill-fated driver of the car, but had so far failed to connect him to any terrorist cells. If the media reports were to be believed, they also had no idea where he got the explosives, where he was taking them, or what triggered the detonation. This lack of knowledge sent spasms of insecurity throughout the security industry, of which Tim and Danny were a small but important part.

The truth was that the buildings under construction could conceivably handle the amount of explosives Vasquez was transporting. The construction mandate was to build a structure that could withstand a powerful explosion from outside, perhaps in a car bomb, with relatively minor damage. If the blast was to take place inside the building, then the essential task was to contain it and prevent it from bringing the building down.

Probably the most unique security feature of the building was its "lockdown" ability. If there were to develop a perceived danger from outside, the capability existed of encasing the building openings with movable steel doors and reinforcements, creating a virtually impregnable barrier to protect the people inside from all but the most overwhelming weapons.

Tim was on site because a number of decisions had to be made, and made quickly, but he was of little value other than that. Danny was far better in these circumstances, with more knowledge of the nuts and bolts of construction. Tim saw the big picture, but Danny knew how to build it.

Danny was in a meeting, so Tim went into the computer room where he knew that Will would be working. Tim hadn't been there since it was finished, and it was a truly extraordinary place. Two entire walls were covered with computer equipment and monitors. Will was hunched over a keyboard, and it seemed as if he were playing an instrument, as the machines were responding to his commands.

"Damn . . . it looks like you could control the world from here."

Will looked over and smiled. "Probably. But right now I'd rather be out in the world and let somebody else do the controlling."

"Having a rough time?"

Will shrugged. "Just the usual. It'll be ready."

"Can I help?" asked Tim, a question they both knew to be ridiculous, since Tim barely had the technical expertise to master e-mail.

Will smiled. "I'll call you if I need you."

As Tim was getting ready to leave the site, he saw that Danny was out of his meeting. "Are you sure you need me here tomorrow?" he asked. "There's plenty for me to do at the office, and you've got things under control."

"Damn straight I need you," Danny said. "Without you, I'd have to bring the doughnuts."

Once Tim got in the car, Meredith called him to say that Eden Alexander had called, and wanted to take him and Kiley to dinner.

"You have her number?" Tim asked.

Meredith gave it to him, and then followed that with an amused, "And who might she be?"

"I didn't tell you?" Tim asked. "I got married yesterday during lunch."

"Are you going to have dinner with her?" Meredith asked, not about to be put off by Tim's sarcasm.

"Bye, Meredith. Take the rest of the day off."

Tim was vaguely surprised by his reaction to Eden's call. He would have expected to be dismissive of the idea of having dinner with her, and perhaps even annoyed by the fact that he now had to turn her down. Instead his reaction was mixed, somewhat unsure. His aunt would see that ambivalence as a cause for celebration.

He called her, and she sounded surprised to hear from him. When he asked why, she said, "I didn't even think your assistant would give you the message."

"Meredith? Why?"

"Have you noticed she's rather protective of you? She was pumping me for so much information . . . there are captured terrorists who've been questioned less."

He laughed. "Sorry. She considers me rather helpless out in the real world."

Eden suggested that they go to a local restaurant called the Firepit, since it allowed dogs. The idea held some appeal for Tim, but he hesitated.

Eden picked up on it. "Tim, relax. I'm not inviting you to a weekend in the Poconos in a heart-shaped tub. It's not even a date."

"It's not that. I—"

"I'll tell you what; we can be at different tables, with a wall between us," she said. "And you can sit in a soundproof booth, under a cone of silence."

"That might work," he said.

"I just thought it would be nice, for us and for the dogs, and I wanted to hear where things stand with the police and that poor woman in Kinnelon."

"Sounds good," Tim said, surprised to be hearing the words come out of his own mouth. "I'll get Kiley and meet you there in an hour?"

"Great," she said, and hung up.

Eden and Travis were waiting for Tim and Kiley when they arrived, and she had already secured two water dishes placed beneath the table.

"Sorry we're late," Tim said. Kiley offered no such apologies, going over to Travis so they could sniff their hellos.

"You're not late. I'm chronically early."

"Why?" he asked.

"I'm not sure; I always assumed it was my wanting to make sure that I wouldn't miss anything."

Tim smiled. "Did I miss anything?"

"Not so far."

Tim ordered a burger, while Eden opted for a vegetable plate, and they both had a beer. They also ordered steamed vegetables for the two dogs; asparagus was Kiley's all-time favorite.

Once they were settled in, Tim recounted to her the phone call from Cashman, as well as his unpleasant encounters with Novack.

"What is his problem?" Eden asked. "You did exactly what you're supposed to do. Would he rather people didn't report these things?"

"He thinks I killed Maggie," Tim blurted out, without really intending to do so.

"That's outrageous," she said. "How can that be?"

"He always has. This just confirms it for him: I'm sure he thinks I killed Sheila as well. Tim Wallace, serial killer."

"So what are you doing about it?" It was a demand; she was outraged, and she expected him to come out fighting.

Tim shrugged. "There's nothing I can do, and nothing I need to do. He can think whatever the hell he wants. He couldn't find any evidence before, and he won't find any now. There's nothing to find. The only consolation to all this is that it drives him crazy."

"You think only guilty people get charged with crimes? You think only guilty people go to jail?"

"I don't really think about it much at all."

"You're in denial," she said.

He smiled. "I won't deny that."

"Tim, I think you should get yourself a lawyer. This guy scares me."

"You think Novack is more dangerous to me than Cashman?"

"Probably, but maybe you should get a bodyguard too. After you get a lawyer."

"You know anyone?" he asked. He had obviously thought about this possibility a number of times in the weeks after Maggie's death, but never came close enough to research attorneys. The only lawyers he had ever dealt with were corporate types, and Tim just couldn't picture them in a room with Novack.

"As a matter of fact I do. My brother is a criminal attorney. Nick Alexander."

"Nick Alexander is your brother? The guy who defended Billy Scarborough?" Scarborough was the CEO of an energy trading company caught in the fraud scandals and charged with what seemed like a thousand counts of fiscal crimes. It was a very public trial, during which the media gave him no chance. Nick Alexander got him acquitted of every single count, and Scarborough walked out the door smiling.

"That's him. He's had some big cases, and he's on television all the time. He can attract enough attention to let people know how unfairly you're being treated."

"The last thing I want is media attention." Tim let it stand at that, without mentioning the danger such attention could cause his business. Someone receiving government money to protect the country from murderous terrorists does not want to be portrayed in the media as a potential serial killer.

Tim decided this was a good subject to change. "So what do you do for a living?" he asked.

She laughed. "You have a driving curiosity about me?"

"What do you mean?"

"I mean we were talking about something that made you un-comfortable, and all of a sudden you asked the first question about me that you've ever asked."

He nodded. "Guilty as charged. I'm afraid I've been a little self-centered this decade. But I really want to know what you do."

"I'm a professor of art history at Montclair State," she said.

"Really?" he asked. "So am I. I'm surprised we haven't run into each other on campus."

They lingered after coffee for more than an hour, talking normal, non-Cashman talk, and they finally decided to leave only when Kiley and Travis made it clear they were getting bored. "I enjoyed this. Thank you," Tim said.

"So I was right not to tell you about my biological clock?" she asked.

"You didn't have to. I heard it ticking."

Novack could feel the frustration
setting in already.

So far everything was coming up empty, much as it had when Tim killed his wife. Novack felt like he was running in place, a hamster in a cage designed by a murderer who was toying with him.

Cashman was nowhere to be found, but that was to be expected. As far as Novack was concerned, Cashman didn't exist. He was created by Tim as part of the game, a game he consistently left Novack no opportunity to win. The fact that Tim was playing this game at all came as a surprise to Novack, and represented a misjudgment on his part. He had Tim pegged as a garden-variety wife killer; this elevated him to a higher plane of evil.

"Are you okay, John?" Cindy asked, as she looked at him sitting at the kitchen table. She was preparing his favorite dish, chicken parmigiana, though if there existed a food that he wouldn't eat, she hadn't yet discovered it. If she served him a plate of horseshit, he would add salt and start chomping away.

He didn't answer, since he was in something of a trance, lost in his own thoughts. It's why she asked the question in the first place.

"John? Earth to John, come in, please."

"What? I'm sorry . . . what?"

"Are you all right? You seem tense and distracted."

"Why do you say that?"

"Well, for starters, you're grinding your teeth and your hands are curled into fists."

He looked at his fists; sure enough, they were clenched so hard his fingers were white. "It's just something at work."

"You're kidding!" Cindy exclaimed in mock surprise. "I thought you were upset that the ballet left town."

"Wallace killed another woman," he said, knowing that she would remember quite well the investigation into Maggie's death. "He's rubbing my nose in it."

She could see how much this upset him, and her instinct was to walk over and put her arm around him. She didn't do it because she knew he hated to be touched when he was upset and stressed. It was one of the hundred thousand ways they were different. "Who did he kill?" she asked.

"We haven't even been able to identify her. But Wallace led us to the body."

"But if he knew where the body was, doesn't that—"

Novack interrupted her with a shake of the head, and told her about Cashman and the alleged conversation on New Year's Eve.

"It couldn't have happened that way?" she asked.

He just stared at her, a frown on his face, and she smiled. "You'll get him this time."

He thought about it for a moment and then nodded. "Yeah, we will. Hey, you want to go get something to eat?"

She smiled. "I'm making dinner, John. That's what I've been doing, in the kitchen where you are currently sitting, for the last half hour."

"I knew that," he lied. "It smells delicious."

Ricardo Vasquez was completely unaware
of just how significant a man he had become.

That lack of awareness was understandable, since his body had
been reduced to a cream sauce spread all over South Jersey. But the
truth was that he had become a hell of a lot more important in
death than in life.

FBI Special Agent Carl White, assigned to Homeland Security,
was in charge of finding out all there was to know about Vasquez. It
was an assignment for which he was uniquely qualified, having
worked undercover on the streets of Miami for three years with
Miami PD before joining the bureau. He knew the area where
Vasquez was from like the back of his hand; he could navigate
through it with ease and get whatever information was to be found.

The last thing Carl had ever expected in his life was to work
undercover. It required an anonymity that superstar athletes simply
could never have, and Carl had superstar athlete stamped all over
him from day one.

ESPN had done a piece on him when he was in the seventh
grade, because he was a phenomenon already drawing attention
from college basketball coaches. His dilemma was not deciding
which college to attend, but which sport to play, as he was every bit
as good a shortstop and running back as he was a point guard.

Among the things necessary to effectively play any of those po-
sitions at the highest level are two healthy knees, and sports history

is filled to overflowing with promising careers cut short by devastating knee injuries.

Carl took his place on that unfortunate list, but he did manage to make his injury unique. It came from an errant drive-by bullet which exploded his eighteen-year-old kneecap as he walked across the street. It took a year before he could jog without pain, and two years before he could walk without any limp. The recovery time necessary to allow him to successfully resume his athletic career would have been measured in decades.

Law enforcement had always been a distant second choice for Carl, but with his first choice not available, he went at it full tilt. Smart, instinctive, and comparatively fearless, he joined the local police force and worked his way up in the department.

Further advancement for African Americans within Miami PD was not only possible, but a departmental goal, yet Carl set his sights on the FBI. He had worked some cooperative investigations with them, and saw it as the big time, the place to make a difference and get noticed on a national scale. When the chance presented itself, he grabbed it.

The Ricardo Vasquez case had given Carl another major opportunity. Homeland Security was in a panic over the explosion, and they were right to feel that way. Vasquez was not carrying garden-variety explosives; this was stuff that the U.S. military used in Afghanistan. No one knew where Ricardo was headed with his cargo, but there is no Afghanistan exit on the New Jersey Turnpike.

Carl was assigned four agents to work directly for him, and was promised whatever other manpower he needed. They spent the four days after the explosion turning Ricardo Vasquez's life upside down.

They came up empty.

Ricardo was simply a small-time punk, with plenty of connections to other punks and assholes, but none to terrorists. There seemed to be no chance that Ricardo could have been a strategist in any plot; he just wasn't bright enough. And any terrorist that would have entrusted Ricardo to transport such a valuable and important cargo couldn't have been very smart either.

But he had had the explosives, and he was taking them some-where. Those are facts that could not be challenged, yet Carl had absolutely no explanation for them.

That, he knew all too well, was a recipe for disaster.

Different people relax in different ways, and
the best way for Tim was to play racquetball.

It required tremendous energy and concentration, and enabled
Tim's competitive nature to kick into high gear. The combination
allowed him to focus entirely on the game, which meant at least a
brief vacation from unwanted thoughts.

He and Danny had a regular game every Saturday morning,
and it was something that Tim looked forward to. Danny was
nearly as good as Tim, and though he didn't often win, the matches
were almost always close. They played at the Englewood Racquet
Club, and kept a standing eight o'clock reservation for court four.
Among the reasons they chose this time was that the court was always empty when they arrived, so if they got there early, they could
just start playing.

This was the first time they had played since Cashman entered
Tim's life, and he made a conscious effort to go all out, both in
physical effort and concentration. After one particularly grueling
point, Danny stopped playing and started laughing.

"What's the matter?" Tim asked.

"Did we bet on the game and you forgot to tell me?"

"What do you mean?"

"You're like a maniac today," Danny said. "Relax or you'll have
a heart attack. You're an old man."

"I'm a week older than you," Tim said, which both of them knew was true. Then he smiled. "Although this has been a long week."

Their normal routine was to play the best of three games, with each game requiring twenty-one points to win. This time Tim won the first two games in record time, yielding only fourteen points combined. It left them with substantial time left over.

"You want to play another one?" Tim said.

"You haven't humiliated me enough?"

"Not even close."

Danny pointed his racket at Tim. "You just made a big mistake, pal. You pissed me off."

Danny played the next game with considerably more intensity, but his reward was merely that he lost by a slightly closer score of twenty-one to eleven. "One more?" Tim asked.

Danny, out of breath and drenched in sweat from the effort, shook his head and said, "No más."

They turned to leave, when Tim noticed something in the compartment recessed in the back wall. It was where players usually put their jewelry, money, or other valuables while they played, and the outside of the compartment was a clear fiberglass. Tim and Danny never used it, because they changed and kept their things in the locker room. "What's that?" Tim asked.

"What?"

Tim pointed. "There's something in there. It looks like a jewelry box."

Danny looked over and saw it as well, and they both walked toward it. Danny reached it first, opened the door and took out the box, which had a Tiffany insignia. He showed it to Tim. "You planning on proposing to me? You buy me a ring?"

"See if there's anything in it," Tim said.

Danny opened the box and looked inside. At first his face took on a puzzled expression, which was followed by a look of pure shock. Suddenly he started to scream, a piercing wail of absolute horror. "AAAAAAYYYYYGGGGGHHHHHH!"

"What the . . ." Tim started to say, but stopped at the sight of the open box dropping from Danny's hand and down to the floor.

The jewelry box struck the floor and its contents fell out in the process. It was not a ring, but a ring could have fit on it.

It was a severed human finger.

The Englewood Racquet Club
never knew what hit it.

Within ten seconds after the finger bounced on the floor, at least half the people in the club came running to see what could possibly have prompted that awful scream. As each person saw the finger, the screams became a chorus, which brought everyone else over to join in.

The latecomers all heard what it was, but still wanted to see it, and then to a person they recoiled in horror when they did. It was as if they had no ability to anticipate what a severed finger might look like, or to predict that they might be repulsed by the sight of it.

By the time the police arrived, at least thirty people had entered the court area, though nobody touched the finger or the box. Tim and Danny were brought back to the manager's office, and the first officers on the scene cordoned off the court.

Stan Mullins of the Englewood police was the first detective to arrive on the scene, and he came in to question Tim and Danny about what had transpired. All too aware of how this was going to play out, Tim asked, "How about if we wait until Novack gets here, so we can do this once?"

"Who's Novack?" Mullins asked.

"He's with the state police. He's the one who'll be taking this case over from you."

Mullins's annoyance was obvious. "Nobody is taking this case from me," he said, and then turned to Danny. "We'll start with you. Tell me exactly what happened. From the beginning."

A shaken Danny said, "Well, we finished our game, and—"

He was interrupted by Mullins's cell phone ringing, which he answered. "Mullins." After a pause, he said, "That's bullshit. You . . . yeah. But it's still bullshit."

Mullins hung up the phone, and without another word, stood and walked toward the door. "I'll give Novack your regards," Tim said, without drawing a response.

It was another twenty minutes before Novack and Anders arrived, and another two hours before Tim and Danny were finally allowed to get their things and leave. Tim and Danny were separated for the questioning, and Tim was surprised that Novack chose to question Danny, leaving Anders to deal with him. Tim figured that maybe Novack was sick of him, a feeling he certainly reciprocated.

Tim had very little to tell other than the specifics of what had happened that morning, but Anders kept asking different questions, which forced him to repeat the story over and over. Even at that, he was finished first, and he waited in the office for Danny to be brought back. Once they were together, Danny started to relate what had happened in his session with Novack, but a glance from Tim told him to wait until they were alone, and he picked up on it.

As soon as they got in the car, Danny said, "Tim, Novack is trying to pin it on you."

Tim nodded, not at all surprised to hear that. "What did he say?"

"All he wanted to know was stuff like, were you ever alone on the court, did you carry anything in with you that could have concealed the jewelry box, that kind of thing. He was hoping I'd nail you, and got pissed when I wouldn't."

"You didn't have to. Cashman is doing it for him."

"Tim, this is moving way past weird. You are dealing with a serious sicko."

"Yeah."

"You think he came after you . . . maybe followed you to the bar that night? Or were you just in the wrong place at the wrong time?"

"He came after me; he knows too much about me to have put this all together on the fly. He may even have killed Sheila for no other reason than to pin it on me."

"You can't just sit back and let this happen to you."

Tim nodded, having come to that conclusion the moment he saw the finger lying on the court. "I'm not going to."

"What are you going to do?"

"I'm going to get a lawyer."

Danny was quiet for a moment, and then said, "Hey, Tim, I think that's a good idea, and you gotta do what you gotta do, but be careful. We don't need publicity about this, you know? I mean for the company."

"I know."

"I mean, my uncle is way out there on a limb for us, but he'll saw it off if he has to. You remember how he reacted last time."

Tim remembered it quite well; Senator Collinsworth had been upset at the publicity following Maggie's death, and the public suspicion of Tim. Danny had calmed him down, and Tim's subsequent exoneration defused the situation, but it was a close call.

"I'm not hiring a press agent, Danny. I'm hiring a lawyer."

Danny pulled into the circular driveway in front of Tim's apartment. "You know anybody that handles that kind of stuff?"

Tim was surprised to see Eden, standing in front of the building. He pointed to her. "No, but she does."

"Who the hell is she?" Danny asked. "You got a life you've been keeping from me?'

Tim didn't answer, just got out of the car and went over to Eden. "What are you doing here?"

"I heard about what happened at the racquetball club," she said. "I thought you might need some help."

"How did you hear about it?" he asked.

"Are you kidding? It's the top story on the news."

"With my name attached?" he asked, cringing in expectation of her answer.

"No, but when I heard about the . . . finger . . . it wasn't hard to make the connection."

Tim nodded. "Come on up."

As they went into the building, Tim looked back and noticed that Danny hadn't driven away. He was just parked there, staring at them.

When Tim and Eden got upstairs, Tim briefly told her what had happened, which didn't differ appreciably from the story she had seen on television. "I need you to call your brother for me, if you feel comfortable with that," he said.

She nodded, went directly to the phone, and within two minutes had an appointment set up for Tim at ten o'clock Monday morning. Then she wrote out the name of the firm and address, and gave it to him.

Tim was surprised when he looked at the paper. "He works for Hammond, Simmons, and Carcher?" It was one of New Jersey's largest and most prestigious firms.

"Yes, they brought him in to start a criminal law division last year. They paid him a fortune, but it may not be the greatest fit."

"Why not?"

"You'll understand when you meet him."

When Anders came into Novack's office,
he had that look on his face.

Novack had no trouble recognizing it; it said that Anders had something important to tell him. There was no telling whether it was positive or negative, just that it was important.

"Tell me something good, One Ball," Novack said.

"Something good?"

"Yes, as in the exact opposite of bad."

Anders smiled and held up a thin folder. "We got a DNA hit . . . we ID'd Sheila."

This had the potential to be an enormous development, and it was all Novack could do not to jump out of his chair. "Who was she?"

Anders opened the folder and looked down at the paper in it. "Her name was Carol Blair, middle name Sheila. She lived in Carson, Wyoming, but would often go away for months at a time. Apparently that's why nobody even considered her missing."

"Why was she in the DNA registry?" Novack asked. The number of people with DNA on file is a relatively small one, and almost always is as a result of criminal activity on the person's part.

"She had an armed robbery conviction, part of a husband-and-wife team that held up a bank. In this case 'armed' is probably understating the case. He had a bomb that he threatened to detonate if they didn't cough up the cash. She was waiting outside in the car, and they got away. Local cops made the collar three days later."

"So she served time?" Novack asked.

Anders nodded. "No . . ." He flipped through the pages looking for the information. "Just probation. She and her husband, a guy named Roger Blair, copped a plea. She walked, and he got three years. This was about eight months ago."

Novack was very surprised by what he was hearing. "That's all they got for robbing a bank and threatening to blow it up?"

Anders kept skimming the pages. "Looks like it. Not exactly frontier justice, huh?"

"So the husband is still inside?"

"No."

"Where is he?"

"Reunited with his wife in that great bank vault in the sky. He had his throat slit in prison a couple of months after he went in."

Novack smiled. "Saddle up, pardner. We're heading out west."

"You think Donovan will spring for two plane trips?" Anders asked. Captain Donovan was notoriously cheap with the department's money. "Sheila was from Wyoming and killed in Kinnelon. We're not exactly swimming in jurisdiction here."

"Are you kidding?" Novack asked, standing up. "Wait here; I'll be right back. When I get finished with him, he'll throw in tickets to the rodeo."

While Novack went off to talk to Donovan, Anders did more than just wait for his partner. He called Keith Rivers, Senator Collinsworth's right-hand man, to tell him about this new development in Wyoming.

Collinsworth and Rivers had tentacles that reached everywhere, and they had had no trouble getting to Anders, offering him substantial considerations for any information about the investigation. Anders had hesitated at first, but finally came to the rationalization that much of the information would be harmless, and that he would judge it on a case-by-case basis.

The Wyoming information was an easy call for him to make, and he had no hesitation in contacting Rivers and sharing it. He accomplished that before Novack came back with the news that Donovan had approved the trip.

They were going to Wyoming.

Hammond, Simmons, and Carcher had their own four-story building off Route 17 in Ridgewood.

It was a dazzling mixture of glass and chrome, so modern and clean that it appeared as if it must have been detailed every night. Tim had seen less sterile hospital operating rooms, but the overall effect was one of modern wealth and confidence, no doubt exactly what they were trying to project in designing it.

The receptionist in the lobby looked like she came with the building, perfectly put together and a model of efficiency. She juggled four calls while Tim was at her desk, yet within three minutes she had ushered him into Nick Alexander's office.

It was hard for Tim to believe that Nick's office was in the same building. It was a mess, papers strewn everywhere, sports memorabilia hanging at awkward angles on the wall, empty soda cans and chewed Popsicle sticks on the tables. With all of the reflections from the chrome and mirrors, the room felt like a carnival maze constructed out of trash.

Nick looked as at home in this décor as the receptionist did in the lobby. He was in sneakers and jeans, with a pullover shirt half tucked into his pants.

"Hey, come on in," Nick said after they shook hands. "Just move that stuff off the chair and sit down."

"Okay . . ." Tim said hesitantly, since it looked as if the couch hadn't been cleaned since the Ford Administration. "Thanks for seeing me on such short notice."

"No problem . . . any friend of Eden's . . . hey, you want something to drink? I've got Diet Pepsi and Yoo-Hoo." He reached into his pocket and took out something grayish. "Or maybe a mint?"

"No, thanks."

"It's hot in here, huh? They turn the heat up in these buildings so high I lose five pounds a day. And you can't open the windows. You believe that?"

Tim nodded. "A lot of buildings, you—"

Nick interrupted. "I know; it drives me crazy. My old office, I had the windows open all the time. Even in the winter. You could smell the food from the fast-food Chinese restaurant next door starting at ten in the morning. You remember the *Honeymooners* episode where Norton could tell what time it was based on when the egg foo yong smell reached his window?"

"No, I'm afraid I don't."

He looked at Tim in surprise, as if it were hard to believe someone could be unfamiliar with that episode. "Really? It was a classic."

Tim smiled, hoping that the trip through TV Land was over. "I'll have to check it out. So, I'm here because—"

Nick finished the sentence for him. "The police, most notably Detective Novack, think you murdered two people." As he talked, he twisted the top off a bottle of Yoo-Hoo and handed it to Tim.

"How did you know that?" Tim asked. "Did Eden tell you?"

"No. I asked around a bit. Believe me, it's not a major secret."

"With all due respect, I haven't hired you yet."

Nick smiled; if he was insulted he certainly didn't show it. "With just as much respect, I haven't accepted you as a client yet. You can be sure I didn't reveal in any fashion to anyone that I had a professional interest in this case. In fact, I gotta tell you, at this point I don't."

Tim nodded. "Sorry."

"No problem. Tell me your story, leaving nothing out."

Tim spent the next half hour doing just that. It was a story he had by then told frequently, but Nick's occasional probing questions brought out more detail and fresh perspective. It didn't take Tim long to realize that Nick was a lot smarter than his first impression had led him to believe.

In previous recountings, Tim's dominant emotions were frustration and anxiety; this time his primary feeling was a growing anger at what was happening to him.

By the time he finished, he knew he was in desperate need of help, as well as an equally strong need for revenge at whoever was tormenting him. He wanted Nick to provide both, but besides asking questions, Nick had not given any sign that he was interested in doing so.

"Is that everything?" Nick asked.

Tim nodded. "I think so."

"Now tell me about your wife."

"What about her? She has nothing to do with this."

Nick shook his head. "Bullshit . . . of course she does. Her death is the reason Novack is after you. And Novack is the guy I'd be defending you against, at least initially, so I have to know what he knows and what he thinks he knows."

The logic of this couldn't be disputed, no matter how much Tim might have wanted to. "Of course, you're right. It just bugs the shit out of me when people talk about Maggie's death as if it were a murder case."

"I don't blame you."

Tim related the events of that awful day as best he could remember them, as well as his dealings with Novack afterward. "Finally, I let them give me a lie detector test, and never heard from them again. The talking heads in the media stopped jabbering about it as well."

Nick laughed. "I was one of those talking heads; somehow I've gotten on the list of defense attorneys that they call."

Tim smiled. "I never watched the coverage. What did you say?"

"I don't remember, and it doesn't matter; I knew absolutely

nothing about it. That never gets in the way; I just jabber about the presumption of innocence and mention that there are holes in the prosecution's case."

"Were there?"

Nick shrugged. "Must have been; or by now you'd be showering with guys named Bubba. Have you told me everything?"

"I think so. But I do have a question for you."

"Shoot."

"What are you doing here?" Tim asked.

"What do you mean?"

Tim pointed out toward the rest of the offices. "Well, you just don't seem to fit in this place. It's not your personality."

Nick grinned. "About eight months ago the geniuses here decided they wanted to get into criminal law, maybe because most of their corporate clients are crooks. They didn't want to build a department; they just wanted to go out and hire the best. For some reason they thought that was me, so they threw a shitload of money at me and gave me autonomy."

Tim laughed. "Obviously you're exempt from the dress code as well. Every other guy in the place is wearing a suit."

"Hey, I dress up pretty nice when I have to go to court. Which is one place we don't want you to wind up."

"So you'll take the case?"

He thought a few moments, and Tim sensed this was his moment of decision. Finally, he said, "I'll draw up an agreement between us; among other things, it will detail the fee structure. You have money? Because somebody's got to pay for all this chrome."

"It's not a problem."

"Okay. Take the document with you and think about it. If you sign it, I'm your lawyer."

"You're my lawyer," Tim said.

Nick raised his bottle of Yoo-Hoo in a toast. "Cheers."

Carson, Wyoming, was everything that
Anders and Novack expected, and less.

Forty-five hundred citizens were spread out over an area probably
as large as Manhattan, and the closest thing to a high-rise was a tree
house some kids had built in the woods behind their trailer.

Basically, the town was divided up so that half of the residents
were involved in farming, while the other half worked at the state
prison located at Lampley, twenty miles away. The Carson economy was therefore simultaneously at the mercy of the weather and
the state crime rate.

The two detectives arrived at four in the afternoon, tired from
their trip and absolutely frozen from the weather. The outside temperature gauge on their rental car showed the temperature to be
eight degrees, which felt generous. Carson, Wyoming, made New
Jersey feel like Guatemala.

They were initially sorry they had made an appointment for
five o'clock, since they would have preferred to go to their hotel
and rest for the night. That was until they saw their hotel, a dive
out near the highway that for some reason had fourteen tractor
trailers in the parking lot, even though there were only twelve
rooms. The parking lot was unpaved, just loose dirt, and if there
were a rainstorm it would likely be left to archaeologists to someday unearth the sunken tractor trailers.

They dropped their bags in their tiny room and left, arriving promptly at the police station, a two-room building that had them longing for the spacious luxury of the hotel. The entire police force was there when they arrived, consisting of a receptionist, deputy, and the chief himself, Matthew Drew.

If Novack and Anders were expecting Andy Taylor and Barney Fife, they were in for a surprise. Chief Drew was an experienced police officer, having spent eleven years in Reno PD. Born in Carson, he'd come back to care for his ill mother seventeen years ago, and though she died six months later, he never left.

"This is a nice, quiet place to live," Drew said after the hellos. "But I guess you guys have come to change that?"

Novack shook his head and smiled. "Nah . . . we're just working the job. One of the perks is that we get to visit nice, quiet places like this."

Novack had sent information ahead for Drew to review before their arrival, including the sketch of Cashman. "I showed the sketch around a bit," Drew said. "Nobody here has ever seen that guy."

"What can you tell us about the victim?" Novack asked.

"Born and raised here; a little wild by our standards but no real problems. She got bored and left to go to L.A. when she was nineteen."

"To be a movie star?"

Drew smiled. "A cocktail waitress. We set our sights pretty low around here."

"When did she come back?" Anders asked.

"About two years ago. She brought a boyfriend with her."

"Roger Blair?"

Drew nodded. "Right. I think he was originally from back East . . . Maine or New Hampshire or something. They lived in a trailer, about five miles out on the road. Pretty much kept to themselves. He was a mechanic, but he made most of his money blowing stuff up."

"What does that mean?"

"He was an explosives expert; learned it in the army. The guy was amazing; give him a glass of water and a tube of hair gel, and he could incinerate South Dakota."

"He made that into a business?" Novack asked.

"You'd be surprised how much use there is for explosives. Irrigation, clearing land, demolishing unwanted structures . . . he seemed to do okay for himself."

"What did she do?"

"She was like his assistant," Drew said, and smiled at the recollection. "You should have seen them; it was like he was a chef and she brought him the ingredients."

"How come he and his wife got off so easy? What the hell is armed robbery out here, a misdemeanor?" Novack asked.

Drew shrugged. "Yeah, I was pretty surprised at that myself. Judge said it was a first offense, nobody got hurt . . . bullshit like that, but I was pissed off when I heard the sentence. He may have been pressured, but I don't have a clue where it could have come from."

"What did the wife do when Blair went inside?"

Drew shook his head. "I don't know, but whatever it was, she wasn't doing it here. Far as I know, nobody had seen her since."

They spent the better part of another hour asking Drew questions. He answered them as best he could, but had no information getting them any closer to Sheila's killer. "Do you know the warden at Lampley?" Novack asked.

Drew nodded. "Sure. Name's Luther Marshall . . . I know him real well."

"Any chance you could get him to meet with us?"

Drew smiled and called out to his receptionist, a forty-two-year-old woman named Bryna Keller. "Hey, Bryna, they want to know if I could get Luther to meet with them."

She laughed. "That depends. You guys like beer?"

"On occasion," Novack said.

"You guys like buying beer?" Bryna asked.

"Less so . . . why?"

"Luther and I are having a few tonight," Drew said. "If you bring your big-city wallets, you can come along."

Danny's drive to Montclair took only about forty-five minutes, but if he had his preference it would have been forty-five days. He had been summoned to meet with his uncle, Senator Collinsworth, back for a few weeks while the Senate was on one of its frequent recesses.

The invitation came in the form of a phone call from Collinsworth's chief of staff, Keith Rivers. That in itself was fairly ominous. When the senator had good news to share, he picked up the phone himself. When it was bad, Rivers would make the call. And there was no third choice; the senator wouldn't be inviting him over unless he had some message to impart. "Gee, can't a guy just want to chat with his favorite nephew?" simply wasn't the senator's style.

The invitation was for six o'clock, and for a drink, not dinner. Based on Danny's experience, this was another danger sign. This was going to be quick, probably one drink, since otherwise the senator would have sent a car to pick him up. It would be extraordinarily unseemly for his nephew to be picked up on a DUI after leaving his house.

Danny was concerned that Collinsworth had learned of Tim's current involvement with the police. The senator had provided federal business for their company, and didn't want to be in any way linked to a suspected murderer. Whether Tim was guilty of anything was of secondary importance; public perception was the crucial factor.

The senator always referred to his home as "the estate," and it was that and much more. The property itself was so large that it could have been an actual "state"; Rhode Island would have fit in one of the walk-in closets.

For entertainment, the house included a screening room, tennis court, swimming pool, and a pair of bowling alleys. Unfortunately,

Danny wasn't summoned for entertainment, nor was he told to bring his bowling shoes.

The only positive to all this was that the senator's third wife, Danny's step-aunt Elaine, wasn't in town. She was in Chicago at a fund-raising dinner for one of the charities she spent her time pretending to be interested in. Danny considered her a pompous pain in the ass, and that was giving her the benefit of the doubt.

When he was brought into Collinsworth's study, Danny was not surprised to see Rivers standing unobtrusively off to the side. Rivers was well over six feet and two hundred twenty pounds, so unobtrusiveness was not his forte, but he knew when to blend into the background. There were very few times that Danny had ever seen the senator that Rivers was not around, so he barely took notice of him.

Danny started with, "Uncle Fred, it's great to see you. You're looking terrific." He didn't expect him to believe it, or to think much about it either way.

Collinsworth was sitting behind his desk in his spacious study. He spent a great deal of time there, though in Danny's recollection he had never seen so much as a piece of paper on that desk. He did sip from a glass of chardonnay, as he seemed to do twenty-four hours a day. Danny had occasionally watched him speak on the Senate floor on C-Span, and was struck by the absence of the wine glass. He assumed it was hidden behind the lectern, but the senator seemed undressed without it.

"Danny, my boy, this is nice . . . you and I communicating like this."

Danny had no idea where he was going with this, but it couldn't be good. "I always enjoy talking with you, Uncle Fred."

"That's good, because I'm easy to chat with, aren't I?" Collinsworth asked, swooping in for the kill.

Danny nodded. "Very easy."

"Then why the fuck didn't you mention to me that the police are after your psycho partner for another murder?"

"He didn't do it. He—"

The senator interrupted him. "Oh, so you only figured I would care if he actually did it? Maybe if he got convicted? You were waiting for the jury to come in before telling me? Or maybe you were holding back until the appeals court refused to overturn his conviction?"

"I'm sorry, but this time it's really ridiculous. There was a murder, but he knows who did it. The guy confessed to him."

The senator waved this off. "I heard the whole bullshit story. The police don't believe it, and I don't blame them."

"Uncle Fred, I swear, they don't have anything on Tim, because there's nothing to have."

"Is that right? You're up on the case?"

"I think so," Danny said, cringing. This was going to be painful; the senator was said to be pondering a run for the White House, and anything or anyone that stood even a remote chance of derailing him was going to be dealt with severely.

The senator shook his head sadly and turned to Rivers for the first time. "I wish I didn't have a weakness for family." Then, to Danny, "Did you know they identified the victim?"

Danny's silence indicated that he didn't.

Collinsworth decided to reveal an important piece of information in order to scare Danny, but of course without revealing that Anders was his source. "Did you know that Novack and his partner are out in a place called Carson, Wyoming, right now, following up on it? Does that sound like cops who are floundering around?"

"I swear, this will blow over. I know Tim as well as I know myself; there's no way he could kill anyone."

"Let me tell you something. Right now he's in the process of killing your career."

They shouldn't have agreed to buy the beer.

That's the first thing that went through Novack's mind when he and Anders met Warden Luther Marshall. They were at a bar/restaurant that was called the Big Barn, which seemed aptly named, since at one time it could easily have been a home to horses and hay. It was one enormous room, with wood-burning stoves positioned strategically to warm patrons at more than thirty tables.

Luther was sitting at a table with Drew, and even though the detectives were not late in arriving, there were already four empty beer bottles on the table when they got there. Luther was slightly less than six feet, about Novack's height, which was particularly significant because he was sitting down. When he stood up to shake hands, it seemed to take twenty minutes to unfold his entire six-foot-eight, two-hundred-ninety-pound frame.

It was unlikely, thought Novack, that there needed to be guards working at Luther's prison. Not even steel bars or cell doors would be necessary. No prisoner would dare piss Luther off by trying to escape.

But Luther proved to be an affable sort, and he and Drew were good guys to drink with, so much so that by the time they got around to talking about why the East Coast detectives were there, Luther had enough beer in him to flood an average-sized basement.

In fact, it was Luther himself who finally brought it up. "So I hear you guys want to know something about Roger Blair?"

Novack nodded. "Whatever you can tell us."

Luther shrugged his shoulders, which at his size represented a seismic shift. "I can't tell you much; he pretty much stayed to himself while he was inside."

"Did his wife come to visit him?" Anders asked.

"A couple of times early on, but after that, nothing. Nobody else came either."

"What about phone calls? In or out."

"Hard to know," Luther said. "Nothing on the prison phone, but they get cell phones in there, so there's no sure way to keep track."

"Any idea why he was killed? Or who killed him?"

"No, but it was a contract job, that's for sure. Chances are the guy who did it didn't even know who was paying him, or why."

"Sounds like a nice place you've got there," Novack said.

"Yeah . . . it's a real pleasure to go to work each day," Luther said. "Warms my heart."

Anders took out Cashman's picture, and he noticed that Novack frowned slightly, considering it a waste of time. Nobody knew Cashman, Novack had said repeatedly, because there was no Cashman. "You ever see this guy?" Anders asked.

Luther looked at it intently for a few moments, then shook his head. "Looks sort of familiar, but . . . no. Don't think so."

More to annoy Anders than anything else, Novack took Tim's picture out of his folder. "What about him?"

Luther looked at it and said, "No, can't say as I have."

Novack starting putting Tim's photo back in the folder when Drew grabbed it and put it back on the table. "I know that guy."

"How?" a stunned Novack asked.

"He was here in Carson. Last year."

Novack looked across the table at Anders and smiled. "Small world, huh?"

As soon as Danny told him the news, Tim called Nick Alexander. It was comforting to him that he had somebody who was unequivocally on his side, someone used to fighting the same system that was rapidly becoming Tim's enemy.

"I think we have a problem," Tim said. "Novack is out in Wyoming. They found out who the victim is; that's where she's from."

"What's her name?" Nick asked.

"I don't know. All I know is that she is from a town called Carson."

Nick couldn't imagine Novack having shared the information with Tim, so he asked, "How did you find this out?"

Tim hesitated. "I'd rather not say."

"I probably should have already explained this more clearly, but now is as good a time as any. It doesn't matter at all what you would rather say or not say. What is important is that you tell me everything, or this is not going to work. Once I hear it, then I'm the one who can't talk about it, or I would be violating my oath of confidentiality."

"Okay. My partner Danny's uncle is Senator Collinsworth. He told Danny about it, and Danny told me."

"How did Collinsworth get the information?"

"I don't know," Tim said. "But he has ways of finding out pretty much everything."

"Why was he interested?"

"He's been helpful in getting our company some major projects, including some work on the Federal Center in Newark. If it turned out that he was getting the work for a murderer, that wouldn't look great for him. Especially if he wants to run for president."

"Okay, let's back up for a minute. You said that Novack's being in Wyoming was a problem. Why do you see it that way?"

"Carson is a small town about three hours from Laramie. I was there last year. This just seems like another one of those things that can't be a coincidence."

"What were you doing there?"

"There's a stone quarry about twenty minutes outside of town.

We had gotten word that some of our competitors were getting materials from there . . . better quality at a lower price. We're in a very competitive business, so we have to check these things out. Carson was the nearest town with a hotel, so I stayed there."

"Do you usually check them out yourself?

"Sometimes, but not too often. Maggie had died a couple of months before that, and Novack was still on my case, so I thought it might be good to get away for a few days."

"Was it worth the trip?" Nick asked.

"No, not even close. There was nothing special about the stone or the price. And then my car was vandalized; I was stuck there for a day while it was being fixed."

"So people in the town would remember you?"

"I would think somebody might. I even went in and filed a police report. God, this is unbelievable. Why are they doing this to me?"

Nick was wondering the same thing, but he didn't express it. Instead he spent another ten minutes questioning Tim about his time in Carson, and whether anything unusual happened.

"Not that I remember," Tim said. "I mostly stayed in the hotel, and when the car was ready the next day I was out of there. As far as I know, they never caught whoever vandalized the car."

"And you still don't remember seeing anyone who looked like the woman on the flyer outside your apartment?"

With Carson as the context, Tim once again racked his memory for any trace of "Sheila." "I don't think so."

"I want you to think some more about your time in Carson. Write down everything you can remember . . . what you did, what you ate, who you spoke to. Every detail, no matter how small."

"Okay," Tim said. Then, "You think we should be worried about this?"

"I find that generally the best approach is to be worried about everything."

Novack and Anders were back
in Chief Drew's office at nine A.M.

They weren't there to talk to Drew; he'd told them the little he knew the day before. Rather they wanted to question Bryna Keller, Drew's receptionist/assistant, who he'd said had dealt with Tim Wallace when he was in Carson the previous year.

A single mother of three boys, Bryna could best be described as unflappable. A lifelong resident of Carson, she knew, and was friends with, everyone in town, a fact which made Drew's job considerably easier. Bryna could handle and mediate disputes between citizens better than he could, and often problems were solved without ever having to involve him at all.

Bryna had also slept with about half of the adult citizens of Carson, but only a very unlikely switch to bisexuality could ever get her past that threshold. No one, including Bryna, had the slightest idea who her son's natural fathers were, and no one, including Bryna, spent any time worrying about it.

When Bryna arrived at nine-fifteen, she noticed Drew, Anders, and Novack staring at her. "Let me guess," she said, "none of you could figure out how to make coffee."

"That's true," Drew said. "But it can wait. These gentlemen need to talk to you."

"What about?"

Anders handed her the picture of Tim. "Him."

She looked at the picture with no sign of recognition. "Who is he?"

"That's what we were hoping you could tell us," Drew said.

Bryna looked at the picture again, and suddenly brightened. "Wait a minute . . . that's the guy who was here last year, right?

Drew looked over at Novack and smiled at the confirmation of his recollection. Of course, Novack was delighted that Drew was right.

"Why was he here?" asked Novack.

"I'm not sure . . . he was on some kind of a business trip . . . but I don't remember what his business was. Anyway, he came in here because his car broke down, and Roger said it was vandalized. Something was poured into the gas tank, I think . . ."

"Roger Blair?" asked Novack.

Bryna looked surprised. "Right, the mechanic. It was before he went to jail. You knew him?"

Novack shook his head. "That isn't what's important. What's important is whether Wallace knew him."

"Well, he serviced his car."

"So you can definitely place them together? You saw them in the same room?"

"Yes. In fact, it was this very room."

Tim spent an hour writing down everything he remembered about that stay in Carson, although after fifteen minutes he had pretty much finished the job.

It was just not a very eventful experience. He had gone out there to check out the quarry, although he could not remember how he had heard about the place. In any event, it wasn't particularly impressive, and he was preparing to leave when his car broke down. Vandals, probably bored teenagers, had put some foreign material in the gas tank, and the entire system needed to be cleaned out.

Tim remembered the mechanic, though he had no idea what his name was, and he had a firm recollection of filing a police report. The car wasn't ready until the next day, so he had stayed in the hotel an extra night. He remembered it as being a small dump near the highway. He had dinner at a local steakhouse, went to sleep early, and left the next afternoon, when the car was ready.

The only woman he recalled meeting worked at the police station, and she'd taken down his information. He knew it was possible that he had spoken to a waitress, or a female hotel clerk, but if he had, there was nothing memorable about the exchange.

And if he met anyone named Sheila, he certainly had no recollection of it. Yet apparently the murder victim lived in Carson, and if Novack went out there, there could be no doubt that he was trying to connect her to Tim.

Tim knew one thing for sure; events had gone way past the possibility of coincidence. Someone, probably Cashman, had diabolically and brilliantly set out to destroy Tim's life, and so far was enjoying great success.

There was no reason to think it would stop now.

"We've got enough, Captain.
We've got more than enough."

Novack and Anders had gone directly from the airport to the precinct, with Novack calling ahead to make sure that Captain Donovan was there to meet with them. He was hoping for a positive reaction to his request to arrest Tim, but wasn't getting it.

"You've got logic," said Donovan. "You don't have evidence."

"What does that mean?" Novack asked.

"It means that Wallace's story about Cashman, his knowing where Sheila was buried, his showing up with the flyer, and his having been in Carson all logically say that he did it. But there's no tangible evidence that he did."

"What about the finger?"

"You got anybody that saw him plant it? Or walk into the racquetball place with it?"

"Come on, if it walks and quacks like a fucking duck, it's a fucking duck," Novack said. "And the three of us are standing knee-deep in duck shit."

Donovan nodded. "Right, but you've got to prove it's a fucking duck, beyond a reasonable doubt. And there's no way that McDermott would think you're there." He was talking about Lee McDermott, the district attorney who would make the ultimate decision about whether to bring the case to trial. McDermott was widely known, and generally scorned by the police, for his refusal to take anything but sure things before a judge. The truth was that in most cases Donovan approved of McDermott's caution; it helped remove the chance that Donovan would approve a very public arrest that went nowhere.

"He's killed two women, Captain. When he kills a third, you gonna tell the victim's family that McDermott would have given you a hard time?"

Donovan was annoyed. "Don't hand me that crap, Novack. McDermott would be right; there is not enough to take this to a jury." He then turned to Anders, who had been largely silent throughout, letting Novack make the case. "What do you think?"

"I think we need to get him off the street, Captain. Things are starting to break our way, and we'll come up with more. But as the pressure mounts on him, I don't want to give him a chance to do something stupid."

Donovan was surprised at Anders's about-face; he thought that Anders still disagreed with Novack's certainty of Tim's guilt. That caused him to pause and briefly reconsider his decision, but there was still no upside to be found in moving precipitously.

"No, not yet. But we're close. Get me something else and we take it to McDermott."

Novack was not about to let it drop. "Something else? Wallace gave us the body, then he gave us the missing finger. If you go to my house and find somebody's head in my freezer, you can arrest me."

"Arresting you is something I would look forward to," Donovan said. "Now get the hell out of here and nail the bastard."

The New Jersey state crime lab was state-of-the-art, and it owed a good deal of its fine reputation to Dr. Robin Miller, who ran the DNA department. The Simpson case and subsequent FBI lab failings shone a bright light on the importance of impeccable lab procedures, and Dr. Miller was considered to be as good as they come.

New Jersey law enforcement liked to use the state lab as much as possible, rather than relying on the FBI, and for that reason Dr. Miller and her staff were constantly in a state of work overload.

She was known to be totally about the science, and showed no interest in the particulars of the cases. She ran her tests without any prejudice or interest in the outcome; like a good scientist should. Her job was simply to determine the facts and report them.

Dr. Miller's administrative assistant, Stephen Cowlings, was left to handle all the other parts of the job, like prioritizing which samples would be tested in what order, and dealing with the law enforcement agencies that submitted the samples for testing. Since in most cases the authorities were eagerly waiting for the results, as their cases often depended on them, it was a position of some importance and power that Cowlings occupied.

Cowlings was, in fact, the main reason that the finger found at the racquetball court was tested before other samples that had come in earlier. Novack's people had put in their request on an urgent basis, but that was becoming standard procedure. Cowlings had another reason for rushing this particular one through . . . a more personal one.

Dr. Miller had completed the tests, first determining the type of preservative used to keep the finger in such pristine shape. She then achieved a DNA type, which was run through the computers to see if a match could be made with samples already in the database. If no match was found, it would then be run through the larger FBI database, which could take up to three weeks.

The results would come to Dr. Miller's office, but since they were of no interest to her, Cowlings would read them and be responsible for reporting them to the authorities that had submitted the sample.

Cowlings was out to lunch when the results of the computer match on the finger were sent to his office, and it was the first thing he looked at when he got back.

Reading it with delight, he knew that the police needed this information right away, but he also knew that somebody else needed it first.

Somebody who would pay for it.

"We need to talk. Immediately."

Nick Alexander's words sent waves of panic through Tim's gut. This could not be good news. "Why? What's the matter?"

"Not over the phone."

"You want to come here, to my office?" Tim asked. "Or should I come there?"

"Where do you live?" Nick asked, and when Tim told him, he said, "I'll meet you at your apartment in twenty minutes."

Tim left the office hastily, and was waiting at the elevator when Meredith came into the hallway.

"Tim? Are you all right?" she asked.

"I'm fine. Something came up that I have to deal with."

"Anything I should know about?" she asked. "When should I tell people you'll be back?"

"I'll call you."

She nodded uncertainly, and as Tim got on the elevator, she went back into the office.

When Tim arrived at his apartment building, Nick was waiting in the lobby. They rode up in the elevator without saying a word, and by the time they got into the apartment, Tim was beyond worried.

"Please tell me what's going on," he said.

"I just learned the results of the DNA tests on the severed finger," Nick said.

"From Novack?" Tim asked, and was immediately sorry he did. It would only delay his hearing the news.

Nick shook his head. "No, I have someone on my payroll at the state lab; it often comes in handy. Like now."

"What did the tests show?"

Nick didn't pull the punch. "It was your wife's finger."

This time there was no internal debate.

Within five minutes of getting the news of the DNA match, Captain Donovan had agreed to Novack's request to arrest Tim. Less than an hour later, DA McDermott had signed on, and a half hour after that they had secured a signed arrest warrant, and another warrant to search Tim's office and home.

Plans were drawn up for the actual arrest. Since it was still morning, Tim was assumed to be at his office. Undercover officers were sent to confirm that, and Captain Donovan started to rearrange his manpower so that the arrest would be done with a sufficient number of officers. No chances were to be taken.

Novack and Anders were to lead a group of six officers into the office, and all exits and stairwells were to be guarded by other personnel. He and Anders went over every detail, utilizing a diagram of the building, and then presented it to Donovan.

Donovan looked at it from every angle, trying to poke holes in it, and finally conceded there were none. "It works for me," he finally said. "Just don't screw it up."

"It'll go down perfectly," Novack said, smiling. "By this time tomorrow you'll be the new commissioner."

"And my first act will be to fire you."

At that moment a call came in from one of the undercover officers saying that Tim was not, in fact, at his office. Pretending to be a potential client, the officer was told by Meredith that she expected Tim back shortly.

The decision was made not to change the plan. They would wait until Tim got back to his office, and then move in.

It was unlikely that any news could have devastated Tim as completely as the news that the finger was a match to Maggie. When Nick said it, he sank to his knees, swamped by his feelings and unable to speak.

It was his worst nightmare.

"It can't be," he said. "It just can't be."

"I'm sorry, but it's a fact. The chance of these things being wrong is one in billions."

"Maggie died in the explosion. I was there."

"But you didn't actually see it. You said you saw a flash of white, and then you lost consciousness."

"We were alone out there in the water," Tim said. "It's not possible."

"We'll need to talk this out, but this is not the time. We've got more pressing shit to deal with."

Tim was not hearing him; he was lost in his own thoughts. "Are you saying she survived, and then she was tortured?" The words came out as a plaintive plea, as if begging Nick to say that there was another explanation.

Nick said, "I'm not saying anything. What I'm—"

Tim interrupted, trying to fully process the thoughts as they flooded into his head. "Could she be alive? If that is her finger, and her body wasn't lost at sea, could she still be alive?"

This time Nick's response was firmer; he had to get through to him. "You need to listen to me, Tim. You are going to be arrested; there is no doubt about that."

"What?" Tim heard the words, but had trouble understanding them.

"You are going to be arrested. So it's best to turn yourself in. That way we'll try and avoid some of the press coverage, maybe cut out the perp walk."

"When . . . when do you want to do this?"

"Soon . . . in an hour."

Tim was responding slowly, still trying to make sense out of this in his mind. "What should I do?"

"Pack a bag, get someone to take care of your dog . . . whatever else you need to do around here. You won't be coming back for a while. Once you're ready I'll call Novack and offer to bring you in; I'll be back here in an hour."

Tim nodded. "Okay."

Nick left, and Tim was alone with his agony. It was a good half hour before he could start thinking clearly, and even then he was tortured with the realization that he was living a nightmare he couldn't begin to understand.

His phone rang, and he briefly considered not answering it, in case it was Novack. He checked the caller ID and saw that it was his office. "Hello?"

It was Meredith calling, and she sounded extremely scared. "Tim, there are police all over the building. They think I don't know who they are, but I'm not stupid."

"It's okay, Meredith." He didn't want to have to take the time to console her.

"No, it's not okay. Tim, I overheard two of them talking. One said he hoped you'd try something, that he'd love to take a shot at you. Then the other one talked about what would happen to you in prison."

"Meredith, just stay in the office. I have to go."

Meredith's call had further shaken him, if that were possible. One thing was all too obvious; whoever was doing this to him had won. It was planned and orchestrated to perfection, and when he was taken into custody he would never come back.

He knew absolutely nothing about his enemy, or how they had done this to him and Maggie. The worst pain of all was that he was the only person who could avenge whatever happened to Maggie, who could bring her justice, and he had no idea how to do that.

He was positive of only one thing.

He had to run.

Lucia Angelos had no idea that two cameras and three agents were watching her every move.

No one had been around when she arrived at Ricardo Vasquez's apartment, and since she had a key, there was no commotion involved. Besides, this downtown Miami apartment did not exactly have a concierge or doorman; even the janitor had quit two months earlier in a pay dispute.

Entering Vasquez's apartment was neither particularly poignant nor upsetting to Lucia. She had stayed overnight dozens of times in the months before Vasquez had been blown to bits near the New Jersey Turnpike, but it had not been an idyllic romance. Vasquez had punched her on more than one occasion, and she had feared that if she dumped him he would have done much worse. Of course, at this point he no longer represented much of a threat.

Lucia took her time in the search; she knew that if Ricardo had hidden something of value there, he would have done a very good job of it. Burglaries were commonplace in this neighborhood and Ricardo knew that better than most people, since he committed many of them.

In watching Lucia search the apartment for over two hours, FBI Agent Carl White was showing remarkable patience. Ever since he had been assigned the case because Miami was his home turf, he had gotten nowhere in figuring out what Vasquez was doing with the Cintron 421. His instincts told him that Lucia was going to change all that.

There was no harm in letting Lucia search the apartment. It wasn't like there was any chance she would find anything; the FBI forensics people had long ago turned the place upside down. But Carl finally sent the agents in because it was better to raid the place and frighten her, rather than simply take her into custody as she was leaving. Carl needed her to talk, and scared people are far more likely to do so.

Six agents burst into the apartment, guns drawn and screaming at Lucia to hit the floor. After shrieking a few times, she did so, and then started yelling that she had done nothing wrong. Carl had the agents cuff her and read her her rights, though the truth was that she hadn't done anything to warrant arrest.

Carl could easily have questioned her there, but he knew she would be more uncomfortable in a downtown holding cell. He arranged for the appropriate accommodations with Miami PD, and they took her possessions and cell phone, and then let her stew in the jail cell for four hours before having her brought into an interrogation room.

Carl would have been surprised to learn that Lucia was more annoyed than afraid. She knew she had not done anything seriously wrong, and that the overreaction of the agents had more to do with the circumstances of Vasquez's death than her own actions. Besides, this was a young woman who had already had a very difficult life; as negative events went, this did not rank very high on her list.

"What were you looking for?" Carl asked, the moment he walked into the interrogation room.

"My stuff," she said.

"What kind of stuff?"

"Just stuff; clothes and things. A pair of shoes. Stuff, you know?"

"You were looking inside the mattress. That's where you keep your clothes and shoes?"

"Jewelry . . . I hide stuff in there," she said.

"Let me see it," he said.

"See what?"

"The jewelry 'stuff' that was in the mattress . . . let me see it."

She shrugged. "It wasn't there. Must have been stolen."

Carl smiled a cold smile and pulled up a chair next to her at the table. He leaned in very close to her and spoke softly. "Here's the thing, Lucia. You think this is no big deal, that you'll jerk me around for a while and then I'll let you go. But this is the biggest deal you'll ever be involved in. And it's a much bigger deal than you can handle."

For the first time, Carl's manner and tone started to cut through her confidence. He could see it, and he continued.

"Whatever your friend Ricardo was doing, it was a threat to this entire fucking country, the country that I'm going to protect. And if you don't make me think that you are helping me, I am going to bury you so far down that you will never come up for air."

"I didn't do nothing wrong."

"Then it's a shame that the next time you'll see your little Carmela she'll have three grown kids and grey hair." He leaned in closer and smiled that chilling smile. "You understand what I'm saying?"

Lucia understood very well; if in just a couple of hours they already knew about her infant daughter, they weren't fooling around. She was afraid of them, but not as afraid as she was of the man who'd sent her to the apartment in the first place. "Does my mother know about this?" she asked, since her mother was caring for the little girl.

Carl looked at his watch. "The agents will be at her house in twenty minutes. Is she afraid of guns?"

Game, set, and match. The FBI was an entity that Lucia might be able to stand up to; her mother was not. Even if she hadn't been told to give in, she would have done so at that point anyway. "I was looking for money."

Carl gave a slight nod of satisfaction and approval and said, "Which money might that be?"

"Ricardo's money. He said he was being paid a lot of money, and he would buy me stuff with it when he came back. It was promised to me, and since he ain't around to use it, I went looking for it." When Carl didn't look convinced, she added, "I earned it, you know? I took enough shit from him."

"Who was paying him?"

"I don't know his name; Ricardo never talked to me about it. He thought it was this big secret, that I didn't know nothing about it." She shook her head in disapproval. "The asshole."

"So you never saw this guy?"

"No," she lied, "but Ricardo was scared shit of him, I can tell you that. Every time he talked to him, he got all nervous."

"You were there when they talked?"

She nodded. "A couple of times. He talked soft into the phone, and I pretended like I was asleep."

"Where was this?" Carl asked.

"At his place."

Carl was not happy to hear that, since every call from the apartment phone and Ricardo's cell phone had been checked and rechecked, turning up nothing suspicious nor apparently related to the explosives.

"What phone did he use?"

"A cell phone. He thought they wouldn't be able to connect him to it."

"We checked all the calls he made," Carl said.

She nodded. "What do I have to do to get out of here?"

It was time for Carl to appear sympathetic to her plight. "Lucia, you didn't start all this; you got caught up in it, that's all. So we don't want you; we want what you know."

She nodded again. "Okay. Ricardo . . . he didn't use his cell phone."

"Which one did he use?"

She pointed out into the hallway. "He used mine. The one your people took from me. I told you he was an asshole."

Tim had to take deep breaths
and tell himself not to panic.

He instinctively knew that the actions he took now would set the
stage for all that would follow, and he didn't want to make any stupid mistakes. He had to think and act deliberately, even if he were
operating in an area in which he had absolutely no experience.

His estimation was that he'd have at least a five-hour head start.
Nick said he'd be back to get Tim in an hour. When he realized
that Tim had left, it was unlikely that he'd immediately pick up the
phone and notify Novack. Surely he'd give Tim time in the hope
that he would come back.

But Tim would not be back.

Tim usually behaved logically, often to a fault. But while logic
right now told him that running was foolish and self-destructive, it
was no match for his gut feeling that it was his only chance. Meredith's phone call had confirmed that feeling. Since the moment he
had met Cashman, everything had gone according to some diabol-
ical script, and somehow he had to rewrite it.

He quickly filled two suitcases with clothes and put them in his
car. He also took what he had come to think about as simply "the
file." He had never opened it, and thought he never would, but he
recognized the possibility that it could be crucial to his current situation.

Tim went back in to get Kiley and write a note to Nick, which he left in an envelope on the door. It said that he needed a little time to think, and anything Nick could do to arrange that would be very much appreciated. He knew that it would lead Nick to believe that Tim might come back, and he regretted deceiving him that way, but he had no real choice.

Just before he left, he made a final, crucial decision. He went to the top of his bedroom closet and opened a box he kept up there, a box which contained only a handgun. Tim had gotten it after Maggie's death, when the media uproar resulted in his receiving a number of death threats. He hadn't touched it since, but thought he should take it, though recognizing that it might prove more dangerous than helpful to have it.

With Kiley in the back seat, Tim's first stop was his bank to get money. He knew that once he was considered a fugitive, his credit cards and other financial instruments would be cut off. For now, though, the bank would have no reason to think there was anything wrong.

Tim had twenty-one thousand dollars in his checking account, which he withdrew. He had to fill out an IRS form, which was required for any cash deposit or withdrawal over ten thousand. He didn't hesitate; tax issues were not exactly his primary concern at the moment.

He also took the maximum cash advances off his credit cards, smiling and telling the obviously curious bank assistant manager that he was headed to Vegas. By the time he left, he had almost thirty-five thousand, which would tide him over for a long while if used carefully.

Half of the bank employees were staring at him as he walked out the door. Tim knew that the police would soon be talking to each and every one of them, and that their recounting of his actions would serve as further proof that he had become a fugitive.

The next issue was Kiley. Much as he wanted to, he couldn't take her with him. It would inhibit his movements and call attention to him, neither of which he could afford. But he certainly couldn't leave her behind; to do so would almost guarantee her a trip to the county animal shelter. He was not going to run away from a prison cage by putting her in one.

He briefly considered asking Danny or Will to care for her, but decided that Eden would be a better choice. He felt that he could trust her to be responsible, and that Kiley would enjoy being with her and Travis more than alone in Danny or Will's apartment all day. Eden would provide Kiley with a loving, permanent home if that was how this all turned out, and odds were it would be.

Tim did not think that leaving Kiley with Eden would result in any legal difficulties for her. He was not yet technically a fugitive, and she could say with some truth that she was simply doing a favor for a friend. She had no way of knowing that the friend was about to be a wanted, and hunted, man.

Tim headed for Eden's house, hoping that she was home. If she wasn't, Tim would probably change his plans and keep Kiley with him. He had an obligation to make sure she was safe.

Not only was Eden home, she saw him coming through the window and came out on to the porch to greet him. The look on his face told her that something was very wrong, and she said, "What is it?"

"Can we go in the house?" he asked, and she nodded and brought him inside.

Once they were inside, he said, "I was hoping you could take care of Kiley. I'm going to go away for a while."

"Where are you going?" she asked.

"I'm not sure. Will you watch her?"

"Of course I'll watch her. But please tell me what's going on."

"The finger . . . the finger in the box . . . it was Maggie's."

Eden put her hand to her mouth, and her knees seemed to sag. "Oh, my God. No . . ."

"They're planning to arrest me, but I can't let them do it. If they take me in, I'll never get out."

"How could they know it was . . ."

"The DNA test. According to Nick, there's no doubt about it."

"But how could that be?"

"I don't know. It doesn't make any sense, but if it's really her finger, then I don't see how she could have died in the explosion. But that raises other possibilities that are terrible." Tim no longer had any real hope that Maggie was somehow alive; logic told him that she had suffered the same fate as Sheila.

Eden knew he was talking about the possibility of Maggie being tortured, but she wouldn't voice it. "Oh, Tim, I'm so sorry."

"Thank you. And I appreciate your doing this more than you know. If they find out about this, just tell them that I asked you to watch my dog, which you've done before. You had no way of knowing I was running from the police."

"But where are you running to?"

"I honestly don't know. Someplace out of the way, and private, where I can think about what to do next."

"Stay here."

Tim's answer was immediate and firm. "No. Thank you, but no."

"They would have no reason to look here. Nobody except Nick even knows we're friends."

"Eden, you could go to jail. This is not a game."

She got angry. "You think I consider this a game? Two people have been murdered, and I think this is a game?"

"I cannot involve you in this any more than I already have."

"I'm not talking about you staying here permanently. Just until we can figure out a safe place for you to be. It would give you time to think about your next step. Because you need to do more than hide. And I can help. You're going to need someone to help."

He knew she was right. He had to learn who was behind this nightmare, and what they had to gain from it, because he couldn't hide forever. As a fugitive, alone, it seemed an impossible ask.

He nodded. "Just for tonight. One way or the other I leave here tomorrow."

Nick knew even before he saw
the note that Tim had run.

It was an intuition he had, the kind that was always right. He sometimes wistfully thought that if he could harness that kind of instinct
and apply it to something more useful, like the stock market, he'd
never have to spend another day in court.

Tim's running was understandable, logical even from his point
of view, but Nick knew it to be ill-advised. Tim was not Osama bin
Laden preparing to hide out in the mountains in Afghanistan. He
was a businessman from New Jersey, and Nick figured his only out-
door survival experience was probably sitting in the upper deck at
Giants Stadium for a December game against the Redskins.

In this case Nick's instinct had served Tim well. He had decided not to call Novack until he had Tim in hand, ready to turn
himself in. Since neither Tim nor Nick had officially been notified
that there was an arrest warrant issued, Tim's not being available
would not immediately lead to his being classified as a fugitive. A
person cannot be avoiding an arrest he does not know is being attempted.

But in the real world that was a short-term respite, and either
way Tim would eventually be taken into custody. Whether he tried
to contact Nick in the meantime was obviously up to him, but if he
did, he wouldn't like what he would hear.

Nick had nothing to gain by hanging out at Tim's apartment, so he drove back to his office. On the way, he called Tim's home phone, of course knowing that Tim was not there. When the machine picked up, Nick said, "Tim, Nick Alexander here. When you get a chance, give me a call. Nothing important, I'm just checking in to see if anything is going on. Thanks."

Novack and the prosecutors would eventually come into possession of that taped message, and it would appear that Nick had no knowledge of anything urgent regarding his client, and that it was therefore more likely that his client also was unaware of his imminent arrest. It was a small advantage, but one that would be wiped away when Tim's flight from law enforcement became obvious.

Once back in the office, Nick called Eden at her house. She was sitting with Tim in her living room when she saw on caller ID who it was. "It's Nick," she said to Tim before picking it up.

"Please don't tell him you've seen or talked to me."

She nodded and picked up the phone. "Hello?"

"It's Nick. Has Tim contacted you?"

"No. Why?"

"Eden, if you talk to him, tell him to call me. Tell him it's not too late, but pretty soon it will be. Do you understand?"

"Yes."

With that one-word answer, he knew that Eden had in fact seen Tim, and might be with him at that very moment. If not, she would have questioned Nick about his cryptic message, and asked him what was going on. But she didn't ask any questions, which meant she already knew the answers.

"Eden, stay as far away from this as you can. Don't make the worst mistake of your life."

"Thanks, big brother."

"I mean it. You can wind up in prison." He could have added, "or worse," but he didn't. The fact was, based on the evidence Nick was aware of, Tim was very possibly a killer of women, and an unusually sick one at that.

As unconventional an attorney as Nick was in a lot of ways, at his core he was a loyal servant of the system. It was the job of a defense attorney to provide the accused with the best possible representation, so that a jury could fairly decide guilt or innocence. Nick spent no time at all wondering whether his clients had committed the crime of which they were accused; the knowledge would have no impact on his work.

But this time, now, it was different. It was personal. If Tim was guilty, Eden was in more danger than she could handle.

Nick got off the phone feeling more afraid and less in control than at any time he could remember. His client was perched on the edge of a cliff, and his sister was out there with him.

And it was a long way down.

By three o'clock, it was apparent that Tim was not coming back to his office, and Novack was in a foul mood. A dozen cops had wasted hours on what should have been a simple arrest, and Novack felt it was his fault.

"You want to pick this up again tomorrow?" Anders asked.

Novack shook his head. "No way . . . the guy is screwing with us. He's going down tonight."

"You want to take him at his house?"

Novack nodded. "Yeah, and we don't need this goddamn army with us. We take a couple of guys with us, and he's posing for a mug shot."

"Or we could call Nick Alexander and give him the opportunity to bring his client in."

Novack shook his head; there was no way he was going to extend that courtesy to Tim or his lawyer. He was not going to tip Tim off a second sooner than was necessary.

For Novack the search warrant they had was the key. It would allow them to enter Tim's apartment if he wasn't home, and look for incriminating evidence. Maybe if they were lucky they'd find a drawerful of fingers and a bottle of preservative.

Either way, one thing was certain. Tim Wallace was going down that night.

"I know where you can stay," Eden said.

"I can't believe I didn't think of it before."

She said it after an hour of their discussing what might be the best steps for Tim to take to maximize his chances of at least surviving. Their conversation was punctuated by lengthy, periodic silences, as each tried to grapple with the predicament Tim was in.

It was a bizarre feeling for both of them; they were sitting in her den, petting the dogs as they talked. It could have been a perfectly normal scene, except what they were discussing couldn't have been further from normal.

"Where?"

"There's a house in Lincoln Park; it's fairly isolated . . . set in the woods. The school owns it; we usually use it for visiting professors, graduate exchange students, that kind of thing." She stood up to go through her desk for her address book.

"And it's empty now?" Tim asked.

She nodded. "For at least the next six weeks. A colleague of mine has been living there, but he's on sabbatical."

"If I was found there it would be obvious to the police that you arranged it."

She had already thought of that. "No, I could have told you about it long ago. We could even have visited my friend there. Look, it's the perfect situation; there aren't many neighbors, but anyone who lives nearby would be used to seeing different people in the house at different times. There's even a car there that you could use."

"That's good, because people would see me. I can't just hole up in there, I'd have to come and go."

"Why?"

"Because I can't hide forever. Somehow I've got to figure out who has done this to me, and I'm not going to be able to call suspects in to be interviewed. I'm going to need to be out there."

She looked dubious about the prospect. "You have any experience at things like this?"

He shook his head. "Of course not."

They lapsed into another period of silence, broken by her saying, "I can help."

"You're already doing much too much."

She shook her head. "I can help you check things out, talk to people, it depends on what you need."

He couldn't help but smile. "You have any experience with this?"

"About the same as you."

He shook his head. "No, you're way too far out on a limb on this already. The more you do the more jeopardy you're in. I'll bet Nick told you that when he called."

"He did."

"He's right."

"I know he is, and I'll be careful. But you need help, and I seem to be the only chance you've got. Now we don't have a lot of time, so we can debate it some more, or we can make concrete plans."

They continued to make plans, figuring out everything from how they would contact each other without risking detection, to how they would change his appearance so as to reduce the chance of his being identified.

By the time Tim went to sleep, he had closely cropped light brown hair, drugstore, non-prescription glasses, and a plan to grow a moustache and goatee. Even without the facial hair, the difference was surprisingly dramatic, so much so that he stared at himself in the mirror.

Eden came up behind him. "Your own mother wouldn't even recognize you."

He nodded. "That's the good news."

"What's the bad?"

"Novack's not my mother."

At that very moment, the man who was not Tim's mother was in Tim's apartment, directing a thorough search of the place. After determining that Tim was not at home, Novack and Anders had presented the warrant to the superintendent, who had no choice but to let them in. Novack had been in there once before, after Maggie's death, for one of his sessions questioning Tim.

The search had so far turned up nothing of obvious value, though forensics was still busy doing their thing. Novack was by this time all but certain that Tim was on the run; there were no suitcases to be found, and even the toiletries had been removed from the bathroom.

Novack made the decision to call Nick at home. "I'm at your client's apartment, counselor."

"Let me speak to him." Nick said this knowing full well that Tim was not there, but hoping to maintain the ruse that neither he nor Tim had any idea he was a wanted man.

"That would be difficult," Novack said. "He's not here."

"Then what the hell are you doing there?" Nick asked, though he knew the answer all too well.

"Looking for your client, and exercising a lawful search warrant."

"I'm coming over. I don't want you stealing any towels."

"Bring Wallace with you, so I can arrest him."

"On what charge?"

"The murder of Margaret Wallace." McDermott, the county prosecutor, had made the correct decision to only charge Tim with Maggie's murder, not Sheila's. They had much more evidence, circumstantial and otherwise, in Maggie's case, and they could hold the other charge in reserve.

Nick could have argued with Novack, disputed the charge and protested Tim's innocence. But none of that would have done any good, or had any effect at all on Novack's actions.

Soon, if they hadn't done so already, they would come to realize that Tim had fled. At that point the manhunt would begin in earnest, and Nick would be rendered even less relevant than he already was.

If that were possible.

The media was enlisted in
the hunt for Tim at six A.M.

Novack held a hastily arranged news conference on the steps in front of the state police headquarters. The decision to do so had actually been made six hours earlier, but it was felt that an early morning announcement would generate more heat, and at a time when the audience would be awake to feel it.

Generating heat would have been good for more than one reason. The temperature outside as the conference was about to begin was sixteen degrees, and one of the reporters who got there early saw Novack arriving at the location and asked him, "Why the hell did you pick this place to do it?"

"Because the Rose Garden wasn't available," Novack said to the shivering man, before going inside.

At the appointed time, Novack walked out of headquarters and strode to the microphone. He was not wearing a coat, just his sports jacket. It made him feel superior to the reporters, who were shivering and huddled together to ward off the cold.

Like the police at most such conferences, Novack adopted the attitude that he was there reluctantly, as if his attendance were compulsory. This was of course despite the fact that the reporters had not convened the gathering, and didn't even know why they were there. Nonetheless, Novack treated their questions as if they were unwanted intrusions, and the questioners as if they were there to defeat the cause of justice.

The truth was that Novack hated these moments; public speaking of any kind made him uncomfortable, which made him irritable, which made him sullen and uncommunicative. Since the entire purpose of the event was to communicate, the situation was not ideal.

"Timothy Wallace is wanted for questioning as a person of interest in the investigation of the murder of Margaret Wallace. We are asking the public to call the hotline number that has been set up if they see him or have any information as to his whereabouts."

Since many of the same crime reporters had covered the investigation soon after Maggie's death, this was a jolting piece of news, and prompted a barrage of questions, few of which Novack would answer.

"Why now? Is there new evidence in the case?"

"I can't discuss any of the evidence in an ongoing investigation," Novack said. "You people know that by now."

"Is there a warrant out for his arrest?"

"We are not prepared to discuss the warrant at this time."

"So there is one?"

"Next question."

"Is he on the run? Is that why you need the public's help in finding him?"

"We have no information as to his whereabouts. When we find him, we'll know why we couldn't find him."

Novack showed Tim's picture and passed out copies, and announced the number to call with information. He agreed to answer one or two more questions, incorrectly implying that he had answered the previous ones.

"Do you consider him armed and dangerous?"

"I would advise people not to find out; if you see him, call the number and let the police handle it. Thank you very much."

With that, Novack headed back to the comfort of the headquarters building, not fully exhaling until he closed the door behind him.

The police hunt for Tim was the lead story on every morning's newscast. Ordinarily, a story like it would have been in fourth or fifth position, but the fact that it rekindled a previously hot story, aided by an otherwise slow news day, was enough to make it number one.

By this time Tim was in the Lincoln Park house that Eden had told him about. He had been busy in the preceding hours. Among other things, he had rented a prepaid cell phone at an all-night electronics store, using a fake name and not having to show identification. He put down five hundred dollars in cash on it, fearful that more would attract attention.

Tim had also stopped and stolen license plates off a car at a shopping mall, and put them on his own car, in case he had to use it. Eden had said there was a car at the house, and if there was, Tim would keep his own car in the garage or out of sight. He could determine later which car he would use. Although he was about to be the subject of an intense manhunt, the theft of the plates was the first actual crime he was aware of ever committing in his life.

Tim had called Danny from a pay phone early in the morning. "What's the matter?" Danny had asked, once he got himself awake.

"They're trying to arrest me for Maggie's death."

"What? This is bullshit; you took a goddamn lie detector test, and—"

"It was her finger. At the racquetball club, it was her finger." The thought was so horrifying, that he found it jarring each time he had to verbalize it.

"Oh, no . . . Tim . . . how the hell could that be?"

"I don't know, but I have to find out."

"Where are you now?"

"I'm on the way to Pennsylvania, to a motel outside of Philly." It was a lie, a planned one. Tim wasn't sure he told it because he didn't want to put Danny in the position of having to conceal something from the police, or because he wasn't sure he could trust anyone, not even his partner and best friend. He would sort it out later, but for the moment he wouldn't take any chances.

"Tim, if the cops are after you . . . are you sure this is a good idea?"

"No, but it's the only one I've got."

"So how can I help?"

"Pay my lawyer for me when he comes to you. We can take it out of the company, and—"

"No problem, Tim. I'll give him whatever is necessary. What else can I do?"

"Nothing. You need to stay as far away from this as possible."

"What the hell are you going to do?"

"Figure this out."

Three hours later, Tim hadn't come any closer to figuring anything out. He felt reasonably safe in the house, but he knew all too well that it was only a stopgap measure. Eventually he would be found, unless he did something to prove his innocence and find Cashman, the man who killed Sheila.

And probably Maggie.

"I'm sorry I did that to you,"

Tim said as soon as Nick picked up the phone. He was worried about Nick's reaction; he needed him as an ally.

"You didn't do it to me," Nick said. "You did it to you."

"I just didn't feel like I had a choice."

"You had a choice, Tim. You made the wrong one. I'm sorry to tell you, but you felt the pressure and you threw up a goddamn air ball."

Nick's blunt assessment simultaneously annoyed and scared Tim. "Where do we go from here?"

"I'm under a legal obligation to advise you that you are committing a felony by avoiding arrest, and to advise you to surrender to the proper authorities immediately."

"And if I don't?"

"Then you don't. You're calling the shots here, at least for now."

"Will you continue to help me?"

"Of course I'll help you; I'm your lawyer."

"Thank you," said Tim, obviously relieved. "You don't know how much I appreciate that."

"Before you say anything else, I do not want you to tell me where you are. If you do, I'm obligated to reveal it to the police. I'm not crazy about obligations like that."

"Okay. What am I allowed to tell you?"

"Any ideas you have that might help your situation . . . anything you want me to follow through on. Things like that."

"I've been trying to think that through," Tim said. "I have no idea who would be doing this to me, or why. The only thing I have to go on, the only thing I know with certainty, is that Cashman is behind it. Or at least involved in it."

"But you don't know who he is. Or why he targeted you."

"No. But I saw him; I spoke to him. And I have his picture . . . you have his picture."

Nick could immediately see where he was going with this, and jumped on it. He picked up the Cashman sketch from his desk and looked at it. "The media will eat it up. I've probably had fifty calls already looking for information from our side; when they get this they'll go crazy."

"Somebody has to know him. When they see him they'll come forward. Should we offer a reward?"

"You have access to money?"

"Absolutely. Just contact my partner, Danny McCabe. He'll front the money from the company for this and for your fees." He paused, then asked, "Is he allowed to do that?"

"Sure. Everybody's entitled to an expensive defense."

"Good. At least it's a first step."

"And not a bad one. I'll get right on it," Nick said. He had never met a camera he didn't like, and the prospect of starting what would be a media barrage appealed to him.

"Can I keep calling you?" Tim asked. "I mean, would they tap your phone or anything like that?"

Nick had thought of this and discounted it. "No way, at least not now. The chance that they'd risk destroying their own case by breaking attorney-client privilege would scare them off. They know I'd cut their balls off. Maybe later when they get desperate, but not now."

"Listen, Nick . . ."

"What?"

"I've been trying to look at this a little bit from your point of view. You don't know me, and you probably think I'm guilty. But—"

"You're not going to tell me you're innocent, are you?"

"Actually, I was."

"Save your breath. Believe it or not, for the moment it's irrelevant."

"But as a human being, I would think you'd—"

Nick interrupted. "So you wanted a human being, but you hired a lawyer by mistake?"

Tim smiled to himself. "I guess so."

"You must not be too bright," Nick said. "You have a TV where you are?"

"Yes."

"Then start watching it, because your nonhuman lawyer's good-looking face is going to be everywhere."

"This is Carl White, special agent with the FBI, from the Miami office," Captain Donovan said.

"Good to meet you," Anders said, shaking White's hand.

"Uh-oh," said Novack, aware this wasn't a social visit. FBI agents don't just show up; what they often do is come in and take over cases. "What's going on?"

"Agent White is interested in our investigation of Tim Wallace."

"Why is that?" Novack asked.

"Remember that car that exploded near the turnpike?" Carl asked. "The driver of the car called Wallace's office from Florida twice in the ten days before his death."

"Any idea why?" Anders asked.

"Not yet."

"It doesn't make sense," Novack said. "I don't see Wallace as a terrorist blowing up buildings. He does his killing one on one, up close and personal."

"But I understand his wife was killed in an explosion?" White asked.

Novack nodded. "She was. And we've also connected him to a now deceased explosives expert in Carson, Wyoming."

White reacted to this; it was further confirmation that Tim was somehow involved in the detonation in New Jersey. "How did he become deceased?"

"He had his throat slit in prison. And we believe his wife was Wallace's second victim."

White was clearly surprised to hear this. "Wallace had two victims?"

"At a minimum," Novack said.

"I've agreed with Agent White that we will share all relevant information from both his and our investigations," said Donovan.

"With who determining relevance?" Novack asked. What he saw as Donovan's capitulation to the FBI did not qualify as a major news event; Donovan would have had no stomach for a fight with the Feds. That's not how careers are made.

Donovan let a harder edge creep into his voice. "That will be determined jointly."

"Hey, I'm not looking to step on your toes," White said. "We all want to get Wallace off the street and find out what the hell is going on. The resources of the bureau might even be helpful to you."

Novack thought about that for a few moments, and decided he could probably live with it. He stood and shook White's hand. "They might at that," he said.

"This is the man we are looking for.

He goes by the name of Jeff Cashman, but that is probably an alias." As Nick said this, he was holding up the sketch of Cashman so that Larry King's audience could get a good look at it. It was his fifth television appearance of the day, so if anyone had not seen Cashman's picture by now, that person likely was one of the few remaining Americans still resisting the advance of cable television.

Nick was sitting in a studio on West Fifty-fourth Street in Manhattan, from where he had done all of the interviews with the various networks. He had not actually met a single person he was questioned by all day.

"And why are you looking for him?" asked Larry, a man who could always be counted on to follow the script and lead the guest to a comfortable and desired place.

"Unlike the police, I do not intend to talk publicly about the evidence, but it would be very fair to say that Mr. Cashman is a person of interest in this case."

"Is he of interest to the police as well?" King asked.

"He should be," Nick said, frowning his disdain for the other side. "They've known about him for weeks, yet they've refused to release this sketch publicly and put out the request that I am putting out today. If anyone has any information at all about this man, if they have ever seen him or know who he is, please call me at 201-525-3176. We are offering a reward of twenty-five thousand dollars for information which leads to our finding him. Do not approach him; we consider him armed and very dangerous."

"Your client, Timothy Wallace, has an arrest warrant out for him. Do you know where he is?"

"I don't have the slightest idea," said Nick. "I'm very worried about him."

"Worried about what?"

"His safety. There are very dangerous people out there who have targeted him, and he is justifiably frightened."

"So you've spoken to him?"

"As I said, I have no idea where he is. As to whether I have spoken with him, that is not a question I would answer whatever the facts were. It starts to get into the area of attorney-client privilege. I just can't go there; I know you understand that, Larry."

Both King and people who subsequently called in tried to press Nick for more information, but he was a master at providing evasive answers. He left satisfied that he had accomplished his main goals. He'd got Cashman's face in front of the public and also conveyed to that public that there was definitely another side to the story, even if he wouldn't come close to revealing what that other side was.

For Tim, sitting in a strange house watching Nick on TV, the feeling was totally surreal. Hearing himself talked about on national television, in a predicament that was at the same time bewildering and overwhelmingly frightening, was almost too much to bear.

He turned off the television and got into the strange bed, trying to force himself to think his way out of this disaster. Concentration was hard, mostly because he had never felt so alone. He missed Maggie more than ever, and now feared for her in death as much as he ever had in life. What had she endured? How much had she suffered? How could he have left her so unprotected from whatever evil it was that had entered their lives?

With Maggie gone, there was really no one he could fully trust. Someone with an intimate knowledge of him might very well be conspiring against him right now. How else could his life have been so thoroughly destroyed other than by someone who understood it?

Someone had known which boat was his and when he would be on it. They'd known where he would go on New Year's Eve, and where he lived. They knew that he'd been in Wyoming, and where and when he played racquetball.

Someone knew as much about his life as he did.

It was disconcerting to Tim that the only person he could think of who fit that bill was Danny.

The facts were clear; Danny knew all or most of the things necessary to have pulled off the plot. He and Will had practically dragged him to the Purple Rose for New Year's, and he would have known when Tim would be out on the boat. As his partner, Tim would certainly have mentioned where he was going on a business trip, and Danny clearly would have known exactly where to post the flyer. As for the placing of the finger at the racquetball court, Danny's ability to have done that was obvious.

But what would he have to gain? Could it somehow have to do with the business? Perhaps Danny was stealing money, or using the company for illicit purposes? But why go to such lengths to do this to Tim? For instance, why kill Sheila?

Tim knew that there were many questions like this that he just did not yet have the answer to. He also simply could not imagine the Danny that he knew doing any of this. But the truth was that he could not comprehend anyone doing it, yet somebody obviously was.

It pained Tim to even consider it, but Danny had to be at the top of the list of suspects.

A list that at the moment included only one name.

Lucia Angelos was glad it was over. She'd done as she was told, the FBI was gone, and Ricardo was out of her life. And she'd even gotten some money out of it in the process.

It was time for her to take that money and start living, which was what she told her sister Maria on one of their endless phone calls. "I'm going to move to New York and get a job."

Maria, who had been advocating such a move for five years, and who lived in New York herself, said, "You always say that, but you never do it."

"This time I will," vowed Lucia. "There's nothing to keep me here. In New York at least I have you."

"But I have Orlando." She was referring to her husband, with whom she did not have a marriage made in heaven.

"So you can leave him, and we'll move in together."

Maria laughed at the absurdity of it. "Of course. We'll go to Park Avenue and have servants."

Lucia was not familiar with Park Avenue, and she was about to ask about it when there was a knock on her door. "Hold on a sec . . ." she said, then put the phone down and went to answer it.

She opened it and saw the man she hoped never to see again. "Hello, Lucia, nice to see you. You're looking well."

"I did what you wanted. I told the FBI everything you said."

He nodded. "I know you did; you did a very nice job. I'm just here to make things clean and neat."

"What . . ."

He moved toward her, and as he did she looked directly into his eyes. Suddenly she knew exactly why Ricardo had been so afraid of this man.

But by then it was too late.

By ten o'clock in the morning, over a thousand
tips had come in to Nick's hotline.

It was far more than the firm's investigative arm was equipped to
handle, and therefore it was likely that more than twice that number could not even get through to leave a message. The hope and
expectation was that anyone with legitimate information would be
persistent.

Techniques were in place for screening the tips, in order to
eliminate the obvious fakes and focus on those likely to really have
information about Cashman. Some were easy to ignore, like the
man who claimed Cashman was her reincarnated great-uncle, or
the woman who was positive he was the man who had seduced her
last summer aboard his spaceship.

Nick could only passively wait for something to develop on the
Cashman front, and passive waiting was never his specialty. He
wanted to know all the evidence the prosecution had against Tim,
but at this stage of the case they had no obligation to turn over anything in pretrial discovery. That wouldn't come until Tim was in
custody and arraigned.

Nick had his sources within the department, and he worked
them vigorously for information. Novack was not about to reveal
anything, but there were plenty of people privy to the case who just
might. Nick had no doubt he would eventually find out what he

needed to know. Whether it would help to know it was an entirely different story.

Eden Alexander, who by her own estimation hadn't watched more than ten hours of television in the previous year, sat glued to the set. Tim hadn't contacted her since leaving for the house, and she certainly would not contact him, in case the police were somehow watching her. So she followed the coverage, cringing every time CNN broke in with a "breaking news" banner, which seemed like every ten minutes. None of them had anything to do with Tim.

She and Tim had agreed that, even though she knew his new cell phone number, if they had to communicate with each other it would be through e-mail. She opened a new e-mail address on Yahoo with the screen name "Kileysfriend," and checked it repeatedly. To this point Tim had not sent her any messages, so all she could do was wait.

Eden was not taking Kiley and Travis for walks on the street, instead using the yard behind her house. She tried to be alert to her surroundings, to see if she were being watched, and so far had not detected anything. Being new to this kind of intrigue, she had little confidence that this meant much; for all she knew they could be tracking her every move, and she was simply oblivious to it.

Within a matter of hours after his moment of clarity regarding Danny, Tim had reversed himself and decided that it was simply not possible. He knew him too well to believe him capable of anything like this. He consciously put it to the back of his mind, took a deep breath, and opened "the file."

It is a truism in Washington that some of the most powerful people in government are complete unknowns to the public at large. One such person was Gregory Campbell, who had come to Washington from his home in Boise, Idaho, as part of the congressional page program. He never left, attending Georgetown University and then immediately securing a job as a low-level minority staffer on the House Appropriations Committee.

In the intervening twenty-five years, Campbell had made absolutely no effort to shed his cloak of public anonymity. Working fourteen-hour days, longer if one were to factor in business lunches and dinners, he became a crucial cog in the workings of government. He advanced to the position of lead minority staffer on the Senate Appropriations Committee, which is where he came under the wing of Senator Fred Collinsworth.

If one had to come under a wing, that was about as good as it could get. Collinsworth could make things happen for people he really needed and pretended to care about. In Gregory Campbell, he found such a person. The senator, with his myriad contacts and influence in the financial world, gradually and secretly made Campbell a very rich man. There was no outright bribery, no envelopes under the table, just the occasional amazingly prescient stock tip, or a fortuitous land purchase in an area that would soon be adjacent to new highways.

The senator had eventually arranged for Campbell to move over to the executive branch, specifically the General Services Administration. From there he could be even more influential in steering large contracts to places the senator wanted them steered.

It was an ideal relationship, and one that would come in handy for the senator in dealing with the potential political disaster that Tim Wallace's fugitive status represented.

As soon as Gregory got the call that he was to meet with Keith Rivers, he knew Senator Collinsworth had a problem. Since people as rich and powerful as Collinsworth rarely solved or confronted problems personally, Rivers was always his chosen solver. He was as good a solver as Gregory had ever been around.

They met at a restaurant in northern Virginia, though they could have dined anywhere in Washington and not attracted attention. They would not be seen as a "power couple," in fact, neither would likely be recognized by anyone but their friends and associates.

Soon after they sat down, the waiter came over and asked, "Would you care for something to drink? Or would you like to hear our specials?"

"No," said Rivers.

The waiter seemed not to know what to make of this direct-ness, so he mumbled, "I'll give you a few moments," and beat a hasty retreat.

Once he was gone, Rivers asked, "Have you heard about the man wanted for murder in New Jersey?"

Gregory had no idea what he was talking about; he was not a watcher of television, nor did he read about crime stories in the newspaper. Besides, a story about a murderer in New Jersey would not have attracted his attention anyway. There were enough mur-ders in Washington. "I don't think so . . ."

"Daniel McCabe's partner is currently a fugitive."

It started to click into place for Gregory, since he remembered that Collinsworth had dealt with this potential embarrassment once before. "Is that the guy whose wife died on the boat?"

Rivers nodded. "It is. There have been a number of develop-ments in the case; you should familiarize yourself with the media coverage."

"I will," he said. Gregory was now fully aware of the purpose of the dinner, but he knew that Rivers, never a master of subtlety, would state it explicitly. It was somewhat insulting, since Gregory had certainly shown over time that he was savvy in matters like this. But it was the way Collinsworth instructed Rivers to operate, and that was not about to change anytime soon.

Gregory didn't have long to wait for Rivers to hit the nail on the head. "It can never become public knowledge that the senator had anything to do with the awarding of the contract to that com-pany. He didn't even know about it until long after the fact."

Gregory nodded in solemn agreement with what was in reality a total fantasy. "Of course."

"The grand strategy of awarding the contracts to small-business people was his; then he left the details to people like your-self."

"Right."

"He doesn't micromanage; he lets people do their jobs."

"Absolutely. That's one of his greatest strengths."

"Enjoy your dinner."

Rivers got up and left the restaurant without eating. Gregory wasn't sure that he had ever seen him eat, or that the senator even allowed it.

Gregory signaled for the waiter to come over. He wanted to hear the specials, and he sure as hell needed a drink.

Sitting in that strange house, reading
the file, Tim had never felt so alone,

not even in the weeks and months after losing Maggie.

The file included newspaper stories about Maggie's death and
the subsequent investigation, the coroner's report, the Coast Guard
report, and the other official documents that such an event always
produces in bulk. Once Tim had been cleared of the murder, he
was deemed entitled to see these records, and he received them
without making a request.

Tim had never wanted to read anything about that day, but he
had requested that Meredith prepare a file, should he one day decide that he was ready. The "readiness" day had never come, but
now he felt he had to go through it in the hope he might learn
something relevant to what he was going through.

It was beyond painful, and the worst part was the lack of hu-
manity that Maggie was granted by the cold type of the documents. In this paper world she was an object, without her smile,
without her personality, without her dreams. Page after page was
about Maggie, and yet they had nothing whatever to do with who
she was.

It was eerily awful to read about that day out on the boat, in
newspaper articles that were written while Tim had still been in the
hospital. At that point he was of course the only one who had real
knowledge of what had happened, so the stories were basically

speculation, albeit informed by the Coast Guard information office.

It was another jolt for Tim to realize that he, in fact, may not have had full knowledge of what really took place that day. If it was Maggie's finger that was found at the racquetball club, then it was entirely likely that she had not died in that explosion. It destroyed the only consolation that he had held on to, that her death was instantaneous and painless.

Tim was finding himself consumed by doubt. Had he not seen what he thought he saw? Could he have been wrong all these months about the events out on the water?

Tim tried to force himself to read the information dispassionately, approaching everything from a logical perspective. The story that the newspapers presented was a simple one; Tim had apparently left the boat to go into the water, and while Maggie was alone the motor caught fire and blew up.

A private plane traveling overhead saw the fire, though based on the size of the blaze it was believed that by the time the pilot spotted it, between five and ten minutes had passed since the explosion. The pilot had called in the emergency, and a Coast Guard cutter was quickly dispatched. By the time they arrived, the boat and Maggie were gone, dispatched by the force of the explosion and resulting fire into the sea. There were small pieces of the boat still floating and able to be retrieved, but Maggie's body was presumed to have been blown apart and washed away. Tim was found floating unconscious, alone, held up by his life jacket. No other boats were in the area, so there were no witnesses besides Tim to the actual event.

The Coast Guard report presented basically the same story, and Tim moved on to the police reports.

Suddenly, the realization hit him between the eyes. No other boats? There was an Oceanfast not far in the distance when he went into the water for the hat. It was close to them all day; he and Maggie had both admired it. And it was certainly close enough to see the explosion; there was no way they could have missed it.

How could the people on that boat not have reported it?

Tim quickly tried to answer that question for himself in a number of ways. Perhaps they were asleep, or they didn't want to be involved, or they were out there for a reason, having nothing to do with the explosion, that they didn't want anyone to know about.

But none of those answers rang true. They had to have witnessed, or at least heard, the explosion, and it was impossible to imagine that in such a situation they would not have tried to help.

Unless they were out there watching Tim's boat.

And waiting for it to blow up.

Anders and Novack went into Captain Donovan's office completely unprepared for what he had to say.

"There's a tip that came in from a guy who claims to know Jeff Cashman. I want you to check it out."

Novack was immediately skeptical, since he had long been convinced that Cashman did not exist. "Why is he coming to us? Why isn't he going after the reward?"

"Because he must want something else more than money," Donovan said. "My guess is he's looking for a 'get out of jail free' card."

"He's inside?" Anders asked in surprise, since the fact that the tipster was in prison would obviously make him even less credible.

"Captain, we're pretty busy on this, and—"

Donovan interrupted. "He said Cashman was his cellmate, and that Cashman is not his real name."

"What's his real name?" Novack asked, annoyed at this waste of time.

"I don't know. That's something for you to find out from this guy when you talk to him."

"Isn't there somebody else you can put on this?" Novack asked.

Donovan shook his head. "Not on something this important."

Novack and Anders made eye contact, conveying their mutual agreement that this was ridiculous. "Important?" Anders asked. "A prison informant? What makes him so important?"

"There's something you haven't told us yet?" Novack asked.

Donovan nodded. "There is. According to this guy, they were cellmates at Lampley Prison, just outside of Carson, Wyoming."

Despite Nick's stated assurance that
his phone would not be tapped,

Tim was reluctant to contact him too often. This time was worth
the risk, though, since he needed Nick's help to check out the
boat.

Nick's secretary answered the phone, and Tim asked to speak
with him, telling her that it was Jerry Koosman calling. It was a signal they had arranged: as a huge Mets fan, Nick had suggested using the name of the former Mets left-handed pitcher.

"Talk to me," Nick said immediately, not wanting these calls to
last too long.

"I read through all the reports on the day Maggie died. There is
no mention of another boat that was nearby. I saw it; it was definitely there, but the people on board apparently never reported the
explosion. The fire was seen and called in by a pilot flying over, five
to ten minutes later."

"So?"

"So people out on the water take care of each other; it's like a
private fraternity. They should have reported it, and there would
have to be a damn good reason if they didn't."

"Did you mention it when they questioned you back then?"

"I don't think so . . . I'm not sure."

"Why not?"

"I don't know . . . I guess I just assumed the people on the boat had been the ones to report it. I never thought to make the connection until now."

Nick didn't think much of this news, but it wasn't like he had anything better. "Anything distinctive about the boat? Maybe a skull and crossbones and a sign that said REALLY BAD GUYS ON BOARD?"

"Not quite, but here's where we catch a break," Tim said. "It was an Oceanfast 360, worth way over a million. Maggie and I were admiring it that day; we even joked about it."

"How many of them would there be around here?" Nick asked.

"No way for me to know, but I'd guess less than five. But this one was painted an ugly green . . . like the color that army khakis used to be. It also had two white stripes all the way around. I even mentioned it to Maggie. It would be the only one of its kind, if it hasn't been repainted."

"So let's find out who owns it," Nick said.

"How do we do that?"

"We take one of our investigators off the bullshit hunt for Cashman and put him on this."

"I definitely think it's worthwhile." Then, "So nothing is happening on Cashman?"

"The only thing happening is that every fucking crackpot east of Maui is trying to get the reward."

"He's out there, Nick," Tim said. "I'm not making him up."

Nick could hear the obvious frustration in Tim's voice. "Okay. I'm on this boat thing. You all right? Not taking any unnecessary chances?"

"I'm not doing anything. I'm sitting here watching my life disappear."

"We'll get you out of this."

"How?" Tim asked.

"Beats the shit out of me. But we'll think of something."

Sitting at a corner table at Spumoni's, a fashionable, overpriced D.C. restaurant, Jimmy Lee Curry was sort of glad Professor Richmond wasn't there to see him. Richmond was the man who took Jimmy under his wing at the University of Alabama, and who basically shepherded him all the way to a master's in journalism. Richmond had seen in Jimmy the makings of a crack investigative reporter, and he had instilled in him the need to be unbiased, ethical, and relentless.

The lessons had taken, and twenty-five years later Jimmy Lee Curry's byline was respected and feared. But as he became more and more successful, the very qualities that got him there became less essential.

Jimmy Lee was not the first reporter this happened to, nor would he be the last. And as far as Jimmy Lee was concerned, not a single one of them had complained.

The basic truth was that there were maybe a dozen journalists big enough to limit the extent of their investigative efforts to picking up their phone, and Jimmy Lee was one of them. People who had news to spread called him, and if he found it interesting enough, he wrote a column on it, and people fawned all over him as if he had uncovered a gem.

At this stage of his life, Jimmy Lee figured, the "relentless" trait was way overrated. Sitting in this restaurant, waiting for Susan Moreno to show up, buy him a great lunch, and slip him an important story, was pretty much as good as it got.

Susan was in her mid-thirties, a tall, strikingly beautiful woman who reminded Jimmy Lee of one of those great-looking football sideline reporters, who had nothing to offer except some prepackaged drivel, but who were still terrific to look at.

But Susan was not the "drivel" type. In fact, she was just about the best-looking shark Jimmy Lee had ever met. The top assistant to Walter Evans, the superstar junior senator from Ohio, Susan had the reputation around town as his enforcer. When Senator Evans wanted something to happen, he sent Susan Moreno to make it happen.

She performed basically the same function for Evans that Keith Rivers did for Senator Collinsworth; she just weighed a hundred and fifty pounds less and had a higher-pitched voice.

Susan always waited until coffee was ordered before delivering her message, and this time was no exception. "Have you heard about Tim Wallace, the guy in New Jersey who the police are after for killing his wife?"

"Of course." Jimmy Lee spent about six hours a day either poring through newspapers from around the country, or watching cable news, and the Wallace story was national in scope.

"Did you know his company was doing construction work on the Federal Center complex in Newark? They've been handling a lot of the security aspects of the buildings."

"Why is that important?"

"Because he got the work through Senator Collinsworth."

"Really? What is Collinsworth's connection to Wallace?" Jimmy Lee asked. "Why get him the work?"

"Wallace's partner is Collinsworth's nephew," she said.

This was moderately interesting to Jimmy Lee, but not the kind of bombshell that someone like Susan Moreno would spend an entire lunch waiting to detonate. "I assume there's more to this? Something that more directly benefits you and your boss?"

She smiled. "Pending our negotiations; we have to come to agreement on the terms."

"Which are?"

"You write this story, and then in two weeks, the day after the Federal Center opens, you write the follow-up piece."

He nodded; here it comes. "And that includes . . ."

"You of course remember the explosion on the Jersey Turnpike a while back?"

"Come on, Susan." Jimmy Lee was having trouble concealing his annoyance at these obvious questions.

"The driver of the car that blew up had called Wallace a few times in the week before he died." She waited a moment for this to sink in, and then added, "So what we have here is Collinsworth getting major security construction work for someone who in turn is dealing with a guy with a truckload of Cintron 421."

This was, in fact, a potential bombshell, and the question of what Susan's boss would gain from this story was now amply answered. Evans and Collinsworth were bitter rivals, a situation exacerbated when Collinsworth got the nod as head of the Senate Appropriations Committee. Evans was a disgruntled number two. They were also expected to play out their rivalry in the presidential election just two years away.

Jimmy Lee smiled. "Now you're talking."

Susan took a leisurely sip of her coffee, then put the cup down and returned the smile. "So, Jimmy Lee, you think this might be a decent story?"

"Do I need a second source on this?" It was common journalistic practice not to go with a story unless it was double-sourced, but Jimmy Lee occasionally waived that requirement when his single source was someone who had proven totally reliable in the past. Susan was such a person.

Susan shook her head. "This is rock solid."

"Why wait the two weeks for the second piece?" he asked.

She leaned forward, lowering her voice. "It's just been decided that the dignitaries the night of the opening will include the president of the United States. Now security will be tripled because of this, so there's no danger. But your story will say that President Markham just spent the evening in a building built by Senator Collinsworth's mad bomber."

Maybe Professor Richmond wouldn't approve of this kind of journalism, but it sure worked fine for Jimmy Lee. "Why don't you stay and get the check?" he asked, standing up. "I've got a story to write."

"You have no idea where he is?" Danny asked.

"Of course not," said Meredith. "You think he would tell me and not you?"

"I don't think he would tell anybody. But that's not what I mean. I mean, can you figure out where he might be? You run his life, for Christ's sake."

"Not this part of it," she said. "This part scares the hell out of me."

"He's going to be fine. He didn't do anything wrong and he's going to be fine."

"Is it having any effect on the business?" she asked.

He nodded. "Probably. The FBI has been down at the site, and Homeland Security has been going over the place as if Osama bin Laden were the architect. Although they might have been doing that anyway."

"Any chance they're going to cancel the opening?"

"Zero. Too many big shots are going to be there."

"Have the police talked to you?" she asked.

"Twice, the FBI once."

"What did you tell them?"

"That I don't know where he is, and that he would never do anything like they're saying."

Meredith nodded; she had pretty much said the same thing to the same people. Of course, if she knew where Tim was she would never tell the police anyway. She was not sure she could say the same for Danny.

"There was this woman . . . I saw him with her recently. Tall, blond hair . . . you have any idea who she is?" Danny asked.

"No," Meredith lied. "He never mentioned anyone." She neglected to say that Eden Alexander had called and invited Tim to dinner, and that he had accepted.

Eden Alexander. That was a name she was not about to share with Danny.

Georgie Silvers had no illusions about the opportunity that had presented itself. You don't spend twenty-two years, slightly more than half your life, in prison without knowing what you can and cannot get away with. What he had to say might get him some special considerations, but there was no way it was going to let him walk.

He wasn't sure he even wanted to walk. He had adjusted to life in this New Jersey state prison, and it had adjusted to him. Besides, even if he got out, he'd wind up back there anyway in a relatively short time. So he might as well just stay; that way he avoided the packing and unpacking.

These cops didn't even seem that interested in him, which also was no great surprise. They weren't the ones looking for the guy, and they hadn't been the ones to go public with his picture.

Novack put the sketch on the table. "So you know this man?"

Georgie nodded. "Yeah. I know him. I was on the inside with him up at Lampley."

"What's his name?" Anders asked.

George couldn't help laughing, even though he knew laughing at cops was not necessarily the best way to handle them. "What's his name? Come on, you guys know that ain't the way this works."

"You want something in return for the name?" Novack asked. "Is that it, Georgie? What can we do for you? Maybe a villa in the Caribbean? A suite at Caesar's Palace?"

"Come on," Georgie said. "I'm a reasonable guy. I got the name, you want it, we can make a deal."

"Who said we want the name?" asked Anders.

"You're here; you didn't come to shoot the shit with me, right? I don't remember you visiting me before. So you want it. I could have gone to that lawyer and collected the reward, but I'm trying to be a good citizen." The truth was the reward wouldn't do nearly as much for him as the cops could, even if he collected it. Georgie had no family on the outside, and little use for money on the inside.

"Your country salutes you," said Novack. "What the fuck do you want?"

"I want a job in the library. Right now they have me in the kitchen, and I'm sweating my ass off."

"You think we're here from the employment agency? We don't assign the jobs here, Georgie," said Anders.

"No, but you can convince the people who do. And in July, when they do the prisoner reassignments, I want to go to Milford." He was referring to Milford Federal Prison, a major step up in comfort level from his current accommodations, but not a place where repeat breaking-and-entering offenders like Georgie Silvers would wind up.

"Milford?" asked Novack, making no attempt to conceal his amusement. "That's minimum security. You want to go there? Run for Congress and take a bribe."

It was a long shot, and Georgie knew it. "I'll tell you what; if this guy turns out to be somebody important to you, then try and get me to Milford. Is that fair? Meanwhile, you can get me the library job."

Novack thought for a few moments and then nodded. "Okay . . . deal. Now what's his name?"

"Billy Zimmerman. We used to call him Dollar Bill, 'cause he was in for forging checks."

Novack and Anders made eye contact with each other at the possibility that "Dollar Bill" renamed himself "Cashman." It rang slightly too true for comfort.

"And he looked like this?" Anders asked, pointing at the sketch.

"Nah, not too much. There's a bunch of stuff that's different. But I can tell it's him."

"How?"

"That's what he told me he was going to look like, if he ever had to go into hiding. You know?"

Novack shook his head in annoyance. "No, we don't know. Why don't you tell us?"

"His girlfriend was a makeup artist or something; I think for one of those Broadway shows that goes on the road. She—"

Novack interrupted. "What was her name?"

"Denise. I don't know her last name. She was working upstate in Buffalo at the time on that show about the French guys. It was a musical."

"*Les Miz?*" Novack asked, since it happened to be the only Broadway show he had seen in the last ten years. He remembered looking around and realizing that he was the only person in the audience who was on the cop's side.

"Yeah, I think that was it. Anyway, she taught Billy how to do the makeup, but they arrested him in bed in the middle of the night. He said if he ever escaped, or if the cops were after him, he was going to change his appearance. He even had his girlfriend draw a picture of what he could look like."

Novack pointed to the sketch. "And that's it?"

Georgie nodded. "That's it."

The man who had killed Jeff Cashman didn't much care for his latest assignment.

Following someone was tedious work, the kind of work that dumb cops were invented to do. And following Eden Alexander was way beneath him; the only thing worse than leading her boring life was watching her lead that life.

It also made no sense at all. If they wanted to know where Wallace was, the way to go about it was not to wait for this broad to lead them to him. The way to do it was to grab her and start inflicting some pain and fear. His professional estimation was that it would take him less than four minutes to find out whatever she knew. That would be the productive way to do it, and that way he'd also have some fun in the process.

The worst part was when she went to school to teach whatever the hell it was she taught. He didn't want to follow her on campus; he would look too out of place. So instead he parked near the front gate and waited the five or six hours it usually took for her to come out. And he couldn't even pass the time by watching good-looking women; the ones passing by were so wrapped in coats and sweaters they looked like dark grey beach balls.

The only positive that he could think of was that he wouldn't have to do this for more than two weeks. That's when his employers needed to know where Wallace was hiding, and if she hadn't led him to Wallace by then, he would simply grab her and extract the information. It gave him something to look forward to.

After that he would make his own move. Instructing him to kill Cashman and the broad in Florida was a mistake his employers would come to regret. It showed him how they treated their partners, and led him to believe they probably had the same fate planned for him.

They thought of themselves as all-powerful, a force that could not be stopped. But no matter now much money and power they had, when it came to both smarts and deadly force, they would soon find out that they were not in his league.

Eden Alexander had never seen the car nor the man behind the wheel before. It was a grey minivan parked at the end of her street, and the man was blond, early thirties, and so large that the inside of the car seemed filled to capacity.

She knew she was being watched, and that he was watching her. It was an instinct she had, and she trusted it completely.

Eden avoided staring at the car or the man, as she went to her own car. She drove to her job at the university, waving to the guard at the gate as he let her in. She did not see the minivan behind her at any point, but she would have bet a week's pay that it was there.

With an hour before her class, Eden went straight to the faculty room. She was relieved to see Andy Miller, a colleague and friend, having coffee, and she approached him.

"Andy, I need a favor."

"Shoot."

"I'd like you to walk out past the main gate. If a grey minivan is near there, I want you to get the license plate number. Don't make it obvious that you're looking; don't write down the number, or anything like that."

"What's going on?" he asked.

"I'm sorry, but I can't say."

His concern was obvious. "You okay, Eden?"

She smiled. "I'm fine. Really."

He nodded and stood up. "Okay. Grey minivan, get the plate number. I'm on the case."

Andy left and was gone about ten minutes, during which time Eden prayed that the minivan was not there, though she was positive that it was.

Andy came back and said "WKT-535."

"Was there anybody in the car?" she asked.

He nodded. "Big guy . . . blond hair. I didn't look too closely at him because I didn't want to alert him. Is that okay?"

She forced a smile. "Great, Andy. Thanks, I really appreciate it."

"Is there anything else I can do?"

"No, thanks."

"And you're sure there's nothing wrong?"

"Really, Andy, everything is fine," she lied. Everything was not fine, and Eden was fighting to avoid panic. That had to be a police officer in that car, and he would only be following her if he thought she might lead him to Tim.

Which meant they were both in big trouble.

He watched the geeky guy pretend not to stare at his license plate, and immediately knew that the woman had made him. She had known she was being followed.

It almost made him laugh out loud; clearly he had been so annoyed at the idea of having to waste time following her that he had been careless. He had let himself be made.

The fleeting, pleasant thought of putting a bullet through the geek's head flashed by him, but he knew that would only complicate things.

He would instead stop following the woman for a couple of days, no big loss since she wasn't leading him anywhere. Then he'd start back up, and if he was lucky she'd spot him again. If that happened he'd grab her, and she'd be only too willing to tell him everything she knew.

It would be a hell of a lot more fun that way.

———

Tim was going crazy.

Just sitting around the house was getting him nowhere, and by now his grown-in facial hair had made him confident he wouldn't be recognized by a media-alerted citizen. So he was willing to go out; the problem was he had nowhere to go.

Tim decided he would make his first foray into the outside world by going to the library. He wasn't in need of reading material; he wanted to use the library computer to contact Eden. He had neglected to bring his laptop with him, which was a mistake, but he couldn't go back and get it now. He also didn't want to cut into his cash reserve by buying a new one.

Tim didn't want to call Eden. He had no reason to believe that the police were watching her, but it was certainly a possibility. If they were, it was far more likely that they would tap her phone than his lawyer's.

Just walking out the door of the house was an uncomfortable experience for Tim. His mind flashed back to some old movie about John Dillinger, and the hail of bullets that gunned him down when he casually walked out of a movie theater. Tim knew the police were not out there waiting for him; if they were they would have long ago barged in. But he still looked around warily, and continued doing so even after he pulled away.

The Lincoln Park library was surprisingly large, and even at this early hour had close to fifteen people in it. He was relieved to discover that he did not have to have a library card to use the computers, all he had to do was sign in. He did so, using a fake name.

Tim had asked Eden to create a hotmail address for him, and he signed on to it. Once he did, he was surprised to see that he had seven e-mails waiting for him. As it turned out, six were spam, and one was from "Kileysfriend," the address Eden had created for herself.

He opened the e-mail and read:

```
I'm being followed. I don't know who it is, but
I'm afraid it's the police. I have the license
number of the car. What should I do?
```

Tim was stunned by the message. He had the sensation of wanting to get up and pace, to relieve some of the pent-up anxiety and perhaps think more clearly. But he couldn't do anything that might attract attention from the other patrons.

He typed a return e-mail, hoping that she was near a computer to receive it:

```
Go see Nick. Tell him what you think and give
him the plate number. Not over the phone.
```

He pressed send and waited for a reply, knowing full well it could take a very long time if she were not at home. Less than a minute later, her reply appeared:

```
I will; I'll write back after I do and tell you
what he said. Are you OK?
```

He wrote back:

```
Yes. If you ever get into danger, tell the truth
about where I am. This is not your problem.
```

Her reply:

```
I'll be careful.
```

That wasn't good enough for him, so he wrote:

```
I'm worried about you. Please don't take any
unnecessary chances.
```

Her reply:

Same to you, buddy.

It made Tim smile, something he would have thought impossible under the circumstances. He wished he could be with her, to spend a normal day, but that was something that really was impossible under the circumstances.

Denise Wagner's career was not exactly taking off.

She was no longer working on theatrical road shows; for some reason the fact that her drinking caused her to miss an average of three shows a week had made her less than sought after.

Denise was now in the ignominious position of working for her sister, who managed a large beauty salon in Manhasset, Long Island. Denise was a makeup consultant, and her function was to teach customers how to best apply their makeup in order to enhance their appearance. She didn't have the greatest attitude for the job; she told her sister that the best way for most of her customers to enhance their appearance would be to put a bag over their heads.

But she needed the work, and even followed orders by attempting to hawk the crummy makeup that the salon was selling.

The place was called Salon 37, apparently named simply for the fact that it was on Thirty-seventh Street. Denise figured it wasn't named for the average age of its patrons; that would have more likely dictated Salon 77.

As far as Novack could remember, this was the first beauty salon he had ever been in. It was a relatively frightening sight, women camped under enormous machines, and others sitting around reading magazines while sporting a head full of tinfoil. This was not the place to be in a lightning storm.

Novack stopped at the desk in the front of the place, and asked where he might find Denise Wagner. The receptionist pointed toward the makeup section near the back of the store, but said that Denise was busy at the moment.

"Aren't we all?" asked Novack, heading for Denise and not waiting for an answer.

Denise was applying eye shadow to a customer when she saw Novack coming. He noticed the flash of fear in her eyes, followed by resignation. This woman knew why he was here.

"Denise Wagner?" Novack asked, taking out his shield to show her.

"Yes."

"I'm Detective Novack," he said, before turning to the customer. "I think she's done as much as she can for you."

The customer was rendered momentarily speechless; Novack often had that effect on people. Denise more gently suggested that she go have her hair worked on, and they could conclude the makeup later. The customer obliged.

"This is about Billy," Denise said, a statement, not a question.

"Yes."

"I saw his picture on television."

"Did you contact anyone about it?" Novack asked.

She shook her head. "No. I haven't seen him in over a year; I never want to see him again. He's out of my life."

"But you're sure it was him?"

She nodded. "I'm sure."

"Do you know where he is?"

"No."

"What can you tell me about him?" Novack asked. "Any relatives, hometown, previous jobs . . ."

"I'm sorry, but I really don't know anything. I met him in a bar when I lived out west. At first he seemed really nice. Then he started beating me, and I wanted to leave, but he wouldn't let me. We were together less than three months before he went to jail on some kind of parole violation."

"And you showed him how to make himself look different?"

She nodded, an anxious look on her face. "He made me show him. I didn't do anything wrong."

Novack questioned her for another fifteen minutes, but got few details that might lead him to Billy Zimmerman, the man that Tim Wallace knew as Cashman.

This was very disconcerting to Novack. He had been positive that Cashman did not exist, and he had been wrong. What else had he been wrong about?

Such were the extent of Nick's connections with the police department and prosecutor's office that he knew about Billy Zimmerman three hours after Novack did. He did not yet know that Denise had confirmed Cashman/Zimmerman's existence for Novack, but he'd know that before long.

Either way it was the first piece of good news that the defense had gotten since this whole thing had started. Nick didn't expect Novack to do anything with it; he was out to nail Tim to the wall no matter what. But Cashman's existence, and especially his incarceration at Lampley, confirmed a piece of Tim's story. Unfortunately, that brought the total of pieces of Tim's story that had been confirmed to one.

But for now it would have to do.

Nick was a little uneasy, if not nervous, over the phone call he'd received from Eden a few minutes earlier. She sounded scared, and said that she needed to talk to him in person. Eden's involvement in this case, peripheral or otherwise, was a cause of great concern for her brother. Nothing good could come from it.

When Eden arrived, she looked even more worried than she had sounded. "I'm being followed, Nick. I'm sure of it."

"Do you know who it is?"

She shook her head. "No, but I got a look at him; it's a big guy with blond hair. He's driving a grey minivan, and I have his license plate number." She took it out and handed it to him.

He walked over to the window and looked down at the street, though from that height it was difficult to see much. "Did he follow you here?"

"I didn't see him, but I didn't want to be too obvious in looking around."

"And the guy you saw was alone?"

"Yes. Do you think it's the police, thinking I might lead them to Tim?"

"I doubt it. They usually travel in pairs. And the grey minivan doesn't fit." Then he said pointedly, "Eden, why would anyone think that you might lead them to Tim?"

"I don't know, Nick. I haven't mentioned Tim to anyone but you, ever. And I don't walk his dog out on the street. The only thing I can think of is that maybe they saw him bring the dog over that day, but then they could have followed him themselves when he left."

"Have you had any contact with him?"

She thought for a moment before deciding whether to tell the truth. "We've e-mailed."

"Shit."

"Is that your considered legal opinion?" she asked, not backing down at all.

"Eden, have I mentioned that you are digging a hole for yourself that you may not be able to climb out of?"

"Yes, repeatedly. Now, will you try and find out who is following me?"

He nodded with resignation. "Yes."

"Thank you, big brother."

"So Cashman is real?

I thought you said he was bullshit . . . someone Wallace made up."

Novack could have responded defensively to what amounted to a challenge by Captain Donovan, but he didn't. "That's what I thought, but I'm not so sure any more."

Anders was in the room as well, but wanted no part of this conversation. He was going to let Novack take the heat.

"So where the hell does this leave us?" Donovan asked. Uncertainty was disconcerting to him, and coming from the usually supremely confident Novack, it was particularly unnerving.

"In exactly the same place we were before. There's absolutely no evidence or reason to make us believe that Cashman set Wallace up on this. It doesn't make any sense."

"But Cashman is real."

Novack nodded. "Right, and it's possible that he was involved somehow in this. It's more likely that he helped Wallace in some way, and Wallace then turned on him. But Cashman sure as hell wasn't out on the water with Maggie Wallace; her husband was. And it was her finger at the racquetball club."

Donovan seemed far from convinced. "I don't like this. We're acting like we know what's going on, and we don't know shit."

"When we find Wallace, it will fall into place," Novack said, without fully believing it.

"And when might that be?" Donovan asked. "I've got the brass coming down on me about this."

Anders felt like he should say something, and this seemed to be a slightly safer area than the Cashman discussion. "It'll be soon."

"You a fortune-teller, or have you seen something I haven't?"

"This is not a guy at home on the streets," Anders said. "He's holed up somewhere, but eventually he'll have to come out, and when he does, he won't last twenty-four hours."

Unconvinced, Donovan turned back to Novack. "We're starting to look stupid for not being able to catch Wallace. But it's nowhere near as stupid as we're going to look if he's not our man, if Cashman set this up."

"There's nothing to worry about," Novack said.

"Then why the hell am I worried?"

To say the Passaic River was not as polluted as it once was is to damn it with faint praise. The truth is, a lot of effort over the years had taken what was once not much more than an aboveground sewer and turned it into an acceptably clean waterway. There wouldn't be any Coors commercials filmed there, but it was no longer an embarrassment.

There were even a few stretches where people went to fish, though the chance of catching an old boot was marginally higher than something edible. One such place was the Morlot Avenue Bridge between Paterson and Fair Lawn, and that was where Jason Durant took his eleven-year-old son Robbie early on Saturday morning.

This was not exactly *A River Runs Through It*; they stood on the bridge, dropped the bait in the water, and leaned forward so as not to be too close to the cars passing behind them. Robbie was not a big fan of the entire procedure; his video games at home had far more appeal. But he liked hanging out with his father, so he went along with it and even pretended to like it.

After an hour of nothing happening, Robbie said, "Doesn't seem like our day, huh?"

Jason looked at his watch, which read seven-thirty. "It's early."

"You think the fish are still asleep?"

Jason nodded. "Could be. But they'll wake up hungry, and that's when we'll get 'em."

After another forty-five minutes of no action, Robbie figured the fish must have forgotten to set their alarm. "I don't know if the fish are hungry, but I am . . . you want something?"

"Might as well. I'll go get the food." They had parked the car about a hundred yards away, near the riverbank.

"What did Mom make?" Robbie asked.

"I don't know, but I'm sure it's good. Wait here . . . call me if you get a bite."

Jason walked toward the edge of the bridge, occasionally glancing back to make sure Robbie was okay. He was filled with love for his son, but knew that days like this were numbered. Robbie would soon have other interests that would seem more appealing than spending a day fishing with his father. In fact, he probably had them already.

He reached the end of the bridge and took a final glance back; it would be hard to see Robbie from the car. Jason quickened his pace, so that he could reduce the time that Robbie was out of his sight.

Jason reached the car, and opened the door. He took out the cooler of food that his wife had prepared, and closed the door. He couldn't see Robbie up on the bridge from there, and it worried him a little. "Robbie? You okay?" he called out.

Robbie didn't answer, though it was possible he didn't hear him. Jason moved quickly, but slipped on a stretch of mud. The cooler fell from his hands, and tumbled the ten feet down toward the edge of the river.

He debated for a moment whether to get the cooler or go back and check on Robbie, so he called to him again. This time Robbie answered. "I'm okay. You bringing the food?"

Relieved, Jason made it down to the edge of the river, balancing himself so as not to slip. He reached the cooler, which had not gone into the water because it was wedged up against something.

A human arm.

Jason screamed, loud enough so that if there were really any fish still asleep, their day had officially begun.

"He should not be there. Can I say
it any more clearly than that?"

Carl White was making no effort to conceal his exasperation, and
did not care that the person he was talking to was his boss, FBI Re-
gional Director Tucker Anderson. Carl was already in a bad mood,
having had to fly down to Washington for this ridiculous conversation, when it could have been conducted over the phone.

"He's the president of the United States. He can go wherever
the hell he wants," Anderson said.

"Why is he choosing this building on this particular night? If
he's into danger, why not go out on night patrol in Afghanistan?"

"The president considers these Federal Centers a good way to
protect federal property and federal employees. He's also invested a
good deal of political capital in it. And with the press out in force,
he wants to be there to take the credit he deserves. I assume you're
familiar with the basic workings of politics?"

"Sir, I consider it potentially dangerous."

"How so?" Anderson asked.

"Parts of these buildings, areas concerned with the potential
dangers of terrorism, are being constructed by Tim Wallace's company. It seems clear that he has had at least some involvement with
terrorists, including the explosion on the New Jersey Turnpike."

"Every square inch of that complex will be checked a dozen
times. On that night, it will be the safest place on Earth."

White knew that what Anderson was saying was completely true. The Secret Service was relentless in protecting their number one client, and on that night they would be triply vigilant. He just didn't see it as a chance they should be taking.

"It's a mistake, sir."

"A mistake? It's designed to be the safest building in the country, and it will have absolute maximum security on that night. The president went to the World Series last year; you think that was safer?"

"I understand what you're saying, but I still want you to know that I believe this to be reckless and unnecessary. And I feel an obligation to put my concerns in writing."

Anderson was dismissive. He stood up, a sure sign the meeting was coming to an end. "You do that. In the meantime, you'll be required to download what you know to the Secret Service."

"That will be a short download, because right now I don't know shit."

"What have you been doing up there, taking in some Broadway shows?" Anderson said, deliberately putting a touch of amusement in his voice. White was one of his best agents, and he wanted to end the meeting on a friendly note.

White wasn't much in the mood for banter, but he knew he had to play the game. "Mostly musicals."

"Don't try and expense it; I'll be watching."

Nick was starting to feel slightly better about the case. It was a vague feeling, not brought about by any particular good news, but simply because some news was at least starting to flow in.

There were six Oceanfast 360s in the New York area, and two more that were there at the time of Maggie's death, but had since been sold to buyers in other parts of the country. Additionally, two of the boats currently in the area had changed hands since that day.

Nick had the preliminary investigative report that listed the owners of the boats, then and now, some of which were owned by corporations and some by individuals. None of the names meant

anything to him, and he would have to rely on subsequent reports
to tell him if the names had any particular significance for this case.
He made a mental note to describe the list to Tim if he called in
again, just in case any of the names might ring a bell to him.

Within an hour of his receiving the list, Tim did call. Nick could
hear the frustration in his voice as he asked if there was anything new
to report, and he was glad that he could answer in the affirmative.

"The police know who Cashman is. His real name is Billy Zimmerman, and he was in prison in Lampley."

"That's great! Do they know where he is now?"

"Apparently not, though that could be changing at any time."

"Do you think they'll look for him? Novack wouldn't be too
anxious to learn anything that might help me."

"I'm not so sure; I think he'll go after it." Nick was well aware
that Novack had long ago decided Tim was guilty, but in his experience Novack was a good cop who would follow the evidence even
if he didn't like where it led.

"So we wait?" Tim asked.

"No, our people are all over it. But the cops have more resources and easier entry. Meanwhile, I've got the list of boats in
this area."

"How many are there?" Tim asked.

"Six, although there were eight at the time. Two have gone out
of state." He then proceeded to read the names of the boats, as well
as the owning people and companies.

"I've never heard of any of them," an obviously disappointed
Tim said. "How long is it going to take to check them out?"

"Can't say; we don't really know what we're looking for. It's not
like we're going to get a bio of one of the boat owners which says,
'spent the last six months framing Tim Wallace.'"

"I understand," Tim said. "Can you find out where the boats
are? I can check them out."

"What good will that do?"

"I've seen the boat; I'm pretty sure I'll recognize it if I see it
again."

"You want to take that chance?" Nick asked.

"I look different; I think I can get away with it. And I'm not going to do anything to call attention to myself."

"If you're wrong, and you encounter the police, do not resist arrest. They consider you armed and dangerous."

"I am armed, but I'm not dangerous."

"You have a gun?" Nick asked, his surprise evident.

"Yes." When Nick remained silent, Tim added defensively, "There are murderers after me. I'm not going to use it against the police. It's not even loaded yet."

"Don't bring it with you when you check out the boats," Nick said.

"I won't. I'm afraid of it."

Carl White received the information first, which reflected his higher status as a federal agent.

It was another jagged piece of a puzzle that did not seem to fit anywhere. He had his assistant place a call to Novack and ask him to come right over. Novack seemed much closer to the facts of the case than did White; and White would willingly exchange information for anything Novack knew but might not yet have shared.

Novack was not the type who liked to be "summoned," especially by an FBI agent, and he only agreed to go to White's office when the assistant assured him that there was some significant news.

He and Anders drove over there, and were ushered right in. White didn't spend any time on small talk, a small fact which Novack appreciated. "On Saturday morning, a resident of Fair Lawn found the arm of a white male while fishing in the Passaic River. Divers located the rest of the body, and DNA testing was done."

Novack had to suppress an instant annoyance that White obviously had been made privy to evidence of a local crime before Novack. "And?"

"And it was determined to be Billy Zimmerman, aka Jeff Cashman."

"Do we know when he died?" asked Novack.

"Too soon to tell, but it's been a while," White said. "Autopsy is being done today."

"You could have told us this over the phone," said Anders.

White nodded. "I could have, but then I wouldn't have been able to pick your brains."

"About what?" asked Anders.

"The Federal Center opens a week from Wednesday night with a big dinner, speeches, the whole bit."

"We've known that for a while," Novack said.

"Did you know the president of the United States is going to be there?"

"No," said Novack. "Lately he hasn't been checking in with me when he's making up his schedule."

The comment annoyed White. "So you don't see this as your problem?"

"I gotta be honest," Novack said, "I don't even see it as your problem. Because I don't see Wallace as a terrorist. I see him as an asshole who kills women for fun, not a guy with a political agenda."

"So Billy Zimmerman was a woman that Wallace killed for fun?"

"I don't know where Zimmerman fits in," Novack admitted. "But if Wallace was going to blow up the Federal Center or assassinate the president, he wouldn't have walked in and told us the story about Cashman and Sheila."

"Right," Anders chimed in. "He would have laid low and drawn as little attention to himself as possible."

White was unconvinced. "Unless he was an asshole who also kills presidents for fun. By the way, there's one other piece of information you might be interested in."

"What's that?"

"We questioned the girlfriend of the guy blown up on the turnpike . . . the guy who called Wallace in his office."

Novack nodded. "Yeah. We saw the interview report."

"But you didn't know that an agent later went back to her apartment to ask her a few more questions. She was gone, but all her clothes and things were still there. She had been talking to her sister on the phone, got up to answer the door, and hasn't been heard from since."

"So she's dead," Novack reasoned.

"I wouldn't want to be her life insurer, that's for sure," White said.

"There's no way Wallace went down there; it would be far too risky," Novack said. "He's in hiding."

"And I don't see how he could have known about her in the first place," White said. "So it was somebody else. Which means it looks like you've got more going on here than you think."

Novack nodded; he had known that ever since learning that Cashman was not a creation of Tim's imagination. "Yes, it does."

Considering the circumstances, both Danny and Will found it more than a little weird to be at the Purple Rose. They had only gone there twice since Tim's disappearance, and that was more out of a desire to try and restore normalcy to their lives, rather than a hope that they might have fun.

Will had been helping by filling the breach in Tim's absence from the business, much as he did when either Tim or Danny went on vacation. His real and very extraordinary expertise was in the computer security systems that were integral to modern buildings in general, and these federal buildings in particular. But he also had general contracting experience, and Danny relied on him to help out.

The two friends agreed in advance not to talk about Tim's situation, but that resolution broke down before the first beers arrived. "I just wish there was a way to help him," Danny said. "If I knew where he was, I could get him money, or something."

"It said in the paper that he cleaned out his checking account," Will said.

"Yeah, I know. He must be scared shitless."

"He should be. The cops are acting like he's Al Capone. They've questioned me three times."

Danny nodded. "I'm one ahead of you. You speak to the FBI agent? White?"

"Yeah. He had a million questions about the buildings." He

shook his head in amazement. "Like Tim's gonna show up with an army and attack it."

"The security down there is unbelievable," Danny said.

"I know . . . I've been going through it every day. I spent five hours last week teaching the computer setup to a government guy. You know who's coming to the opening?"

Danny shook his head. "Not really . . . just what I read. A bunch of congressmen, my uncle . . ."

"He giving you grief about Tim?"

Danny nodded. "Every hour on the hour. He has his right-hand guy, Rivers, call me. Like there's something I can do about it."

"If one of us finds out where Tim is, we tell the other, okay?" Will asked. "And we figure out a way to help him."

Danny held out his hand and Will took it. "It's a deal."

According to Nick's list, the Oceanfast 360s were spread out through the metropolitan area.

Three were at different piers on Long Island Sound, one was on the Hudson River, north of the city, and the remaining two were docked at various locations in New Jersey.

Tim knew some of the locations; they were upscale, high-end piers which charged exorbitant fees and provided excellent service and access. This made perfect sense; you wouldn't spend the money for a boat like that and leave it in some dump. It would be like owning a Ferrari and parking it on city streets.

At this point the listed owners meant nothing to Tim, Nick, or the investigators, and Tim did not want to wait the time that more digging would take. He was fairly confident that he'd know the boat if he saw it, providing it wasn't repainted a different color and design.

So Tim set out to check the boats himself, fully understanding the risks involved. Those risks were heightened by the fact that he was at least casually familiar with many people in the boating community, and they with him. The chances of him being recognized and reported to authorities went up accordingly.

Working in his favor was the fact that the boats would not be used in the winter, and many would be in dry dock. Not many owners would be around, unless they were doing work on their boats. The flip side of that, of course, would be that with fewer people there, Tim would stand out even more.

Though the Jersey piers were significantly closer, Tim decided to check out those on Long Island first. He had seen it that day on Long Island Sound, and though it could have been there simply because that's where Tim was, it seemed more likely than New Jersey. And Tim wanted as little exposure as possible.

Two of the boats were said to be on the North Shore and one on the South Shore. Since the North was on Long Island Sound, where Tim's boat was that fateful day, he decided to head there first.

Even the drive there was an intense experience for Tim. He was sure that everyone in each car was staring at him; when one of the drivers alongside him took out his cell phone, Tim considered pulling off and turning around. It took all of his self-control to realize that he hadn't been spotted, and that he would likely know it when he was. He was glad he used the car at the house, and not his own.

The woman taking the tolls at the George Washington Bridge looked at his face as she took his money. He thought she might have recognized him, but there was nothing he could do, and he wouldn't be sure either way until it was too late. He literally cringed for the next couple of miles, but the lack of flashing lights and sirens, to say nothing of bullets, convinced him that he was okay for now.

His first stop was at Mill Neck, a place that Tim had considered using when he first got his boat, but decided against because it felt too crowded. He parked as close as he could to the pier, believing that the less time he spent walking around in public the better.

Tim got out of the car, leaving it unlocked in case he wanted to leave quickly. It was almost thirty degrees out, relatively balmy for this area, but he still pulled his ski cap low on his head and bundled his coat slightly upward, as if trying to ward off the cold. It left only a relatively small amount of his face exposed, and Tim felt fairly confident that few people could recognize him.

The dock area was fairly desolate. Most people worked on their boats either right after the summer, or just prior to spring. Since this was neither, there were only a few people around.

There were at least four hundred boats, some in and some out of the water. There was a fence around the entire property, but three gates were open. Security was lax; most of the boats were locked, and there was little chance that someone would stick a boat in their briefcase or jacket pocket and walk off.

Even though he didn't see anyone around, Tim tried to make it appear that he knew where he was going, as if he had his own boat there, and that was his destination. The boats were set up in aisles, and Tim figured that walking quickly he could weave in and out and see all of them within five minutes.

Tim walked down the first aisle, didn't see the Oceanfast, and turned to walk back up the second aisle.

"Hey, can I help you?" The words sent a wave of panic through Tim that he attempted to conceal as he turned to answer a short, stocky man, mid-fifties, who seemed to be an attendant at the pier. The man looked none too pleased to have his morning nap disturbed by this apparent intruder.

Tim smiled, trying to catch his breath. "Nah, just looking around. I'm gonna buy a boat, and I'm trying to get some ideas."

"This ain't a showroom, pal."

Tim laughed, as if the man had made a joke. "I know . . . but I heard there was an Oceanfast 360 here, and I wanted to get a look at it."

"You know what those things run?"

"Pretty steep, from what I hear. Me and a couple of friends, we're thinking of going in on it together."

The attendant thought about that for a moment, then finally shrugged and pointed. "Third aisle, near that end. But don't try and board it."

Tim nodded. "Gotcha. Thanks."

Tim walked away, literally shaking from the encounter. He could feel himself drenched with sweat under his clothes, not a normal occurrence in weather like this. Tim knew he would have to get himself under control; if he was going to react this way to what was basically a nonincident, he would likely die of stress when he had a really close call.

He wasn't halfway down the aisle when he saw the Oceanfast 360, and he instantly felt a wave of disappointment. It was the smaller version, as the boat was made in two basic lengths. This one was a seventy-footer, and while it was an extraordinary vessel, it was not the one Tim was looking for.

Tim put his head down and walked briskly back to the car. There was no use giving anyone an extra moment to recognize him. This part of the trip was a waste; in fact, the entire idea might well be ridiculous. There had been people out there on a boat that day who didn't want to get involved; it could be as simple as that. And here was Tim pinning his hopes, his life, on finding it. The whole thing was pathetic, and he knew it.

But he had nothing else to do, no other way to move forward, so it was on to the next one.

The license plate on the car
following Eden was stolen.

It had been the property of Roberta Cassell, an eighty-one-year-old grandmother of six in Cherry Hill, New Jersey. The thief had chosen well; the woman had not used her car in almost two years, and had not yet even noticed the plate was missing.

The report confirmed to Nick that Eden was correct in believing she was being followed, and that it was not the police doing the following. It did not, however, give him a clue as to who it might be.

He called Eden to tell her what he had learned, but she sounded less worried than she had been.

"I haven't seen him in a couple of days, Nick. He probably got bored."

"Or maybe he's just being more careful."

"Is it the police?" she asked.

"Not unless they're into stealing license plates."

"So who is it?"

"I have no idea, Eden. And maybe he won't be back. But if you see him again call me immediately. And only go to very public places."

"Okay . . . thanks, Nick."

"When you're home, make sure the doors and windows are locked and the alarm is on."

"Will do, big brother."

———

Tim knew it was the same boat the moment he saw it. Not just the color, but the stripe design. It was highly unlikely that there could be two such boats.

It was one of at least a hundred boats at the pier in Southold, but it was the only one surrounded by its own fence, a silent statement that it was more expensive and more important than the others. Which it was.

The boat was in the water, and Tim could see a jet underneath it, which was merely a machine to keep the water it was sitting in from freezing.

Tim had an instant regret that he had not stopped to pick up a disposable camera, so that he could get a picture to send to Nick. Then he realized that a photo wasn't important, that there was really nothing that Nick could learn from it. The important thing was that he had identified which boat it was, and Nick could focus his investigation on the ownership.

From Tim's vantage point he could make out only a small part of the name on the hull; the last three letters were *e-a-s*. He imagined the last word was "seas," but couldn't be sure. There was also no way to determine the boat's serial number, since boarding, or even closely approaching, was impossible.

So Tim basically just stood there, staring at the boat and letting the memory of that day on the water once again roll over him. This boat, and the people on it, had been out there with him. At the very least they did nothing to help, at worst they were the cause of Maggie's pain and death.

"Not bad, huh?"

Tim turned and saw a young woman dressed in work coveralls under a ski jacket. She held in her hand what Tim recognized as a sander; she was obviously there working on a boat. She had a welcoming smile on her face, and obviously did not consider Tim any kind of a threat.

She was referring to the Oceanfast, and Tim gave it another quick glance. "Beautiful, though I might go with a different color."

She laughed. "That's for sure. Have you ever been on one?"

"In a showroom once. That's the closest I'll ever come. Is it yours?"

Another laugh. "Afraid not. Mine's over there. You could fit mine in one of the bedrooms on this one, but that's okay. They both float, and the sun shines on both of them."

Tim didn't want to appear too interested in the Oceanfast, but then realized that none of the TV coverage on him would have had any reason to mention it, so there was no reason for this woman to make the connection. "Do you know who owns this one?"

She shook her head. "Nah . . . I tried to talk to a guy on it the other day, but he blew me off."

"People come on this time of year?"

She nodded. "Yeah, but he wasn't one of the owners, he was there doing work. The owners are definitely big shots."

"Because it's so expensive?" he asked.

"Well, sure, but also because of the people that have been on it. A lot of Washington types, even some senators and congressmen."

"Is that right? Which ones, do you know?" He smiled, not wanting to appear too anxious. "I'm sort of a political junkie."

She thought for a moment. "Well, I definitely know Senator Collinsworth was on it at least once, 'cause I recognized him. But I'm sure there were a bunch of others."

The news that Collinsworth had been on board was jolting to Tim, and instantly reestablished his suspicions about Danny. "Wow," he said. "When was Collinsworth on?"

"Last summer. There were a whole bunch of people in tuxedos; I saw them as they were sailing out. Can you imagine having to put on formal clothes to go out on a boat?"

"Hard to believe," he agreed. He gently tried to coax more information out of her, but she didn't seem to have any. He extricated himself from the conversation, even politely declining her invitation for him to see her boat. She wished him a good day and went back to her work.

Tim was going to go back to the house, the only place where he felt remotely safe. He had a lot of thinking to do, about Danny, and Collinsworth, and the boat that was out there the day that Maggie died.

Out there for a reason.

Jimmy Lee's story didn't set the world on fire,

but that didn't concern him in the least. People in Washington, and those interested in politics elsewhere, read the column and took some note of the fact that Senator Collinsworth had apparently engaged in nepotism in arranging for his nephew to get federal contracting work. The fact that the nephew's partner, Tim Wallace, was a man wanted for the murder of his wife made it more delicious for Collinsworth's political enemies, but had no real effect on the public.

There was an obvious reason that Jimmy Lee was not upset that his story wasn't received as a bombshell. He knew that when he published the second part, revealing that Wallace had had multiple contacts with the man transporting all those explosives, the reaction would be far greater. Especially since the president and many other dignitaries would have spent the previous evening in the building the fugitive helped build.

Jimmy Lee had no problem with sitting back and waiting for that payoff. He knew that timing was everything, and this timing was going to be perfect.

For Senator Collinsworth, the story was a potentially major problem. Not so much because he had steered work to a company owned by a relative; while embarrassing, that was understood to be business as usual in Washington. Besides, there was no allegation that the company was incompetent or unable to perform the work they contracted to do.

Collinsworth was upset because of what it portended for the future, and for the plans he had laid so painstakingly. Once the Federal Center in New Jersey was finished and judged a resounding success, it would be duplicated in virtually every state of the union. Hundreds of billions of dollars would be involved, and with Collinsworth's plan of spreading the contracting work to many mid- and small-sized businesses, he would be able to build a network of beholden contributors that could fill his campaign war chest to overflowing.

If the story about Wallace caused any damage to that plan, if it shone an unfavorable light on Collinsworth's involvement and jeopardized the future, it would be an unmitigated disaster.

Collinsworth was not a big fan of unmitigated disasters, at least ones in which he was personally involved, so he did what he could to minimize this one. He had Keith Rivers plant a competing story, one which said that while Collinsworth had had the grand idea for these complexes, he stayed out of choosing contractors.

The planted stories also included quotes from Gregory Campbell, the lead bureaucrat at GSA, affirming that Collinsworth was not involved in the awarding of contracts. Campbell claimed only a passing acquaintance with Collinsworth, conveniently leaving out the fact that he would do virtually anything Collinsworth told him to do, since the senator had made him a very wealthy man.

One call Collinsworth did not bother making was to Danny, the nephew at the center of all this. There was nothing to be gained from that; Danny would be smart enough to know that the days of his uncle getting him work were officially over. He might as well disappear along with his murdering partner, because as far as dear Uncle Fred was concerned, he no longer existed.

The first call Tim made when he got back to the house was to Nick. He was not in his office, but when Tim said that "Jerry Koosman" was calling, his assistant told Tim to call him at home.

Before Tim could say why he was calling, Nick mentioned the story about Collinsworth that had broken that day. It was of little consequence to Tim; the last thing on his mind at the moment was future business prospects.

"I've got more interesting news about Collinsworth," he said.

"Oh?"

"I found the boat that was out on the water that day; it's the one docked at Southold. And I found someone who told me that Collinsworth has been out on it."

Nick checked through his paperwork and saw that the boat Tim was talking about was owned by Bennington, Inc. "You ever hear of them?" Nick asked.

"No, I don't think so."

"I haven't either. I'll have them checked out. In the meantime, I've got something else to tell you, which you are very definitely not going to like."

Tim braced himself. "What is it?"

"I found out from my sources that there's an FBI agent up here from Florida, assigned to this case."

"FBI? Why? And why Florida?"

"Remember the car that blew up on the Jersey Turnpike?"

"Of course," Tim said. "It was carrying Cintron 421. Danny and I were worried about it."

"Well, now you've got a bigger reason to worry about it. The driver of that car apparently called your office a few times in the week before the explosion. They think he talked to you."

Tim exploded. "Jesus Christ! Now they think I'm a terrorist? What'll it be next? Maybe I killed Kennedy!"

"So you know nothing about it?"

"Of course not. I—"

Tim paused for a few moments, and Nick heard only silence. "What's going on?" he asked. "You still there?"

The frustration in Tim's voice was suddenly replaced by excitement. "It all fits! Damn . . . it all fits!"

"Enlighten me," Nick said.

Tim went on to explain his suspicions about Danny, since only Danny would have known the details of Tim's life necessary to pull off this operation, and at the same time have access to places like the Purple Rose on New Year's Eve and the racquetball club. "So this guy may have called our office, but he didn't talk to me. He must have talked to Danny."

"What would Danny have to gain by all this?"

"I'm not sure, but it has to involve the business. He must want me out of the way."

"But you don't know why."

Tim was firm. "No, but I'll figure it out. First, he tried to have me killed, and then—"

"Tried to have you killed?" Nick asked.

"Absolutely, that's something else I've thought about. I was the only person who knew Maggie was going out on the boat that day; she had never been out there before. I never even told Danny. That explosion was meant to kill me, not her."

"Then how did her finger wind up at the racquetball court?"

A few moments of silence from Tim, and then, "Shit. I don't know; I just don't know. There are a lot of pieces we don't have, but every one we do have involves Danny. And Collinsworth has to be involved as well."

"You somewhere safe?" Nick asked. "Without telling me where that somewhere is . . ."

"I'm somewhere safe."

"Then sit tight and call me tomorrow. I'll be in court on another case until about noon, call after that."

"Is that other client innocent as well?" Tim asked, trying to lighten things a bit.

"Pure as the driven fucking snow," Nick said.

Tim smiled, the first time in a while, then steered the conversation back to his own situation. "Have you got any idea what you're going to do?"

"To tell you the truth, I think it might be time to talk to Novack."

Cindy could tell that something
was bothering Novack.

This didn't qualify as a particularly stunning insight; something had been bothering him pretty much every day for as long as she had known him. It always had to do with his work, but she had never really gotten used to it, and was always frustrated by her inability to really make him feel better.

On this particular night though he seemed more troubled than usual, so she decided to try and talk to him about it. She did so as they were sitting in the dining room after a dinner during which he had hardly said anything. He was drinking coffee, and she was clearing the table. "Is it the Wallace case?" she asked.

"What?" he asked, obviously distracted.

"Is it the Wallace case?"

"Is what the Wallace case?"

"Whatever it is that has you so upset."

"I tried to hide it."

She smiled. "Good job."

"It's the Wallace case," he confirmed. "I don't like where it's going."

"I saw the story today about the senator getting him the contract. Was that a problem for you?"

"Are you really interested in this?" he asked. "Or just trying to make me feel better?"

She smiled. "Both."

He nodded. "Okay, but it won't work. I simply refuse to feel better."

"I know."

"I couldn't care less about the story today. That's just political bullshit."

"Then what's wrong? Is it the fact that you haven't found Wallace yet?"

"That ain't helping, but there's something else. The FBI thinks he's a terrorist; they've tied him to that car that exploded on the turnpike." Novack was able to tell her this without fear of it coming back to haunt him; he had long ago learned that he could trust Cindy completely.

"A terrorist?" she asked, surprised. "Are they right?"

He shook his head. "No way. I'd bet anything it's a load of crap. It just doesn't ring true."

"But you still think he killed his wife?"

He half whirled to face her. "He killed his wife. No doubt about it . . . none. And he killed that woman in Kinnelon."

She was surprised by his reaction. "Okay . . . okay . . . don't take it out on me."

"Sorry."

"What about that guy Cashman?" she asked. "Did Wallace kill him too?"

Novack thought about that for a moment. "I don't know. I don't know where the hell he fits in." Then, "There's too much about this case I don't know."

"And that bothers you," she said.

He smiled. "No shit, Sherlock."

"I think we should go into the bedroom and make love," she said.

He shrugged. "Might as well . . . nothing else to do," he said, then ducked as she threw the expected dish towel at him. He knew that she would understand he was kidding; the next time he would turn down a chance to have sex with Cindy would be the first.

———

Eden sensed that the grey minivan was back even before she saw it. She was in the supermarket, and as she walked back down an aisle toward the front of the store, she looked into the parking lot. There it was, parked in a space near the back, with a vantage point to the front exit of the store.

She thought she had been rid of him, and now was upset that she hadn't asked Nick to provide protection for her. If she had, maybe they could confront the man, and find out what he wanted. And maybe that answer could help unravel the mystery of what had been done to Tim.

Eden left her cart in the corner of the store, where she could not be seen from the parking lot. She went into the restroom and called Nick's office from her cell phone. His assistant said that he was in court and couldn't be reached.

Eden then went to a pay phone, still out of sight of the person in the minivan, and called Tim's cell phone. They had decided to communicate only through e-mail, but she felt that this was enough of an emergency to take a chance, especially since she was not calling from a phone that the police might be tapping.

Just the ringing of the phone scared him; he had never even heard it ring before. The caller ID showed a number he didn't recognize, and he debated whether to answer it, deciding after the fourth ring to do so.

"Hello?"

"Tim, it's me, Eden. I'm sorry to call you—"

"It's okay," he said, worried that she sounded upset. "What is it?" The first thought that went through his mind was that something had happened to Kiley.

"I'm being followed again."

"By the same guy?"

"I didn't see him, but it's the same car. I'm sure of it. I thought I was finished with him. What do you think I should do?"

"Have you called Nick?"

"I tried. He's in court."

Tim was worried. "I think you should get into your car and drive to the police station and tell them what's going on. Tell them you have my dog, and that the guy following you must have something to do with me."

"Are you sure about that? If they know about me, it might help them get to you."

He thought about it a moment, an idea coming together in his mind, then made a decision. "Where are you now?" he asked, and she told him she was at the grocery store, and that the man following her was at the outskirts of the parking lot.

"Okay. Stay where you are for about fifteen minutes, then get back in your car and drive to Paramus Park," he said, referring to a large, nearby shopping mall. "It won't be crowded now; it's too early. Park in the rear parking lot, farthest from Route 17, and go into any store over there. There's a Men's Wearhouse and I think there's still an Ann Taylor, but any store is fine."

"Then what?"

"Stay inside for at least a half hour, then you can get back in your car and go home. The guy won't be following you at that point. Call Nick and tell him what happened when you get home."

"What are you going to do?"

"I'm going to start taking my life back."

Eden was not happy about
following Tim's instructions.

She wasn't concerned for her own safety; the Paramus Park Mall was a very public place, and she would be in little danger there. But she was very worried about whatever it was Tim had in mind. If he was right that the man would no longer be out there when she returned to her car, then it would have to mean that Tim had intervened.

She had the feeling that intervening with people like this was not Tim's specialty.

But she had no real option other than to do as he requested; it was Tim's life that was at stake, and he had to do whatever he could to save it. So she headed for Paramus Park, and though she didn't see the minivan behind her, she was sure it must be there. At least she hoped so.

Tim had little more confidence in his ability to handle this than Eden. But the clock was ticking on how long he could elude the police, and he still instinctively felt that if he didn't create something positive, his prospects for exoneration were nil. So he too headed for Paramus Park.

And he brought his gun.

He got to the parking lot before Eden, and positioned himself in a place where he would be able to see her drive in, while neither she nor her pursuer would have a reason to look in his direction. It was almost ten minutes before she got there, and she did as she was told, parking toward the front of the rear lot, near the entrance to Ann Taylor.

There were cars parked far from the stores, at the very rear of the lot, bordering the woods. Tim had worked at Men's Wearhouse during one college summer break, and remembered that this was the area in which employees of all the stores were told to park, so as not to take the closer spots from paying customers. Tim assumed that the grey minivan would park among these cars, so as to stay a safe distance from Eden, yet not stand out in an otherwise empty area.

For Tim's plan to have any chance of success, the man would have to park in this area.

He did.

Once the minivan was settled in, and it was apparent that the driver was staying put, Tim waited five minutes and then drove up and parked two rows behind the minivan. He walked up the aisle between cars toward the passenger side of the minivan, remembering that the mirror on that side made objects look farther away than they actually were.

He saw the driver look up when he either saw or sensed Tim's approach. Tim felt a wave of fear, but by then the die had been cast. Pulling the gun from his pocket with his right hand, he yanked the passenger door open with his left. He never considered the possibility that it might be locked, and if it had been, he'd have been in trouble.

It wasn't.

The large, blond man in the driver's seat whirled toward Tim and started reaching for his inside jacket pocket, but stopped when he saw Tim, who was pointing the gun at him with two hands and screaming, "DON'T MOVE! DON'T FUCKING MOVE!"

The man seemed unruffled, but partially raised his hands, palms upward and said, "No problem, pal. Whatever you say."

Tim got into the car and closed the passenger door, keeping the gun pointed at the driver with a shaking hand. Once the door was closed, he resumed pointing it with two shaking hands.

Tim spoke in a firm, calm voice that even surprised himself. "Reach into your jacket pocket really slowly and take out your gun. Place it on the seat toward me. While you do so, make sure it's pointed at yourself. If at any time it isn't, I'm going to shoot you. Believe me, I will."

The man did as he was told, taking out the gun and gently placing it on the seat. Tim pulled it toward himself, but did not pick it up.

"Okay. Drive," Tim said.

"Where to?"

"Drive," Tim repeated, and the man shrugged and pulled out of the parking lot.

Tim directed him up Route 17, getting off at Route 202 and heading toward Rockland County. The ride took almost twenty minutes, and Tim became conscious of his arms aching from holding up the gun. But he was not about to lower either the gun or the almost surreal sense of alertness he was feeling.

Tim directed the man to make a right turn down a long dirt road, to an area where Tim and his friends had played sports and hiked a number of years ago. Finally he had him pull over, in what could have been semiaccurately described as "the middle of nowhere."

"Okay, turn the car off but leave the key in the ignition," Tim said, and his order was followed. "Now put your hands on the dashboard, palms down, with the backs of your hands up against the front window."

Again the order was followed, though the man did not seem at all afraid. In fact, he seemed almost bemused, though inwardly he was embarrassed and infuriated that he had allowed this jerk to put him in this position.

"I'm going to get out and walk around the car. The gun will be trained on you at all times. If you move your hands, I will shoot you in the head. Do you understand?"

The man didn't give an answer, and Tim didn't insist on one. He opened the passenger door and walked around the car at the front, pointing the gun at his captive at all times. When he reached the driver's door, he opened it. "Get out and stand over there with your hands clasped behind your head," he said.

The man got out slowly and did as he was told.

"Why are you following that woman?" Tim asked.

"I wanted her to lead me to you."

"Why?"

"So I could kill you."

"And now look at you," Tim said. "I guess it didn't work out so well."

The man smiled confidently. "There's plenty of time."

"Why do you want to kill me?"

"None of your fucking business."

"Who are you?"

"None of your fucking business," the man repeated, and then made a judgment. "Look, I'm getting tired of this. I'm leaving, and the only way you're going to stop me is to shoot me. And I would be real surprised if you had the balls for that."

"Try me," Tim said, desperately hoping that he wouldn't.

The man took a half step forward, which caused Tim to tense and seem ready to shoot. When he didn't, the man smiled and took another step forward, toward Tim and the car.

So Tim shot him.

He wasn't even sure he did it intentionally; he may have just been frightened and inadvertently squeezed the trigger. That same fear caused him to be inaccurate, and the shot went off to the right, grazing the man's left shoulder.

The man reached for his arm, and put his hand on a small but growing spot of blood. The look on his face was momentarily one of such rage that it made Tim's blood run cold. The man recovered quickly and smiled. "You think things have been bad lately? They just got ten times worse. You will long for the way you felt yesterday."

With that he did an about-face, slowly walking away from Tim and the car and toward the woods. He had by now determined that

Tim would shoot him again if he felt threatened, but would never shoot him in the back.

Tim waited until the man was a couple of hundred feet away, and then got back into the car on the driver's side. He was satisfied but profoundly shaken by the encounter; he hadn't expected the man to tell him anything, but at least now he would find out his identity.

The other significant positive for Tim was that he had met the enemy, and he hadn't been killed.

On the way back to Paramus Park, Tim called Nick and was relieved when he answered the phone. He told him as concisely as he could what had happened, then said, "Go to Paramus Park; there'll be a grey minivan parked near the back of the rear parking lot. It will have a gun on the front seat, which will have the fingerprints of the driver. In fact, both of our fingerprints will be all over the car."

"Where is Eden?" Nick asked.

Tim was pulling into Paramus Park at the moment, and was relieved to find that her car was gone. "I assume she's home; can we get someone to protect her?"

"Yes. Now get out of there quickly; in a little while that place is going to be crawling with cops, one of whom will probably be Novack."

"You think that's wise?"

"Tim, ultimately we are going to have to deal with them. We've got to let them know there are other bad guys in the picture."

Nick knew exactly what it meant when
he got an 8 A.M. call from Novack,

asking him to come down for a meeting as soon as possible. It meant that they had hit pay dirt on the fingerprint, and that Novack wanted to know everything that Nick knew.

Nick had been cryptic the day before, telling Novack about the grey minivan with the gun on the seat, and mentioning that it had a direct relevance to the Wallace case. The police had descended on the place, according to an associate that Nick sent over there, but Nick stayed away. If gamesmanship was professional football, Nick would be chosen for the Pro Bowl every year.

Novack and Anders were waiting for Nick when he arrived, and he was ushered right in. "You want coffee or something?" Anders asked.

"I'll have a Venti vanilla triple shot latte. And a sesame bagel. Toasted."

Novack said to Anders, "You know, we should spend every morning with an asshole attorney. It would make us appreciate the rest of the day."

"I'll have black coffee," said Nick.

Novack looked at the pot. "We've got light brown." He poured Nick a cup and handed it to him. "So . . . tell me where the car with the gun came from."

Nick smiled. "So . . . tell me that Jeff Cashman is really Billy

Zimmerman." He did this to demonstrate that Novack was not fully in charge, that Nick had access to information and was therefore a force to be reckoned with.

"Was," said Novack. "He's dead. His body was fished out of the Passaic River a few days ago."

Nick was surprised to hear this news, but he took it in stride. "I suppose you think Tim came out of hiding to do that? You think he runs a murder factory? The General Motors of homicide?"

Novack smiled. "Let's just say he's a person of interest."

"Okay," Nick said. "Moving on . . . whose prints were on the gun?"

Novack exchanged a glance with Anders, then turned to Nick. "I'll tell you what. For the purpose of this conversation about this car and this gun, we'll share our information. You tell us what you know, and we'll tell you what we know."

Nick nodded. "That works, until it butts up against client confidentiality."

"Fair enough. You start," said Novack.

"Okay. My sister is a friend of Tim Wallace's; that's how he came to call me for representation. Wallace left his dog with her before he ran off. She discovered that someone was following her in recent days, maybe thinking she would lead him to Wallace. Which she could not do."

"Because she doesn't have the slightest idea where he is," Novack said dryly.

"Right. And did I mention she's on my staff, working on this case?" Nick had told Eden he was "hiring" her, so that she could hide behind client confidentiality as well. He set her up at a salary of one dollar a month, payable in advance. It wouldn't legally protect her against helping Tim evade the manhunt, but it might stop the police from questioning her vigorously.

"What a surprise," Anders said. "Keep going."

"I received a phone call saying that the car was there, with the gun on the seat. I have a description of the man as well."

"A call from who?"

"Sorry," Nick said, tacitly citing confidentiality. "But I can tell you that the man was slightly injured in the encounter; a bullet grazed his left arm. Anyway, that's what I know. I believe it's your turn. Who was the driver?"

"His name is Richie Patrick. He's thirty-one years old, born in Bloomington, Indiana. He was wanted in three different states for three different murders."

"A hit man?"

Novack shook his head. "That's too limiting. He's available for hire to do pretty much anything, but murder is his specialty."

"So there's a hit man involved in this case, but you make Wallace for all these murders? How does that make sense?"

"Wallace is charged with the murder of his wife, and he's guilty as charged."

"You said Patrick 'was wanted,' " said Nick.

Novack nodded. "Right. He was identified as killed in a plane crash eighteen months ago in Minnesota."

"Well, he's apparently made a comeback."

"We done here?" said Anders. The idea of meeting and "shooting the shit with a defense attorney," as he put it, was not something he was inherently comfortable with.

"Not quite. There's something else I want to tell you guys. I'm not sure if I should, but I will."

"We're all ears," said Novack.

"There was a boat out on the water that day, not far from Wallace's boat, when the explosion happened. The people on board never reported it, and they left the scene before the Coast Guard arrived." He proceeded to talk in more detail about the Oceanfast 360, and how Tim and Maggie had seen it repeatedly during the day, including moments before the explosion.

"Why should we care about this?" asked Novack, who was less openly skeptical about it than Anders.

"Because I now know which boat it was, where it is located, what company owns it, and most importantly, who has been on it in the past."

"Who might that be?"

"Senator Fred Collinsworth."

It seemed as if there were more dogs than people at the Federal Center in Newark. Every square inch of the building was being sniffed and examined, over and over again.

One of the features of the building in which the dinner party was to be held was an ability to lock it down. What that meant was that in the event of an outside threat, the capability was there to close up the building, turning it into a literally airtight, virtually impregnable fortress.

The computers that controlled such a lockdown, and the ventilation system that was triggered to provide oxygen to the people inside, were checked and rechecked. Again Will was called in to provide a detailed description of the system that he had helped design, in essence repeating a meeting he had two weeks prior, albeit with a different Homeland Security computer expert.

This one's name was Teri Berman, an attractive woman who looked incredibly familiar to Will. He had a hunch that she'd shot him down at the Purple Rose one night, but didn't want to bring it up, in case another opportunity presented itself.

This wasn't such an opportunity. She came into the computer room at the Federal Center building with a no-nonsense attitude, asking that he show her everything about the system, starting at the beginning. "Leave nothing out."

Will was slightly annoyed to be having to go through this again. "Don't you guys ever talk to each other down there?" he asked.

"What does that mean?"

"I went through this with one of your colleagues two weeks ago . . . took half a day."

She shrugged, not knowing who or what he was talking about, and not really caring. Inefficiency in the bureaucracy was not exactly a news event, and she had her job to do. "So you should have it down pat by now."

When they were finished, Teri made it very clear to Will that he would not be on the scene on the big night. She and other government operators would be running the system from the computer room. He was to provide them with all applicable passwords and codes, which he did. It wasn't that they didn't trust Will, it was simply that they didn't trust anyone.

The outside of the building was scrutinized just as thoroughly. There was simply no way a vehicle could get close enough to damage the building, even if it were loaded with Cintron 421.

The air space over the entire area would be off-limits, and fighter planes would be enforcing that restriction. Additionally, security would be fanned out into the surrounding neighborhoods.

Everything was deemed by the Secret Service to be as it should be, and that was to be confirmed repeatedly in the days leading up to the event.

The word was communicated to an anxious White House that all was secure, and that there was no reason to reconsider the president's attendance.

The fact that they were wrong would not be known until it was too late.

"I think we should go to Donovan with this,"

Novack said. In addition to all the other new information they had received, they had just learned that the Oceanfast in question was registered to a holding company whose ownership could not be determined. However, the listed name on the documents, a requirement for a boat license, was Keith Rivers, right-hand man for Collinsworth.

"Why?" asked Anders.

"Because this is way past what we thought. And I'm not sure Wallace is behind it."

"You've got to be kidding. You've been after this guy for months, and now you're letting him off the hook?"

Novack had been slowly moving toward this position for a while, and he was aware that he was moving more toward Anders's original point of view.

"I was positive he killed his wife, I didn't know if it was for money, another woman, whatever, and I could never find anything. But he's not a terrorist, he didn't hop on down to Florida last week to kill that woman, he didn't create Zimmerman out of thin air, and I doubt that he killed him. He also didn't tie that boat to Collinsworth."

Anders, playing the devil's advocate, chose to focus on the last point. "We don't know that. Wallace could have known who owned that boat, maybe Collinsworth's nephew told him, and he made up the story that it was out there the day he killed his wife."

Novack wasn't convinced. "The finger doesn't fit in either. Why, if he was behind all this other shit, would he have saved the finger and planted it? He would have had to know we'd nail him on it."

"Sickamus fuckamus, remember?"

"I don't think so, not anymore."

"Come on, Novack. You saying some mysterious bad guys kill his wife, then wait almost a year to—"

"But that's the point. If he didn't do it, then the wife probably wasn't the target. It was the first time she was on the boat. What if he was supposed to die?"

"Then why not kill him now? Why go through all this stuff?"

Novack shrugged. "Beats me; I'm just a dumb cop." He looked at his watch and stood up. "And I'm outta here."

"Where you going?"

"I've got that departmental physical; I've been putting it off for three months, and personnel said if I don't take it they're going to cancel my health insurance and boil me in oil."

"Good . . . you've been looking tired lately," Anders said.

"The reason you don't get tired like me is you don't have to carry around two balls all day."

"Kiss my ass," Anders said.

"Call Donovan and set up a meeting for first thing in the morning."

"What do you want him to do?"

"Offer to pull back the arrest warrant on Wallace, maybe as a way to get him to come in. I think there might be more to gain by hearing what he has to say than arresting him."

"Donovan will think you're nuts."

Novack shrugged. "It won't be the first time."

Things had gotten a lot more complicated for Richie Patrick. He had been stupid and careless, and he had let an amateur clown get the jump on him. He had little doubt what the repercussions of that would be; the police would have his fingerprints, and they would be looking for him. Worse yet, they would know his supposed death was a hoax. No longer could he do his job with impunity; he had to be aware that he was now both the hunter and the hunted.

Another factor that he now had to consider was his insatiable desire for revenge. Tim Wallace and Eden Alexander were going to die for this. In fact, by the time he was finished with them, they were going to beg him to die.

Richie would finish what he was paid to do, and then he would have his revenge.

On everybody.

For Senator Collinsworth, the worst was apparently over. Jimmy Lee Curry's story had run about his connection to Tim's company, and while it was a short-term embarrassment, the damage appeared to have been minor. Collinsworth had commissioned a poll to be taken on the subject and was relieved to find that eighty-one percent of Americans were not even aware of it.

The best news of all was a phone call Detective Anders had made to Keith Rivers, informing him of recent developments, which were so significant that Novack had actually had strong doubts about Tim's guilt. Putting Anders on the payroll was one of the smartest moves he had made.

Collinsworth would have Rivers contact Danny and tell him the news about Novack's serious doubts, which might even lead to Tim's coming out of hiding. This was dependent, of course, on Danny knowing how to contact him, as Collinsworth suspected he did.

The recent events would allow the senator to focus on the weekend's opening of the Federal Center. As the home state senator and a man directly responsible for the project in the first place, Collinsworth was going to make the welcoming speech. With the president in attendance, every major media outlet in the country would be there as well.

It would be a platform and a moment that Collinsworth would

not let go to waste. He had three speechwriters working on it, and he was torturing them to get it exactly right. It was to focus on the project's concept as a way to defeat terrorism and protect Americans; that was how Collinsworth wanted to be viewed. It also had to demonstrate Collinsworth's gravitas, and therefore his capacity to handle whatever higher office he might seek.

It would be a moment for which he would be ready.

"I need to speak to Novack,"

were the first words Cindy heard when she picked up the phone.

"I'm sorry, but he's not here," she said.

"It's very important that I see him right away. It's a matter of life and death."

"Who is this?" she asked.

"Tim Wallace. Can you please give him a message for me?"

The name sent a shock wave through her, and it never entered her mind to think about or be worried by the fact that he knew her home number, even though Novack did not live there. "Yes, I will," she said, knowing that he was due to come over at any time.

"Please tell him to meet me at Squires Delicatessen in Fort Lee. Tell him to take a seat at a booth in the back, and I'll be in five minutes after he arrives."

Ever a cop's wife, albeit a divorced cop's wife, Cindy asked, "He'll want to know what this is about."

"It's about me giving him information that will blow this case wide open, and then turning myself in after I do."

"I'll tell him," she said. "But I'm not sure how long it will take."

"That's okay; I'll wait. But make sure he comes; he's the only one I will tell this to."

"I'll tell him."

Click. The call was disconnected, but Cindy continued to stare at the phone, only stopping when she heard the front door open.

Novack was home.

He came into the room, and immediately saw the look on her face. "What's wrong?"

"Tim Wallace just called. He wants to see you right away." She proceeded to describe the conversation in as much detail as she could remember, and was very accurate, considering how nervous she was.

"Did he say I needed to come alone?" he asked.

"No, but he said it had to be you. That you were the only person he would tell the information to."

"Did you use that phone?" he asked, pointing to the phone on the desk.

"Yes."

"Don't use it again. Make any calls you need to make on your cell." He wanted to preserve the possibility of calling back the number by using *69, should that become necessary.

Novack took out his own cell phone and called Anders. He quickly and concisely described what had happened, and within three minutes they had a plan to place officers strategically on the blocks surrounding the deli. That way they could cordon off the area on a moment's notice if it became necessary. They would also have two officers in the deli in plainclothes, posing as customers. Anders would arrange it all, and Novack would delay leaving for another fifteen minutes to give it time to set up.

"Are you sure you should go?" Cindy asked when he got off the phone. "You said yourself he's a murderer."

"Maybe," Novack said. "Either way we'll have cops everywhere. We can play by his rules for now."

She managed a faint, worried smile. "How come we never get to play by my rules?"

He kissed her on the head. "That comes later tonight."

The fifteen minutes spent waiting to leave were among the longest Novack had ever endured. He was uncomfortable waiting; there was always the danger that Wallace would change his mind.

The truth was that he was suspicious of Wallace's motives; if he had crucial information to impart, he could have done so over the phone, or more likely through his lawyer.

He briefly considered whether to call Nick Alexander, but quickly rejected it. It was entirely possible that Wallace was doing something contrary to his own best interests, and Novack didn't want Nick talking him out of it.

Novack went upstairs to the bedroom to wash his face and change his clothes. In a few minutes, it was time to leave, and he called Anders to confirm that everything was ready. Satisfied that it was, he went back downstairs.

Then something hit Novack that he hadn't thought about before. "Did he say how he got this number, or why he thought I'd be here?"

Cindy shook her head. "No."

The idea of Wallace knowing where Cindy lived was discomforting at best, and he said, "Make sure the windows and doors are locked. Don't open it for anybody. If I want to get in, I'll call you first."

"You really think he might come here?"

"No, just covering every base."

She hugged him and he left the house, walking toward his car, parked out in front where he had left it less than half an hour ago.

He was halfway there when he heard her calling from behind. "Call me as soon as it's over," she said through the still partially opened door.

He turned to tell her that he would do exactly that, and the turn of his body caused the bullet to miss his heart and hit him below the right shoulder. The bulletproof vest he was wearing did not provide full protection from the "cop-killer" bullet, and he was blown back five feet from the impact.

He heard Cindy scream and saw her rush toward him. He wanted to yell at her to go back, not to risk being shot herself by the additional bullets that he believed certain to follow.

But he couldn't form the words, and she reached him, crying

and holding his head in her hands, sobbing his name. And she stayed that way, as he lapsed into unconsciousness, until the place was swarming with neighbors, and paramedics, and seemingly enough police cars to fill the parking lot at Yankee Stadium.

Tim was watching CNN when he found out that he'd shot Novack.

It started out as an alert, with a "breaking news" banner that had become so commonplace in twenty-four-hour cable news. The early report said that Novack was shot in front of his house, and identified him as the lead detective in the Tim Wallace murder case.

Within five minutes, coverage became wall-to-wall. The proximity to New York made it easy for reporters to get there, and rumors were flying fast and furious. There was open speculation that Tim was responsible, followed by a vaguely worded statement from the state police public relations office that seemed to confirm that Tim had been the shooter. There was no word on Novack's condition, only that he was still alive.

As bizarre as the preceding weeks had been for Tim, this was way beyond all that. He watched as if disembodied, and even wondered if there was another Tim Wallace, an alter ego of himself, that had set out to destroy the world.

None of it made any sense to him. Somebody had done this deliberately, as part of the grand scheme, but why bother? Tim was already a fugitive, already widely believed by the police and public to be a murderer. What did this accomplish, except perhaps ratcheting up the pressure?

And why Novack? If people were set on destroying Tim, then

Novack was their ally. He was the commander of the anti-Tim forces. Why take him out of the picture?

Tim called Nick at home and got the machine, so he didn't leave a message and instead called his cell phone. He was relieved when Nick answered, "Alexander here."

"Nick, what the hell is going on?"

Nick was at that moment standing behind police barricades outside the house where Novack was shot. There were several policemen within a few feet of him, so Nick walked away when he realized it was Tim, and his voice got much lower. "Somebody shot Novack; they think it was you."

"Why?"

"Did you call him tonight?" Nick asked.

"Novack? Of course not. Are they saying I did?"

"Somebody called saying it was you, and asking Novack to meet you somewhere. When he walked out of the house, he was shot."

"I swear, it wasn't me. Can't they trace the call or something?"

"I'm trying to find out more now, but they're saying very little."

Tim was watching on television while talking, and suddenly there was a panning shot of the street, and Tim actually saw Nick on camera. "You're there . . . I can see you on TV now."

"Are they showing my good side? Listen, I gotta go . . . call me later." With that he disconnected the call, leaving Tim with nothing but his television.

Novack regained consciousness within a few minutes of arriving at the hospital. He had lost considerable blood and was immediately given a massive transfusion. It took a few hours for the blood and fluids to stabilize him sufficiently for him to be relatively clear-headed.

At that moment, he was the only person in the police department, and one of the few in America, who did not believe he was shot by Tim Wallace.

His reasoning was simple. Wallace had called Cindy before Novack got home, and the message was for Novack to leave immediately for the meeting. He therefore already had to have been in position at the house, waiting for Novack to leave, so that he could shoot him.

But if he were there, he would have shot Novack in the back, on the way into the house. There wouldn't have been any reason to wait for him to come back out; he couldn't even have been sure that Novack would take the bait to go meet Tim at all.

And Novack finally, instinctively, knew one other thing with certainty. Not only was Wallace not the shooter.

He was not a murderer at all.

Senator Walter Evans could feign outrage with the best of them, and when he took to the Senate floor the next morning, he was in rare form. Evans was only a freshman senator, but his youthfulness and charisma had immediately vaulted him into the group of politicians considered potential presidential timber.

The chamber was mostly empty, but with the C-Span cameras rolling, he could be sure that his words would reverberate on cable news for a number of cycles.

Evans never mentioned Senator Collinsworth by name, yet there was no doubt that he was taking direct aim at him. He acted as if saddened that he had to address the issue at all, and in the process implicitly criticize a member of his own party.

The speech was obviously referencing the Jimmy Lee Curry article, though that was not directly mentioned either. Instead Evans railed against the "old way of doing business," and how that wasn't good enough in "this era of terror." He was taking full advantage of Jimmy Lee's revelation that Senator Collinsworth had essentially put a murderer on the government payroll, knowing that the Washington press would fill in the blanks.

By Washington standards it was a stunning shot across the bow. Evans and Collinsworth were known to be rivals, both because of Evans's second-place status to Collinsworth on the Appropriations Committee, and more importantly as a possible presidential contender.

Susan Moreno watched the speech from the comfort of her office and enjoyed it immensely. She thought that her boss was doing a great job, avoiding specifics to make a very specific point. There was no doubt it would have the desired effect of drawing attention to Evans at the expense of Collinsworth, and she readied herself for the calls asking for Evans's appearance on the various Sunday talk shows.

She couldn't help smiling over the knowledge that her counterpart on Collinsworth's staff, Keith Rivers, must be furious and seeking revenge.

It was just one of the things she couldn't have been more wrong about.

There was a steady stream of visitors to Novack's hospital room during the next twenty-four hours.

A parade of fellow detectives came by to show their support for a downed colleague, and they were delighted to find that Novack was doing very well. So well that by late morning he was being insulted and ridiculed with regularity.

Anders was also there frequently, as was Captain Donovan, though neither had anything positive to report on the hunt for Tim. Novack expressed to both of them his feeling that Tim had not been the one who spoke to Cindy on the phone, or who had shot Novack as he left the house.

"He would have shot me on the way in," Novack said to Donovan and Anders.

"Maybe he wasn't ready to shoot," Anders said. "Maybe you surprised him by showing up before he could get a good line of fire."

"I can prove it wasn't him."

"Then go right ahead," said Donovan.

Novack turned to Anders. "Cindy's out in the hall. Ask her to come in."

Anders went out to get Cindy, who had been at the hospital virtually every moment since the shooting, except for running a crucial errand for Novack.

"Tell these guys what you did this morning."

Cindy nodded. "I went home and listened to some recordings in your Wallace case file." Novack had kept his file on the Wallace case at home so that he could periodically look through it. It included copies of all relevant documents, and copies of the taped recordings of interviews conducted with Wallace around the time of Maggie's death.

Donovan turned to Novack. "You realize you just broke about ten departmental rules by having her do that."

"Oops. My bad," said Novack. Then, to Cindy, "Tell them what you found out."

"It wasn't Wallace on the phone," Cindy said. "Not even close."

"How can you be sure of that?" Donovan asked.

"Captain, she's a speech therapist."

"I can go into specifics about speech patterns and accents, if you want, Captain," she said. "But there's not a doubt in my mind. The person who called that night was not from around here. He was a Midwesterner; maybe Michigan, maybe Indiana. He's also older than Wallace."

"Richie Patrick," Donovan said, since the hit man whose fingerprints were all over the car was from Indiana.

Novack nodded. "That's what I think. I also talked to Kelly in forensics; they think the shooter was in the alley adjacent to the house across the street. It was no easy shot, especially with so little light. There's no evidence that Wallace had any real experience with guns."

"Have we been wrong on this guy all along?" Donovan asked.

"You weren't. I was."

The most worried man in the room at that moment was Anders. He believed it possible that the reason Novack was shot was because he was starting to believe in Tim's innocence, and the shooter did not want his new view to prevail.

But Anders was most likely the only person that Novack had at that point confided in, and Anders had not kept that information confidential.

He had told it to Keith Rivers, which was the same as telling it to Senator Collinsworth.

It had been a while since Eden had heard anything from Tim, and she was going crazy. The media had already tried and convicted Tim of the Novack shooting, and it seemed like there was an update on the manhunt every ten minutes. The fact that the updates consisted of no new developments did not seem to deter the networks at all. They had decided that the public was thirsting for news about Tim, and would drink anything, no matter how flimsy.

Nick had assured her that Tim had had nothing to do with the shooting, and for the first time he admitted sharing her feeling that he was innocent of all the other charges as well. It was comforting to her, and at that point she could use all the comfort she could get.

Eden hadn't been going out much, if at all, out of concern that Richie Patrick might reappear. She hadn't seen him since that day at Paramus Park, and it was quite likely that he was deterred by the police officer Novack had assigned to sit in a squad car in front of her house. Or maybe he was deterred by Tim shooting him. Either way, she hoped and expected never to see him again.

But while Eden felt fairly personally secure, she was in constant fear for Tim, and she checked her e-mail every few minutes, hoping that he would contact her. She would not call him, since once Nick told the police about her friendship with Tim, she understood that there was a possibility that her phone could be tapped.

It was almost dinnertime when Eden received the e-mail. It read,

```
I hate to ask you this, but I need you to tell
Danny that I have to see him. Don't call; they
might be monitoring his phone and/or yours.
Tell him I need his help, and that he should
meet me tomorrow morning at ten o'clock, where
we used to play touch football. He'll know what
that means. Thanks, and be careful.
```

Eden had no hesitation about doing what Tim asked, but there was a practical problem. She e-mailed him back.

Where does he live?

She waited for an hour, but there was no response. She knew at that point that she wouldn't be getting one, since the library would be closed by then. Obviously he had sent the e-mail, but couldn't wait around for a quick reply.

Eden had no way to get Danny's address online or through the phone book; she didn't even know his last name. She had two choices. One was to go to the company office in the morning, and hope that Danny came in early enough to still be able to meet Tim at ten o'clock. This was dubious, especially since there was a chance he wouldn't be in the office at all. They were a construction company finishing a major job; he might well go to the site instead.

The other alternative was to go to the Purple Rose. Tim had told her that he and his friends used to hang out there almost every night, and possibly he was there on this night as well. It was certainly worth a try. If he wasn't there, maybe somebody else would know how to contact him.

Eden debated whether to tell the police officer out front where she was going, thereby allowing him to follow her. It was a double-edged sword; while he was ostensibly her protector, he was also a representative of law enforcement. When he saw that she was talking to Danny, it could result in his having Danny followed the next morning, a maneuver that would lead them to Tim.

She finally decided that personal safety was the priority, and it was unlikely the officer would follow her into the bar, so he wouldn't know who she was talking to. He also did not seem to be a person who was involved in the investigation; he was simply filling a probably boring role of providing protection for her.

She went out and told the officer that she was leaving to have a drink with a friend, and he nodded without showing much interest and said that he would follow her. She got in her car and drove to the Purple Rose, and she noted with satisfaction that the officer just pulled into the parking lot behind her and waited in his car.

The Purple Rose was fairly crowded, and since Eden had never met Danny, she went to the bartender, Frank Lester, for help. "Excuse me, can you tell me if Danny is here? He's a friend of Tim Wallace's."

"Danny? Yeah, I think he's . . ." Frank said, eyes scanning the room. "Sure, he's right over there." He pointed to a table across the room, where Danny was sitting with Will. "In the blue shirt."

"Thanks," Eden said, and headed for the table. She didn't know Will, and there was no way she would convey the message to Danny in front of anyone else.

As Eden approached, she and Danny made eye contact, and he noticeably tensed. He had seen her that day in front of Tim's apartment, after the finger was found at the racquetball club. It couldn't be a coincidence that she was heading straight for him.

He stood up, and she said, "Danny?"

"Yes."

"I need to speak to you about something. In private."

He waited a beat. "Sure . . . of course." He turned to Will. "Can you give us a couple of minutes?"

Will had never met Eden, and it took him a moment to register that he was being asked to leave. Then, "Yeah . . . no problem."

Will got up and took a walk toward the back of the restaurant. "Have a seat," Danny said. "I'm sorry, what's your name?"

"That doesn't matter. I have a message for you from Tim."

"How is he?"

"He's fine. He wants you to meet him tomorrow morning at ten o'clock."

Danny instinctively looked around to make sure that no one was close enough to hear what they were saying. "Where?"

"At the place where you used to play touch football. He wants you to come alone, without telling anyone else about it."

"Why does he want to meet with me?"

"I don't know."

"Do you know where he is? Can I reach him tonight? Maybe he wants me to bring money, or something that—"

She cut him off. "I've already told you everything I know."

She turned to leave, and saw Will watching them with obvious curiosity as he walked back toward the front of the place. She hoped that Danny would really keep her message to himself, but she had her doubts.

Once she left, Will came back to the table. "Who the hell was that?" he asked.

"A friend of a friend," Danny said.

"You want to be a little more specific than that?"

"No."

"This have something to do with Tim?"

"No."

"Thanks for sharing," Will said, reaching for his bottle of beer.

Eden left the restaurant relieved that she had been able to do what Tim asked. She called Nick to tell him what had transpired, thinking that Tim would be fine with her doing so. Nick wasn't in, so she left a message on his machine, conveying the message cryptically and without mentioning the place where Tim and Danny were to meet.

Eden signaled to the officer as she was approaching her car, and he nodded and pulled out behind her. When they finished the fifteen-minute ride, she parked in front of her house, and he pulled in behind her. She walked over to him and spoke through the window.

"Can I get you anything? Coffee? Maybe something to eat?"

He smiled. "No, thanks. I have a trunk full of doughnuts. Besides, someone takes over my shift in an hour."

She returned the smile. "I wish someone could take over my shift. Good night."

"Good night."

Richie Patrick was waiting for Eden
when she entered her house.

He sat calmly on the couch, petting Travis with one hand and casually holding a handgun in the other. "If you scream, it will be the
last sound you ever make," he said.

Her panic was such that she couldn't catch her breath. All she
could think about was the police officer outside, and how she might
alert him. "What do you want?"

He laughed. "More than you've got, but you'll have to do for
now."

"The house is surrounded by police."

"You mean that clown in the black-and-white outside? That's
who you're counting on?"

She didn't say anything, so he continued. "Where is your
boyfriend . . . Wallace?"

"I have no idea."

He smiled. "Sure you do. But we've got time for that later. Let's
go."

"Where?"

"I'll tell you what, let's make some ground rules. You do exactly
what I say, and you don't ask me another . . . single . . . fucking . . .
question."

The sudden intensity with which he spoke was chilling to her.

She didn't respond, and his amiable smile returned. "Good. Now let's go."

He took her by the arm and led her out the back door. They were gone by the time her protector finished his first doughnut.

Nick got Eden's phone message around ten o'clock, having just returned from dinner out. He returned the call, but there was no answer. He assumed that she was still out after her meeting with Danny, but wasn't very worried, because she had mentioned that she was letting the police officer follow her. He left a message for her to call him back, and went to sleep.

Nick woke up briefly at four in the morning, and reflected on the fact that Eden had not called him back. He assumed that she got home late and didn't want to wake him. He still wasn't particularly worried, certainly not enough to call her at this hour.

So he went back to sleep.

It was as uncomfortable a night as Tim could ever remember spending. He could not be certain that Danny would be coming to the meeting alone, so he had to be in position well in advance. That would enable him to see a trap being sprung, and escape it.

The meeting was at the same location in Rockland County where Tim had taken Richie Patrick. He chose it because there was only one entrance in by car, a long, winding road that Tim could observe from a vantage point in the hills above the area. If he were to see that Danny was not alone, he could be out long before they would even know he was there.

The downside to this was that it was twenty degrees that night, so Tim had to stay in his car with the motor running and the heat on. He also felt the need to stay awake, in case his adversaries also had the idea to show up very early to set a trap.

The night went by uneventfully, and approaching ten o'clock there still was nothing to arouse Tim's suspicion. This was an area that would not see any traffic at all, particularly midweek at this time of year. If a car showed up, it would be Danny. If more than one showed up, Tim would be out of there.

At five to ten, Tim saw Danny's car start up the winding road leading toward the meeting place. He saw no other cars, nor could he see anyone in the car with Danny. His vantage point was not the best, and it was a considerable distance, but Danny did seem to be alone.

Danny stopped his car where Tim knew he would, on the field where they had played touch football all those years before. All that seemed part of a different life to Tim, a life that could never be completely repaired, no matter how this wound up.

Danny got out of the car and looked around for any sign of Tim. He kept glancing back toward the road, and whirled in surprise when he heard the words yelled from up above him.

"Start walking up the hill!"

Danny looked up toward the sound of the voice but could not see Tim, especially since the sun was coming from that direction. He shielded his eyes, but the glare was still too great.

"Tim?"

"Start walking up the hill!"

Danny did as he was told, walking up the only path that would take him there. Tim kept his eyes on the car and the road, but saw no sign of anyone but Danny. He let Danny get three quarters of the way up before starting down to meet him.

Danny heard Tim before he saw him, and still was pretty much blinded by the sun over Tim's shoulder. "Tim, is that you?"

"It's me."

Danny again shielded the sun with his hand, which was how he saw that Tim was pointing a gun at him. "What's that for? What's going on?"

"We need to talk, Danny."

"So let's talk; that's what I'm here for. Why do you have a gun? Is that thing real?"

"Why are you doing this to me, Danny?"

"Doing what?" Danny said, his voice cracking slightly, his fear evident. "Come on, Tim, it's just me here."

"You set me up from the beginning. You killed Maggie."

"No, no—"

"Danny, you're going to tell me the truth, or I'm going to kill you right here."

"Tim, I swear, I don't know what you're talking about. Please—"

"I'm talking about you knowing I was going to be on the boat that day. I'm talking about you knowing I was in Wyoming, about you being there at the racquetball club."

"Of course I knew where you were, we're partners. You always know where I am too."

"Danny, I'm not trying to figure out if you did it. All I want to know is why."

"Tim, I swear—"

"There was another boat out there the day Maggie died. I found it. You know who's been out on that boat? Your uncle."

Danny seemed unable to process all of this. "My uncle?"

"Right. The boat is owned by some dummy corporation, but Keith Rivers signed for the license. Were you out there that day, Danny? Just waiting for the explosion?"

"Yours is the only boat I've ever been on, Tim. I swear it."

"What does your uncle get out of ruining my life, Danny? What do you get out of it?"

"Please think about this, Tim. We're friends, since we were kids. Why would I do this to you? Why would my uncle do it? It's making him look bad; he's pissed off about it."

Tim walked toward him, until he was about ten feet away. He was pointing the gun with two hands. "Danny, you're going to tell me the truth by the time I count to three, or I'm going to shoot you."

"One . . ."

"Two . . ."

The fact that Danny didn't confess to anything did not come from some place of courage, or principle. He was so confused, so frightened, that he did not even have the capacity to make up a story.

"Tim, I have told you the truth," he finally said, and braced himself. "Please . . . there's nothing else I can say."

Tim didn't shoot; instead, he lowered the gun. "Danny, I need help."

Eden had absolutely no idea where she was.

Patrick had tied her hands and placed a gag over her mouth and a blindfold over her eyes, then put her in the back of what seemed to be a van. She tried to figure out how far they drove, but that proved impossible. Instead she spent the time trying to get her fear under control.

When they arrived at their destination, he led her out of the van and over what seemed like a short wooden path, almost like a footbridge. He took her down some stairs and into a room, then cuffed her to what felt like radiator pipes. They were hot, uncomfortably so, but it was probably better than being exposed to the freezing weather outside.

She was surprised when he took off the gag but left the blindfold on. Had he taken it off she would have seen little other than that she was in a small room, no more than seven by ten. It was sparsely furnished and had one window, which was covered by a sheet.

"This is gonna be your home for a while," he said. "Depending on your behavior, it could be the last one you'll ever have."

She didn't answer him.

"I'll be back tomorrow. No one can hear you anyway, but there's an intercom system which has a microphone recording any sound in the room. If I find that you've screamed, or even spoken in any way, I will cut open your throat and rip out your larynx with my bare hands. Understand?"

She nodded.

"Good. I'll see you tomorrow, and you'll tell me where your friend is."

He left, and she willed herself not to cry. The microphones would pick it up, and she didn't want to give him the satisfaction.

Nick tried Eden three times between seven and eight in the morning, and then went to her house. He knew by instinct that something was wrong, just like he knew Tim had run that day. What he was there to find out was just how wrong things had gone.

Nick saw the officer parked in front of her house, identified himself, and asked him where Eden was.

"She's inside," he said.

Nick could hear the sound of the dogs barking inside. "She's not answering her phone."

"Maybe she's asleep."

"With that barking going on? Come on."

The officer got out of the car and followed Nick to the front door. They rang the bell a few times and pounded on the door, but there was no response other than an increase in the level of barking.

The officer broke a small window in the front door and reached in, unlocking it. Eden was of course not to be found, and there was no evidence that she spent the night there. Her bed was still made, and it did not appear that the barking dogs had been fed. Nick knew her too well to consider the possibility that there was a benign explanation for this.

She was in desperate trouble.

If she was still alive.

Danny and Tim talked for almost three hours. It was unlike any conversation they had ever had; no sports, no business, no women. They were trying to figure out how Tim's life had been taken away from him, and how to get it back.

Much of the conversation was Tim filling in Danny on what he had learned, about the Oceanfast, about Senator Collinsworth, about Carson, Wyoming, about Ricardo Vasquez calling their office, and about Richie Patrick. He was hoping that it might trigger a thought in Danny's mind, something that would somehow clear up what was a bewildering picture.

It did not.

Danny's reaction was primarily astonishment, especially about Collinsworth's possible involvement. "It doesn't compute," he said. "Your situation only makes him look bad for steering us the business. When that newspaper article came out, I thought he was going to have a stroke."

"He's got an angle we haven't figured out," Tim said. "This somehow gets him what he wants."

"He's got more money than he could ever spend, so that can't be it. What he really wants is to be president, but how can this help him get there?"

Tim had no answer for that, so he once again changed the subject. He was jumping around, trying to stumble on something that made sense. "It's got to be a bigger picture than we're seeing; it has to be much more than just about me. There has to be another shoe that's going to drop. I'm being made the fall guy for something that hasn't happened yet."

"Maybe about the Federal Center?" Danny asked. "The opening is Saturday night; the damn president is going to be there. The FBI has talked to me twice, and the Secret Service once. Maybe that's where the Cintron 421 was going."

"Well, it's not going to get there now," Tim said. "That place will be swimming with security; nothing is getting near there."

"But that guy called our office?"

Tim nodded. "Yeah, I thought he was calling you. What he must have been doing was pretending to be somebody else, maybe a salesman or something, just so my number would show up on his phone. The bastards have covered every base."

"I hope you don't mind my bringing this up, but what I don't understand," Danny said, "is how that could have been Maggie's finger. I mean, you saw the explosion, right? It knocked you out, didn't it?"

"All I remember was a flash of white. I assumed it was an explosion, and I believed them when they said Maggie's body was never found."

"But they were sure? I mean the DNA tests . . ."

Tim nodded. "That's what they said. They said when it matches it's one in billions that it could be wrong. And the labs aren't police labs, so . . ."

Tim's voice trailed off. Something was bothering him, something didn't make sense, and he couldn't quite put his finger on it.

"What is it?" Danny asked.

Tim was still silent, trying to focus on it. It was almost there . . .

"Tim?"

He had it. "Danny, I just thought of something; I've got to go deal with it."

"Okay; can I help?"

"I don't think so, but if you can, I'll get in touch with you."

They walked up the hill to Tim's car, so that he could drive Danny back to where he left his.

As soon as they got in the car, Tim turned the radio on to the local news, and it was the first story they heard. A woman named Eden Alexander was kidnapped, and it was believed to be tied to the Tim Wallace case.

"Oh, my God," Tim said, devastated by what he had heard. "It has to be Patrick . . ."

"What would he want from her?" Danny asked.

"Me."

The ceremony that would officially open the
Federal Center was forty-eight hours away,

and it could be said that the preparations were both complete and
ongoing. Everything had been gone over countless times, and with
construction finished, the place was in total lockdown mode. Yet
despite that, things were being checked and rechecked. With the
level of people that would be there on Saturday night, it was man-
dated that the people responsible for security be ultracareful.

On this particular day, the U.S. Marshal's Office and Secret
Service were running what amounted to a dress rehearsal. Employees of those agencies, as well as staffers from both the White House
and various senator's offices, were there to re-create the next evening exactly as it would take place.

Nothing would be left to chance.

The evening was to be fairly simple. There would be a cocktail
party, lasting for ninety minutes. The president would arrive fifteen
minutes prior to the end of the party, then join the assembled dignitaries as they moved into a large room, which would eventually
hold hundreds of federal workers, separated by cubicles. For now
those cubicles had not yet been installed, and the area would serve
as a large ballroom, where dinner would be served and speeches
would be given.

The building and room where the dinner was to be held was
chosen because of the uniqueness of its security. In the event of

danger, a computer would totally lock it down, closing impregnable metal doors, in effect creating a hermetically sealed fortress that would be resistant to all but the most powerful explosives. The same computer would simultaneously start an emergency ventilation system, utilizing oxygen tanks in the building's basement. There were a total of twelve tanks; each could supply enough air for a crowd this size to breathe for three hours.

The theory was unique, and planned for use in the subsequent Federal Centers to be built around the country. Buildings would no longer have to be evacuated in an emergency, an often panic-filled process which by itself could result in injuries and deaths. In these buildings there was another alternative, creating a safe haven within the structure itself.

Before serving dinner, short speeches would be given by Newark Congresswoman Nancy Fellows, Senator Evans, and Senator Collinsworth. Much focus would be on the two senators' comments because of their open rivalry, exacerbated by Evans's speech about Collinsworth on the Senate floor following Jimmy Lee's article.

As his remarks concluded, Collinsworth was to introduce the president, for a speech that his aides promised would be "short and to the point." Nobody had any confidence that the prediction would be true; the president had a habit of endlessly speaking off the cuff to friendly audiences.

Once dinner was finished, the president and his entourage would leave the room, no doubt to sustained applause, and they would clear the building before the other guests departed. The entire evening was scheduled to take three and a half hours, not a long time, unless you were in charge of security.

Carl White was not in charge of security, that was jointly in the hands of the U.S. Marshals and Secret Service, but he spent virtually all of his time on the scene. His investigation into Ricardo Vasquez had basically run cold, but his instincts told him that Wallace's connection to the case meant it was tied to the Federal Center.

White was rapidly becoming a pain in the ass to Secret Service Captain Steven Radford, the man in charge of security for the evening. Radford had twenty-eight years on the job, and was not about to take anything for granted, so he understood White's concern. But while he recognized the potential threat, he was confident that it had been dealt with effectively.

Nonetheless, he listened respectfully to White; Radford was not a man into the traditional rivalry between their respective agencies. He tolerated White's constant presence on the scene, though he didn't have to. It was just that the moment of truth was getting close, and Radford knew he had things under control.

Tim knew he could no longer go back to the house where he had been staying. He had told Eden that if she got into trouble she should give up his location, and he had to assume that she had done so. He could only hope it would save her, but he knew that if she had seen Patrick and could identify him, he would not have the compassion to let her live.

Tim tried reaching Nick, but was unable to. He didn't bother leaving a message, since there was no way for Nick to call him back.

His focus had shifted completely. Whereas he had spent weeks thinking only about how to extricate himself from his situation, now his main concern was Eden. It was a new kind of agony for him, as bad or worse than any that had come before it.

There was no escaping the plain truth that if not for him, this evil would not have entered her life. Tim could feel the cold fear that she was feeling, and it tortured him. He had to consciously and silently scream at himself to use it as a motivation to find a way out for both of them.

Among the many things he could not understand was why Patrick and the people he was working with were so desperate to get to Tim. They had gone to incredibly elaborate lengths to put him in this situation, so what more could they want? If they still wanted to kill him, as he believed they had tried to do on the boat that day, they could have done so easily at any time in the months since then.

They would only have gone after Eden to get to Tim; she had

nothing else to offer them. If he could figure out why, he believed it would be the key to everything.

Tim checked into a place called the Village Motel in downtown Hackensack. It was the kind of establishment that did most of their room renting by the hour, but it suited his needs quite well. It was surprisingly clean, and most importantly the desk clerk did not require ID or a credit card.

He called Nick again, and this time got through. Nick was distraught, blaming himself for not doing more to protect his sister. Unfortunately, he had little more to offer about Eden's situation than what Tim had learned through the media. She was gone, obviously not of her own free will, but no ransom or demands of any kind had been made.

After leaving Kiley and Travis with his assistant, a dog lover herself, Nick had been to see Novack, who was chafing to get out of the hospital. Novack was of the belief that things were coming to a head, and he wanted to be back in the action.

"For what it's worth, I think he's done a one-eighty on you," Nick said.

"What does that mean?" Tim asked.

"He wouldn't say so directly, but I've got a hunch he thinks you're innocent, that you've been set up for something all along. Too bad he can't convince his captain and the district attorney."

"Will he see me?"

"*Now* you're turning yourself in?" Nick asked.

"No, I mean will he talk to me . . . face-to-face . . . without arresting me? There are things he knows about that day, about Maggie, that I need to know. I think together we might have a chance to figure this out."

Nick thought about it, trying to test his original reaction that the request was ridiculous and impossible. "He might do it," Nick said. "I could talk to him."

"Can we trust him?" Tim asked.

"If he gives his word, we can take it to the bank."

"Then talk to him," Tim said. "And please hurry."

"You want me to meet with him?

Are you out of your fucking mind?" A nurse opened the door without knocking and walked into Novack's hospital room. She heard his last question and turned right around and walked out.

Novack clearly wasn't reacting too well to Nick's proposal. "There's a warrant out for his arrest. Your client is a fugitive, counselor."

"Who you know damn well is innocent."

Novack smiled. "If I confirmed that, any chance you'd mention this conversation to a jury when the time came?"

"That time is not coming, and you know it. Tim Wallace is never going before a jury."

Novack thought it over for a few moments, then, "What does he want?"

"I don't know; it's something about the day on the boat. He thinks together you can figure something out."

"Sounds like a waste of time."

"Time might be in short supply," Nick said. "Especially for my sister."

"If I met with him and didn't arrest him, you know how many laws I'd be breaking?"

"Nobody will know about it. You have my word. When are you getting out of here?"

Novack got out of bed and reached for his pants. "Right now. I got a meeting to go to."

———————

Patrick arrived at 7 A.M., though Eden had no way of knowing what time it was. He untied her, but kept her blindfold on. It wasn't that he was afraid she would see where she was, since he was going to kill her anyway. It was just that he knew she would feel more vulnerable not being able to see, and he wanted her to give him the information quickly, so he could move on.

He had other things to do.

He grabbed her by the arm and told her he was taking her to the bathroom. "If I find out you took the blindfold off, I will take a candle and burn out your eyes," he said, matter-of-factly.

She heard a door closing, and sensed that she was in the bathroom by herself. She felt for the toilet, and for the sink, and did what she had to do.

A few minutes later, the door opened and Patrick led her back out. He sat her in a chair and said, "Here," putting a box of what she discovered were crackers in her hand. She wasn't feeling hungry, but ate a few, and he gave her a glass of water to drink.

She sat there, waiting, not knowing if he had left, and she thought she heard the sound of someone typing on a keyboard. That lasted for about ten minutes, and then the room was silent.

Her fear and hatred were palpable. She had heard about the syndrome whereby kidnap victims identified and even sometimes sympathized with their captors, but at this moment it was beyond her comprehension. She knew that if she had the opportunity she could and would kill him without a moment's hesitation. Unfortunately, it seemed that there was no way such an opportunity would present itself.

"There's a table in front of you," he said. "Put your hands on it, palms down."

She did as she was told.

"I'm going to ask you a question. If you answer it correctly the first time, then we're fine. For every time I have to ask it again, I will cut off one of your fingers."

She started to sob and shake, momentarily gripped in a fear beyond anything she could ever have imagined.

"Ready?" he said. "Where is Tim Wallace hiding?"

Eden had known she was going to be asked that, and even felt some relief that it was the question she expected. Tim had told her that if she found herself in this kind of position, she should reveal what she knew. She would have done so anyway; this kind of fear, this kind of evil, was not something she was equipped to deal with.

She told him where the house was, and answered a few specific questions about how to get there, what else was on the street, et cetera. He could tell she was telling the truth; somehow he always had a built-in lie detector.

"Okay, you can take your hands off the table," he said, when they were finished. He debated whether to kill her then, but decided he didn't have the time. It wasn't the killing itself, that would take only a few seconds. But there would be some cleaning up involved if he did it then, so he decided to wait until afterward, when the cleanup would not be necessary.

The other reason he didn't kill Eden was because situations like this were always unpredictable, no matter how careful the preparation. If things went wrong there might be a need for bargaining chips, and Eden alive was therefore worth more than Eden dead.

He took her back down the stairs, tied and gagged her, and left her in the constant darkness.

Patrick drove immediately to the house in Lincoln Park that Eden had told him about. He no longer expected Tim to be there; once Eden's kidnapping was reported in the press, it would have been a clear signal for Tim to find another place to hide.

Eventually, though, Patrick knew that there would be no place for Tim to hide from him. The moment that he fired his handgun, grazing Patrick on the arm, was the moment that he guaranteed an agonizing death for himself. But there would be time for that later.

Patrick had known he'd waited too long to get this location

from Eden, but he had had other things to do, other plans to make. His employers would be unhappy about it, because having Tim in their custody was vital to their plan.

But Patrick had other plans. Not having Tim would soon be the least of his employers' problems. Things were going to go very wrong for them, were going to spiral out of their control, and for them it would be too late.

It would be much too late.

When Patrick arrived at the Lincoln Park house he was careful, acting as he would have if he believed Tim was inside. He approached cautiously in such a way as to be undetected, and he circled the house, inspecting the inside through the windows. Finally, he jimmied the door and went in, if only to confirm that Tim was gone.

Satisfied that he was, Patrick moved on to more important things.

Nick and Novack quickly negotiated the
terms and details of his meeting with Tim.

Present would be Tim, Novack, and Nick, and all promised in advance that they would not reveal that the meeting ever took place.

The place was to be Tim's motel room, chosen for its out-of-the-way location and the near certainty that Novack and Nick would not be recognized arriving or departing.

The motel was structured so that patrons could park in front of their own rooms, therefore there was no necessity to enter any kind of lobby. Nick and Novack pulled up in Nick's car, and after determining that there was no one around, they parked and quickly went into Tim's dingy room.

Tim was standing ten feet from the door when they walked in, which meant he was almost clear across the tiny room. Nick closed the door behind them, and Novack and Tim just stared at each other for almost fifteen seconds. Both were so used to hating the other that it seemed to take them time to digest that they were there for a common purpose.

"Nice place you've got here," said Novack.

Tim nodded. "Yeah. I appreciate your coming. I've had a lot of time to think about what's happened, and I don't think we have much time."

"Before what?" Novack asked.

"First of all, I'm innocent; I haven't done any of the things you thought I did."

Novack started to react, but Tim cut him off. "Just hear me out. You can believe me or not; I don't really care what you think any more. But I suspect you know that what I'm saying is true, or you wouldn't be here."

"Keep going . . ."

"Nobody would go to all this trouble just to hurt me, just to ruin my life. That doesn't make any sense. Plus I don't have those kinds of enemies. I didn't even know Richie Patrick until the day I shot him. I only wish I was a better shot."

"So why you?" Novack asked.

"Because it's about something much bigger; it has to be. Look, I was supposed to be the one killed on that boat that day. There was no way anyone could have known Maggie would be out there. I was supposed to be blown up, and they were out there on the Oceanfast watching, probably ready to finish the job if I somehow survived. The sun was behind us; they would have been looking into it, and it would have been hard to see. I doubt that they realized I was in the water, still alive."

Nick spoke for the first time. "So why haven't they killed you since?"

"Because they figured out another way, a better way for them. I was going to be killed to get me out of the way so they could do something criminal; I must have somehow been in their way without my knowing it."

Novack had already figured out where he was going. "So instead of getting rid of you so they could do it, they decided to do it and blame you for it."

Tim nodded. "Right. And in some way they dissected my life, manipulated me like I was a goddamn puppet, and set me up as public enemy number one."

"Who knows you that well?"

"That's why you're here," Tim said. "You're going to tell me that answer."

"Good luck," Novack said, obviously skeptical.

"You told me that it was Maggie's finger at the club that day."

Novack nodded. "Right."

"How did you know that?"

Novack looked at Nick as if he could not believe Nick hadn't told his client such a basic fact. Then he turned back to Tim. "We ran a DNA test. It came back conclusive."

"Matched against Maggie's DNA?"

Novack nodded. "Of course."

"Where did you get it?"

"Her DNA? We've had it since we opened the investigation into her death."

"But where did you get it? Maggie's body was lost at sea. And it's not like she was a convicted felon, somebody whose DNA would be on file. Where could you have gotten it?"

Novack slowly nodded his head; the significance of what Tim was asking was clear. "Shit. I don't know."

He took out his cell phone and dialed a number, and when it was answered, he spoke. "Sam, I've got to ask you about the Wallace case. Right . . . I need you to get the file out now. I want to know who collected the DNA, and how we got it. I'll wait."

Novack put his hand over the mouth and said to Tim and Nick, "Sam's our forensics guy. He probably handled it himself; if not, he can tell me who did."

Novack held the phone to his ear for almost ten minutes. Everyone in the room was silent, waiting for the answer that they hoped could be the key to everything.

"I'm here," Novack said, as Sam came back on the line. "What did you come up with?" Another pause, and then he said, "You're sure? Okay, thanks."

Novack hung up the phone. "Sam collected the DNA himself. He checked the file to make sure, but he remembered it anyway. He said it was because she was hot."

"Who?"

"Your assistant, Meredith Tunney. You were in the hospital,

and she took Sam to your house. He got the DNA off your wife's toothbrush. She gave it to him."

"Of course; God, why haven't I seen it? She ran my life. She scheduled our racquetball games, she knew when I'd be on the boat . . . she knew absolutely everything there was to know."

"How long has she worked for you?" Nick asked.

"Since a few months before Maggie died." He sat down, trying to digest it all. His dominant feeling at the moment was incredible relief that Maggie had in fact not suffered or been tortured; she really had died instantly and painlessly on the boat.

"I just realized something," Tim said. "I'm not sure, but I think Meredith may have been the one who told me about the stone quarry near Carson. That's what brought me there in the first place."

"Where they were waiting for you."

"Right. Once Maggie died, and you told the world how guilty I was, they probably figured I'd have more value to them as someone to set up for what they were going to do in the future."

"They were right."

"Yes. But if it wasn't Maggie's DNA, and Maggie's finger, whose was it?"

Novack shook his head. "We'll probably never know. They could have killed a woman just for that purpose. Maybe someone who lived on the street and wouldn't be missed. Killing doesn't seem to be something they're particularly hesitant to do." He was immediately sorry he said that, since Eden was still missing. So he added, "Now that we know how they got to you, we need to figure out why."

Tim nodded. "It has to be about the business, and about Collinsworth."

Novack shook his head. "This is not some white-collar crime we're talking about. We're looking at a bunch of murders, an exploding car on the turnpike, a kidnapping . . . whoever has employed Richie Patrick is not manipulating stock prices. And that would be pretty dirty, even for a U.S. senator."

"It's the Federal Center," Tim said. "Something must be planned for that, and I'd bet it's tomorrow night."

"But everything that's happened has called attention to it. Security will be maxed out."

"Meredith was in a position to give out our passes to get on the site during the construction. She could have gotten her people in there."

"But even so, why plan something and do all this to alert their opposition?"

"Because they're not worried about their opposition. They don't think they can be stopped."

"It's Meredith. I need to talk to you about Tim."

"Have you spoken to him?" Will asked. "Do you know where he is?"

"I don't want to talk about it on the phone, but it's very, very important. I couldn't reach Danny, and I need to talk about it with someone right away."

"Okay . . . sure," he said. "Should I come to the office?"

"No . . . I'll come to you."

Will was in Ridgewood, so they made arrangements to meet in front of a small park on Ridgewood Avenue. "I'll be in my car; it's a red Toyota. Just get in the car and we can talk while I drive. That way no one can listen in."

Will was waiting for ten minutes when he saw her pull up. She reached across and pulled on the door handle, opening it for him. As soon as he got in, she pulled off.

"What's going on with Tim?" Will asked.

She smiled. "Not much. What's going on with you?"

Her answer confused him. "You said you had to talk to me about Tim."

"If I were you, I'd be more worried about yourself."

"What? Why?"

"Well, for one thing, at least Tim doesn't have a gun pointed at the back of his head."

Will turned and saw Richie Patrick pointing a gun at him from about six inches away. "Hey! What the hell is going on here?"

Patrick smiled. "Well, I would say you've got a bit of a problem."

It didn't take more than a few moments for Will to realize where he had seen Patrick before. "You're the guy from Homeland Security, the guy I took through the computer system in the building." As he was saying it, he realized why he was subsequently asked to do so a second time, with a different person. It was because Patrick had been there under a false identity, with a pass provided by Meredith.

Patrick smiled again. "And you have no idea how much I appreciated it."

Novack left Tim in the hotel room with instructions to stay put. He was still a fugitive, officially considered armed and dangerous, and Novack didn't want him getting shot by some cop looking to make a name for himself.

Novack did make the concession that he would attempt to keep Nick informed of developments, and Tim would then be able to be brought up to date by Nick.

He called Anders and Donovan and downloaded them on what he had learned, leaving out the fact that he had actually met Tim in person. Novack then picked up Anders and they went to the offices of Wallace Industries, backed up by four other officers.

Meredith was not there, but Danny was in his office. He told them that Meredith had not been in at all that day, and had not called to explain why. He said it was very out of character for her to do that.

"Where does she live?" Novack asked.

"I don't know. But I can get it for you." He got up to look in the file cabinet. "Any chance you'll tell me what's going on?"

"Zero," said Novack.

"Is Tim okay?"

"The address . . ."

Danny located the file and gave Novack the address, which was in Leonia.

"If she calls in, do not tell her that we were here," Novack said, knowing all the while that she wouldn't be calling.

The subsequent raid on her house also failed to apprehend her, mainly because she didn't have a house. The address she had on file was a vacant lot.

Meredith was long gone.

Donovan took on the job of communicating the recent events to Carl White. Danny provided Novack with a picture of Meredith, taken at a company outing a few months prior, and they supplied that photograph to White, who turned it over to the Secret Service.

Facial-recognition monitors were posted at twenty-one locations surrounding the Federal Center, and the pictures of Patrick, Meredith, and Tim were added to the existing terrorist data bank. If any of them came within five blocks of the location, the authorities would know about it in a split second.

Steven Radford, the Secret Service agent in charge, was not unduly worried by the account that he heard from White. The fact that there were dangerous people who might be intent on killing the president and other high-level people was no surprise; such people are out there in droves. What was important to Radford was that the location was secure no matter what might be attempted, and he felt confident that it was.

Eden heard them upstairs. It sounded like two men and a woman, and she could tell that one of the men was Patrick. She couldn't make out what they were saying, and didn't dare call out.

Their arrival came at a particularly inopportune time. She was making ever so slight progress on loosening the rope that was tying her hands to the metal bar. It was tedious work, made much more so by the fact that she had the blindfold on.

The difficult decision she faced was whether to keep working on it, even though Patrick was upstairs. If he came downstairs quietly and caught her, he would do something horrible.

But Eden was by nature a realist, and she had to force herself to be one now. When this was all over, when Patrick had accomplished whatever he was planning, he was going to do something horrible anyway.

So she continued working on the ropes. She was going to go down fighting.

It would not have been a surprise to anyone to know that Keith Rivers was giving the senator crucial advice. What would have rocked Washington was the fact that the advice he was giving was not to Senator Collinsworth, but to Senator Evans.

The conversation was over the phone; the men could not have taken a chance being seen together. Rivers was making sure that Evans knew every detail of what was to take place, and understood exactly what he was supposed to do. Evans was not as bright as Collinsworth, and Rivers's confidence level in him was low.

"Are you sure you have it committed to memory?" Rivers asked. "The timing is crucial."

"I've got it. Just make sure our friends know what they're doing."

"They're professionals," Rivers said, the clear implication being that Evans was not, at least in matters of this type.

"I hope so," Evans said. "You know what this means for all of us."

"Yes, I do."

"When was the last time you spoke to your boss?"

Rivers knew who he was talking about, and it certainly wasn't Collinsworth. "Last night."

"Is he in Washington?"

"No," Rivers said. "He's out of the country."

"Maybe I should speak with him," Evans said.

"He's not reachable until well after this is over."

"Fine," said Evans, but what he was thinking was that when this was over, he would talk to whomever he wanted, whenever he wanted.

Then even Rivers's boss could kiss his ass.

"The frustrating thing about money is
that it's impossible to own all of it,"

Byron Carthon said, and then waited for the uproarious laughter to
subside. He enjoyed the sound of it, even though he knew that the
reaction was not merited by the joke itself, but rather by the fact
that he owned his audience, lock, stock, and barrel.

There were seventy people in the audience as Byron spoke,
representing the top thirty-five employees of the Franklin Group,
and their spouses. They had come from Franklin subsidiaries all
over the world to this outing, on the Crystal Line cruise ship *Serenity*, as it sailed the South Pacific.

The purpose of the gathering, according to Byron, was to relax,
talk, and strategize about the company's future growth. Byron's
goal was to grow his company over the next ten years at a greater
rate than the previous ten. That would be a tall order, as Franklin's
growth had been meteoric. It had no peer as the leading construction, mining, and oil and gas company in the world.

And the world was Franklin's home base. Originally based primarily in America, Franklin's tentacles had spread around the
globe, and ironically the only blemish on the business at that moment was its American operations.

Franklin had come out on the short end of what Byron Carthon
considered petty American politics. Certain politicians had used
the company as a convenient whipping boy, and government

contracts had become less frequent and lucrative than in the past. Franklin had more than made up for it through its international operations, but that was not good enough for Byron. The U.S. market was still the most important, and Franklin would once again reign supreme.

What Byron did not tell his guests, what he would not tell anyone, was that the real reason for being on the ship was simply to be on the ship. It was the perfect place for him to be when his plan was finally executed.

And it was totally his plan, although history would never record it as such. It would leave Byron Carthon wealthy beyond even his imagination, and in control over everything, including the next president of the United States.

"You all have the agenda," Byron said near the end of his remarks, "and you see that there are no meetings scheduled until Monday. So take the weekend to relax and rejuvenate. For the next two days the world will go on without us."

He neglected to mention that after tonight, the world would never be quite the same. And the transforming event would take place while he and his team were completely carefree, sailing on a ship aptly named the *Serenity*.

It was a source of some annoyance to Richie Patrick that Will was still alive. The plan had called for Will to be captured and brought to the operation's center. That way, if he were needed for some last-minute help with the computer, he could be forcibly coerced into providing that help.

So Richie had done it, since the need to have Will out of commission during the event was obvious. But having to keep him alive was rather insulting. Richie had intensively trained for over a year on this computer, and there was no way he needed help from this geek. He should just kill him now, and if the geek caused any trouble, that's exactly what he would do.

Of course, bound as Will was, there was a limited amount of trouble that he could cause. So Patrick decided to play a little game with himself. He would stare at Will for sixty seconds, and if Will blinked more than twenty-one times, he would break his neck. Twenty-one or less, and he could live to watch everything play out, which would give him another four hours.

So he stared, and Will stared back. And staring back probably cut his blinking rate, Patrick figured. He was upset with himself for setting it up this way. He shouldn't have alerted Will in any way, but it was too late to change the rules now.

In the first thirty seconds, Will blinked eleven times. He was on pace to die.

After forty-five seconds, the total was sixteen. It was going to be close.

Fifty seconds, eighteen.

Fifty-five seconds, twenty.

Sixty seconds, twenty-one.

Patrick shook his head and chuckled to himself at the guy's luck. "You just earned yourself four hours, asshole," he said, and then laughed again.

Tim had the awful sensation that he was being dragged toward the edge of a cliff, a long, slow process that would result in his plunging off the mountain in about two hours. That was when the gala event was to start at the Federal Center building, and Tim instinctively felt that if something weren't done before then, all hell was going to break loose.

If Eden were still alive, Patrick would surely kill her once he got what he wanted. And whatever he wanted was going to be clear that night.

Tim was going insane cooped up in that motel room, but he was not there out of fear of being captured. He was well beyond that now. He just couldn't figure out where to go. The Federal Center would be the most heavily guarded place in the country; there was nothing for him to accomplish there. Yet how could it be so secure, and yet so vulnerable?

Tim came to the conclusion that it had to be something that

was to be accomplished from the inside. Yet everyone, from the highest dignitary on down, would have to go through security screeners to get in.

Unless . . . unless it was an inside job controlled from the outside.

Tim grabbed the phone and called Danny. He didn't answer at home, so Tim tried him on his cell and was relieved when his friend picked up. "Danny, it's me."

"Tim, are you okay?"

"Where is Will? I've got to talk to him."

"I wish I knew. I've been trying to reach him since yesterday."

"Where did you try?"

"Everywhere. Home, cell, even his new girlfriend. I don't understand it."

Tim understood it very well, and in that instant his fears were confirmed. Will would never leave without letting Danny know where he could be reached in case of a business emergency. To do so the day of the big opening was completely inconceivable.

"Danny, keep trying to find him. If you reach him, call me immediately." He gave Danny the number of his cell phone; there was no hiding any more.

Tim hung up and called Nick. "Nick, it's the computer."

"What are you talking about?"

"Will Clampett did the computer security work at the Federal Center. He's been missing now for twenty-four hours and can't be reached."

"Couldn't he be away for the weekend?"

"No, in his position he would always leave an emergency number. One hundred percent of the time."

"So you think he's on the other side?"

Tim had already considered that possibility. "It's possible, but I doubt it. But whoever might want to control the computers could do so through him. And Meredith would know that."

"What is it you're worried about? What might the computer do?"

"Whatever it's told. And it can be operated from a remote location. Nick, I don't know what they're doing, but I know how they're doing it. That building has got to be shut down now."

As soon as Nick got off the phone, he called Novack and told him what Tim had said. Novack had interviewed Will a couple of times during the investigation, and did not see him as the type to just take off without regard to his job.

But where Tim did not believe that Will himself would be involved in anything criminal, Novack was not so sure. He called Danny and asked him to locate a picture of Will as soon as possible, an easy request to handle because the friends had taken many pictures together.

Next Novack called Carl White, who at that moment was in the Federal Center itself. The guests had not yet started to arrive, but they would be soon. Novack quickly filled him in on what he knew.

"They could be making their move through the building computer somehow," Novack said when he was finished.

"I don't see how," White said. "Secret Service techs are running the thing. I was in the room with them a little while ago. Everything seemed fine."

"At least alert them to the possibility that something might happen. And make sure that room is secure."

White was not used to taking orders from local detectives, but this was not the time to stand on ceremony, since Novack was right. "Will do," he said. "And call me if you learn anything else."

"If something happens," Novack said, "I'm afraid you're going to know about it before me."

The president of the United States is the elephant in every room he is ever in.

That's a given. But equally true is the fact that he is also the elephant in every room he is planning to enter.

This was obvious to everyone in attendance at the cocktail party at the Federal Center. The president was not due to arrive until fifteen minutes before the dinner would begin, but everyone in the room was already jockeying for position, so as to have access to him when he did show up.

This little dance was made slightly more complicated by the rivalries in the room, most notably the one between Senators Collinsworth and Evans. They and their chief staffers were determined to stay apart from each other, yet equally determined to be near the arriving president. It made for interesting theater, sort of a senatorial Kabuki dance.

If Evans had ever been more nervous in his life, he certainly couldn't remember when. As great as the rewards would be for his actions in the next two hours, such was his anxiety that he still would have considered backing out, if such an option were available to him.

It wasn't.

So Evans made small talk with people of lesser political stature than him, a category which included pretty much everyone in the room, except for Collinsworth.

He tried to ease his tension and relax by imagining how each of the people at the party were going to react when faced with tonight's crisis. It was not going to be a pretty picture.

Evans pointedly avoided eye contact with Keith Rivers, the only other person in the room who knew what he knew. Rivers was fawning over Collinsworth, pretending to take care of his boss while actually in the process of destroying his career.

Yes, thought Evans, this would be quite a night.

Carl White was getting nowhere with Radford. The Secret Service captain had listened patiently to White for two weeks, but this was showtime, and he had no time for wild theories. The computers were firmly in the hands of men with top security clearances, men whom Radford had long worked with and trusted completely. Besides, what real damage could the computers cause? The building was secure; Radford saw no way that hackers, even in the wildly unlikely event that they were successful, could be any more than an annoyance. Surely there was no way they could pose a physical danger to the guests.

So Radford was too circumspect to say it straight-out, but he basically implied that Carl should have an hors d'oeuvre and leave the Secret Service alone to do their job.

Jimmy Lee Curry estimated that it had been at least two months since he had not gone out for dinner. It was part of his job, as important as the writing itself. Social contact was how he kept the information flowing, and information in Washington was the currency that ran that city's economy.

But tonight was different; tonight he would watch the coverage of the Federal Center opening from the comfort of his own couch. The opening itself was not huge news, but the presence of the president would make it a focal point for the media.

Jimmy Lee was not watching to learn anything; nothing eventful was going to happen. There would be boring speeches, as the politicians rushed to pat each other on the back for bringing the

project to fruition. Rather, he was watching to see how much coverage there was and to revel in it, because the more the public knew
about the event, the more impact his story tomorrow would have.

It was already filed for the morning and online editions, and
would reveal that Senator Collinsworth not only had gotten work
for a company whose co-owner was a wanted murderer, but more
significantly, that the same man had terrorist connections.
Collinsworth in effect had brought the president of the United
States into a building literally built by a terrorist.

So this night might be a little boring, but tomorrow would certainly be a hell of a lot of fun.

For Senator Collinsworth, the evening represented a personal tri-
umph. He as much as anyone was responsible for the Federal Center concept, and he would make that known in his remarks prior to
introducing President Markham. With the significant coverage
that the event would get, this would in effect be the unspoken start
of a two-year campaign to become Markham's successor.

Soon additional Federal Centers would be authorized all over
the country, and Collinsworth would steer the construction money
to hundreds of medium- and small-sized contractors, all of whom
would become beholden to him.

He would have the public image and the war chest that would
make him difficult, if not impossible, to beat.

And it all would start tonight.

Richie Patrick thought it was damn nice of CNN to act as his ac-
complice. There was one pool camera that would cover the
speeches at the dinner, and CNN would be among those to show it
on the air.

The timing had to be just right to provide maximum effect, and
Richie, who would otherwise have no idea what was going on in
that building, could just turn on the television and be perfectly well
informed.

Once he triggered the event, then his computer monitors

would tell him all he needed to know. But for now, CNN would do just fine.

Tim would be watching television as well, but he was watching with a feeling of helplessness and foreboding. He knew in his gut that something was going to happen, something awful, and it would involve the computers.

At that point he would understand what he had been trying to understand for all these months. He would know what they were doing, and how they were blaming him for it.

Of course, by then it would be too late.

President Markham arrived promptly fifteen
minutes before the end of the cocktail party.

Like everything else involving the president, every movement was
perfectly coordinated by his staff. He managed to talk to and take
pictures with everyone he was supposed to during that time.
Markham was a master at this, and made personal comments to
each person, perhaps asking about their family, perhaps reminding
them of something that occurred the last time they met, that made
each person feel good.

The president separately spent a little extra time with Senators
Collinsworth and Evans. They were important to his ability to get
his legislative agenda through Congress, and Markham wanted to
get across the fact that he valued them.

He knew both senators had ambitions to succeed him, and he
had been holding out the carrot of his future support to each of
them. The truth was he considered Collinsworth a pompous ass,
and thought Evans overly aggressive, arrogant, and not very bright.
He had told his wife the night before that if he thought one of
them might someday be moving into the White House, he'd burn
it down first.

The assembled guests moved into the main hall for the dinner.
The room was not designed for this, and it lacked the elegance that
the evening called for, but great strides had been made and no

expense spared. The tables were set ornately, and the flowers alone cost more than any five of the waiters earned in a year.

After all, the nation was watching.

One of the few people not watching was Eden Alexander. She could still hear Patrick and other people upstairs, but it had been so long since he had come down that she felt confident he was not going to.

She was almost out of her bonds; there was only a little more to be done and then she would be free. She hadn't yet figured out what she would do with that freedom, but at least she would be giving herself a chance to survive, where previously she had had none.

It wouldn't be long now.

"I've been in this business a long time," Senator Collinsworth began. "And I've learned time and time again that you have to dream big and then compromise. Nothing happens exactly as you hope; everyone has their own interests and agendas that have to be taken into consideration. All you can do is your best, and hope that the end result includes as much of your original vision as possible.

"But tonight, at this glorious Federal Center, is very, very different. This is exactly how I and others envisioned it just two short years ago. It is the perfect model for other Federal Centers that will rise all over this great country of ours, and will come to symbolize the strength and ingenuity that we are, and the security that we are entitled to.

"In short, this Federal Center is not a compromise, and it is not any less than we imagined. If anything, it is more, and it is truly a dream that has come true."

Collinsworth went on for another seven minutes, claiming full credit for the center while trying to appear gracious and modest. He was a fine speaker, and he managed to pull it off to all those who did not know that he didn't have a gracious or modest bone in his body. There were very few people in the room who fell into that category, but likely the viewing audience at home did. And those were the people to whom Collinsworth was playing.

"And now it is my pleasure to introduce to you the man who ultimately made this all possible. He is a leader in every sense, and without his leadership all the dreams in the world wouldn't have been enough.

"Ladies and gentlemen, please welcome the president of the United States, Christopher Markham."

The crowd rose to its feet in a standing ovation. They had no idea that Richie Patrick had just typed in a code and pressed a button on his computer that effectively gave him control over their lives.

Tim Wallace was not watching television. He had left his motel room long before. He still did not know what was going to take place, but he thought he had finally figured out where it was going to happen.

And that's where he was going.

At first, almost nobody in the hall
realized what was happening.

The noise from the standing ovation, plus the fact that everyone
was facing toward the dais, watching the president make his way to
the podium, prevented people from noticing what was going on behind them.

Large reinforced steel doors were closing in from both sides,
and similarly reinforced steel panels were moving into place and
covering the windows. The first sound that the people in the room
really noticed was the loud locking into place as the steel doors met.

Since it was nighttime, the lighting in the room did not change,
and few of the guests realized that what had happened was out of
the ordinary. Carl White was one of those who did, and he immediately started looking for Captain Radford. He was not about to
find him, because Radford was in an outer hallway, checking
perimeter security. The closing doors locked him out, with no way
back in.

White ran to the computer room, where there was no uncertainty about whether something was wrong. The room was in chaos,
as the computer operators realized they no longer had any control
over the systems.

Their monitors had gone dark for about two minutes, after
which a typed message appeared. White arrived in the room just in
time to read it.

```
This building is now under my control. No one
can get in or out, and those inside will live or
die depending on their actions and the actions
of those that speak for them.
     Specifically, oxygen tank number three con-
tains one fiftieth of one ounce of thallium. It
is enough to kill every single person in the
building a hundred times over. By simply press-
ing a button, I can instantly release it into
the air supply.
     This computer has been programmed to treat
any interruption of power, from any source, as
an enemy attack. It will similarly regard any
attempt to enter the room or·breach the barri-
cades. The response will be immediate and
deadly; in a matter of seconds all present will
be inhaling thallium.
     There is to be no contact between those in-
side and outside my building.
     You will have my nonnegotiable demand in five
minutes.
     I can see through every camera in the room,
so be assured that I am watching.
     Timothy Wallace
```

The message was simultaneously sent to every mainstream media outlet in the country, and Captain Radford himself read it on
one of the media monitors outside the building. He knew all too
well that it would most likely be impossible to violently enter the
building. The entire motive behind creating these enormous steel
barriers was to render it virtually impregnable to outside attack,
creating a safe haven within.

A safe haven that had become a prison, and possibly a tomb.

———

"How am I doing?" Patrick asked Will, who had watched in horror as events unfolded.

"How did you get thallium into that tank?" he asked. Will knew thallium to be a radium poison, deadly in minute quantities. It was said to be the poison of choice when Russian undercover operatives wanted to dispatch someone with certainty. The poison, once ingested, caused a death that was slow and very, very unpleasant.

Patrick smiled. "Same way I got you to show me the computer system. When you have a pass to get in, you can do anything."

Will looked over at Meredith, who had provided the construction passes in her position as office manager. She smiled, obviously not having any second thoughts about her crucial role in this operation. "So how's he doing?" she asked.

Will turned his attention back to Patrick. "They'll figure out a way to take back control."

"You know something?" Patrick said. "They just might. But not in twenty minutes, and that's all they have."

There was obviously no way for Tim to be sure he was right. He knew enough about computers to realize that the people controlling the building could be anywhere.

But when they accomplished whatever they were setting out to do, they would want to disappear, without leaving a paper or electronic trail. And the woman at the Southold marina had said that people had been on the Oceanfast 360 doing work, and that they had blown her off when she tried to be friendly.

The boat was in the water, and there would be nothing to stop it from sailing away, silently and anonymously.

Tim tried to reach Nick, but had to leave a message telling him where he was going and why. He himself had no idea what he would do when he got there, especially when he realized with horror that in his haste he'd forgotten to bring his handgun.

He was still at least twenty minutes away from the pier, and would spend that time listening to hyperventilating radio newscasters tell the world that he, Tim Wallace, was holding the president of the United States hostage.

Inside the building, the guests were only slowly learning what was going on. The Secret Service agents in the room were at an uncharacteristic loss how to proceed. Generally the protocol was to take the president to a safe haven, where they would wait out whatever threat was out there. In this situation they had nowhere to take him; he was a prisoner like all the others. So instead they shepherded him to a corner of the room and hovered around him like human shields, though their bodies would obviously be of no benefit against an airborne poison.

When Senator Collinsworth was informed what was happening, he saw his political life flash before his eyes. He was smart enough to know that even if this turned out well, meaning no injuries and Wallace's capture, it would be the biggest story since 9/11. And the main focus would be on Collinsworth, for providing a terrorist-murderer with the opportunity of a lifetime.

Meanwhile, Senator Evans kept taking deep breaths and telling himself to remain calm. He didn't need any updates; he knew exactly what was going on, and therefore was not worried about any terrorist threats. Instead he stared at a window, fifteen feet up at the east side of the room. He could not see the place where the steel covering was not fully closed, but he knew it was there.

In eleven minutes he would pretend to see it, and climb up to it, in apparent disregard of his own personal well-being. Then he would pry it open and heroically lead the people in the room to safety.

He would be hailed as an American hero, and would be the most popular and admired person in America.

And then there would be no stopping him.

The next set of instructions came exactly on time, as promised:

You will immediately wire five billion dollars
to the Bank of Zurich, account number 327-548-

6999873-24. You will also inform the bank that
the United States Government insists that they
follow the separate instructions I have already
sent them.

All of the transactions must be accomplished
within the next fifteen minutes, or I will release the thallium into the building.

No excuses will be tolerated.

The late-night piano player in the ship's main
bar was better than Byron Carthon expected.

He was doing a long medley of Broadway songs, and Byron had always been a sucker for show music. The man was moderately talented, but not quite deserving of the hundred-dollar bill that
Byron placed in his tip jar.

Byron wanted to be noticed, which was why he had brought a
bunch of his executives to the bar with him. Usually early to bed,
Byron chose to stay up late, so he could be seen having absolutely
nothing to do with the chaos that he knew was going on at that moment, thousands of miles away, at the Federal Center.

His work was finished long ago. He had used his contacts, separated by many layers, to procure the thallium and secure the route
that the money would take. He had placed the best people available
in place, paying exorbitant money to do so. Of course, it wasn't exorbitant when compared to the ultimate payoff, and this was an operation that would never stop paying off.

So Byron ordered another round of drinks and requested a ren-
dition of "If I Were a Rich Man," from *Fiddler on the Roof*. The
idea of Byron Carthon yearning to be a rich man drew a laugh
from the others in his party, and Byron laughed along with them.

It was obvious he didn't have a care in the world, and there was
an entire bar full of witnesses to swear to it, if it somehow ever
came to that.

———

Frantic conference calls were conducted among the vice president, the attorney general, the director of Homeland Security, the chairman of the Joint Chiefs of Staff, and the directors of the Secret Service, FBI, and CIA.

The first thing to be determined was whether the threat was credible. The chairman of the Joint Chiefs and the CIA director both reported that their respective biological warfare experts were confirming that the thallium could easily have gone undetected in the tanks. The quantity necessary to be deadly, encased in those heavy tanks, would have made detection almost impossible, especially since no one would have been specifically looking for thallium.

No one could say for sure that the thallium was there, but more importantly, no one could say it wasn't. And the people that they were dealing with, whether it was Wallace acting alone or with accomplices, seemed capable of anything.

Next to be examined was the likelihood of entering the building by force. This was quickly rejected as impractical. The building was incredibly well fortified, and explosives powerful enough to penetrate it might well kill or injure the hostages. Less than overwhelming force would give Wallace the time to release the thallium into the air supply.

The question of the money was the easiest. Despite President Markham's many pronouncements over the years that the United States would never negotiate with terrorists, since to do so would only encourage them to commit future acts, the decision was made to pay the money. If they could get out of this for five billion dollars, they would feel they got off cheap.

The approval was given and the money was sent.

When Novack got the call from Nick he didn't hesitate. Tim had expressed his fear that something terrible was going to happen at the Federal Center, and this was even worse than they had imagined.

Novack had no role to play there, the federal government was in charge, for better or for worse. If Tim was directing him to this marina, he would go there immediately.

He sure as hell had nothing better to do.

Jimmy Lee Curry stared at the television with equal measures of horror and disbelief. Like the rest of the mesmerized viewing public, he couldn't be quite sure what was going on. But there was one thing he did know.

Life as he knew it was over.

Jimmy Lee had filed the story about Tim Wallace's terrorist connections, and it was slated to run in the online edition of his newspaper within the hour. The story might or not be pulled, since events had now overtaken it. But even if it never ran, it would be a focal point of the investigations that would dominate the country in the coming weeks.

Law enforcement, elected officials, people on the street . . . everyone would point at Jimmy Lee and say, "You knew. You knew and you let this happen, just for the sake of a story." He knew that he would go down in history as the man who could have stopped all of this from happening, but chose not to.

If people died on this night, if the president of the United States died on this night, Jimmy Lee would go down in history as an unwitting executioner.

So as Jimmy Lee sat at home watching, he did not feel sorry for the people in that building facing death.

He envied them.

Senator Evans knew that his moment had come. This was an operation entirely based on precision timing, and he couldn't risk deviating from it in any way. The money had surely been sent and then rerouted by now; he was about to assume the spotlight.

He glanced over and made eye contact with Keith Rivers. He thought that Rivers nodded ever so slightly, but it didn't matter either way. It was time to act.

History was waiting.

Evans looked up toward the window at the side of the room, and pretended to see something. "Look at that," he said to no one in particular, but loudly enough that at least half a dozen people near him could hear.

"What?" someone asked, but Evans did not respond. He was already up and walking toward the window, as if intent on whatever he had seen.

Evans stood under the window, which was about fifteen feet above the floor. "Give me a hand with that table," he said to those nearby, and they helped him drag it over to a position under the window. Evans then pulled over a chair, which he put up on the table.

Richie Patrick laughed in gleeful anticipation of what was about to happen. He was watching Evans's every move on the security cameras which fed into his computer monitors. "Watch this," he said to Meredith and Will. "This is going to be great."

The only regret Patrick had was that he wouldn't be able to see Carthon's reaction when the big man learned that the president he was going to control was dead.

Evans got up on the chair, from where he could barely reach the ledge under the large window with his arms outstretched. He would pull himself up, demonstrating the heroism and athleticism that people would admire in their next president.

Evans thought of it as JFK without the bad back, and he was about to show them a profile in courage.

It was a bit of a strain, probably because of his nervousness, but he had practiced this many times. He would reach the window, then drop back down and secure a piece of metal or tool, which he would take back up. Then he would insert it into the opening he found, pry the panels open, and with the help of rescuers outside, bring everybody to safety.

He made it up there, but then experienced the most crushing moment in his life. All he saw was steel. No opening. No light. No way out. No chance.

He understood instantly that he had been betrayed, stabbed in the back, and he had no way to salvage the situation.

He also understood that he and everyone else in that room were going to die.

Richie Patrick knew exactly what was going through Evans's mind. He had no sympathy for him, because Evans was stupid. He should have realized that in an operation of this magnitude, with the largest law-enforcement effort in history certain to follow, Patrick could not afford to leave anyone alive.

They were all going to die . . . Evans, Rivers, Eden, Will, Tim, and even Meredith, though she didn't yet realize it. She thought they would marry and sail off into the sunset, but she was in for a rather rude, and deadly, awakening.

He would even kill Carthon, though that would be a little more difficult, and much more dangerous.

But he would do it, no matter what. Because the truth, as Patrick knew it, was that you have to kill to stay alive.

It was the cost of doing business.

Tim arrived at the pier and parked on the opposite end, where he could not be seen from the Oceanfast yacht. He realized as he got out of the car that it might well not even be there any more, and may have already gone out to sea. If it had, that would be game, set, and match, and there would be nothing for Tim to do.

He ran toward where the yacht had been and was relieved to find it still docked there. He then cautiously made his way to it, trying to avoid being seen by anyone on the boat who might be watching. It was likely that if Patrick was there he would be too busy to be watching for anybody showing up, but he might have accomplices who could be doing so.

Tim approached the yacht cautiously, but did not detect any movement or activity inside. He recognized the distinct possibility that he was wrong about all of this, but he had to act as if he were one hundred percent right.

Tim quietly walked onto the boat, and for the first time he could hear someone talking. It told him which direction to go in, and he edged across the boat, past a kitchen and two bedrooms, toward the other side, which was where the sounds were coming from.

He reached a room which seemed to be some kind of a den, and he could peer in through the partially open door. Inside he could see Patrick sitting in front of an elaborate computer setup, and Will and Meredith across the room on a couch. Will seemed to have his arms bound behind him.

Tim backed away, trying to figure out how to get Patrick away from the computer and out of the room. He went into the kitchen, where he picked up a knife and a large coffee mug. He then went out into the hall and positioned himself along the corridor in an adjacent bedroom.

Then he held out the coffee mug and dropped it on the floor.

There was no point in waiting any longer.

Patrick knew that the time had come to end this; he had actually delayed it too long. He hadn't held off because he was awed by the historic nature of the moment, it was rather that he was enjoying himself so much he didn't want it to end.

But he had to get moving. At some point they would come after him, and he intended to be long gone. He also had all these bodies to dispose of at sea . . .

Patrick heard a noise that seemed to be coming from near the kitchen; it sounded like something fell to the floor. Since the boat was rocking silently in the water, it was certainly likely that this meant little. Still, he wasn't about to take any chances.

"Go check that out," he said to Meredith.

"Why me?" she asked, obviously worried about the danger.

"Because I fucking said so," he said. Killing her would be the most enjoyable of all.

She didn't argue any more, just left the room and walked down the hall. Tim let her walk by, trying to figure out what to do.

He made his decision while she was on the way back. If he let her return to the room, he would have accomplished nothing. He had to draw Patrick out.

As she walked back down the corridor, he waited until she was at the doorway before coming out just behind her. He didn't use the knife, just punched her as hard as he could in the right temple. The idea of hitting a woman, something that would have previously seemed inconceivable to him, didn't bother him at all. This was a person who had helped to kill Maggie.

Tim caught the unconscious Meredith before she reached the floor.

Patrick didn't need to wait for her return. As Will watched in horror, he pressed the code numbers that would release the thallium-tainted oxygen into the room at the Federal Center.

Only then did he go to find out what the hell was keeping Meredith.

In the Federal Center, the guests had no idea that the poisonous air was slowly making its way into the room. It was as colorless and odorless as it was deadly.

By the time Patrick came down the hall, Tim had pulled Meredith's unconscious body into the bedroom. He heard Patrick coming, and as he walked by, jumped out at him and swung the kitchen knife.

He slashed Patrick in the area between the shoulder and the neck. Blood started gushing, and Patrick staggered a few feet and fell. Tim saw him go down, and started to move quickly toward the computer room.

The bullet hit him in the upper back and sent him sprawling. He fell to the ground and rolled over, an agonizing pain shooting through him. He looked back and saw Patrick raising his gun from his prone position, preparing to fire again.

He also saw Eden come up behind Patrick and smash him over the head with a heavy wooden lamp. It crushed his skull, killing him instantly.

Eden rushed to Tim, who was conscious and alert, but covered in blood. "Untie Will," Tim said, and she hesitated a moment before rushing off to do so.

Once untied, Will went straight to the computer and shut off oxygen tank three, at the same time opening the doors and windows of the building. The guests, not even aware that they had been exposed to the thallium in varying degrees, rushed out of the room and fled the building.

Eden went back to where Tim was lying. He was unmoving, apparently unconscious. She heard a noise and looked up to see Novack, running toward them, handgun drawn.

"It's over," she said. "But Tim . . ."

Novack went to Tim's side and saw that his eyes were closed. He felt for a pulse, as Tim opened his eyes and looked up at him.

"I'm gonna live," Tim said.

"Damn . . . I can't catch a break," Novack said, and then smiled.

He took off his jacket and wrapped it around Tim's back and shoulder to stem the flow of blood. "You owe me for this jacket."

Epilogue

If there's one thing I do not have to educate the public about, it is the devastating effect of thallium. Thirty-one people in that room that night have since died, cruelly chosen by fate according to their unwitting proximity to air vents.

Included in the fatalities were Senator Collinsworth and Keith Rivers, while Senator Evans has suffered but survived, though he surely will live out his days in prison. Among the lucky ones were President Markham and Carl White, both of whom were far from vents and quick to get to fresh air when the doors opened.

Evans and Meredith have provided much of the details of the conspiracy, though they will receive no benefit from the courts of law or public opinion for doing so. The crime was too heinous and too public for deals to be made; justice must be served and the thirst for public revenge must be quenched.

Byron Carthon is living in Venezuela, and for the moment successfully fighting extradition. There is speculation that if the Venezuelan government refuses to send him back to face the American legal system, then Special Service commandoes will be dispatched to render a more immediate form of justice.

Tim Wallace suffered substantial injuries on the boat that day, but physical therapy has gotten him back to almost full strength. He has been properly called a hero by various government agencies, and will soon be awarded the Congressional Medal, the highest honor a civilian can receive. He has not gone public with his thoughts about his experience, preferring to get on with his life.

Amazingly, there are those, conditioned by earlier media reports and current conspiracy theorists, who still believe Tim to have been a participant, even a leader, in the criminal operation. Those in the know are very public and very loud in correcting this absurd allegation, and Detective John Novack has probably been the most vocal of all in defending Tim's role.

Tim and I are spending a great deal of time with each other. We try to live our lives privately, but that is mostly impossible with the media following us everywhere. But we still go to the dog park every Sunday. I socialize and Tim throws the tennis balls, though not as far as he used to because of his injury.

We're planning on moving in together next month. Kiley and Travis seem very much in favor of it; they wag their tails whenever the subject is mentioned.

Tim is upbeat and looking forward to the new life we are starting together.

The nightmare is officially over.